Nicole Locke discovered her first romance novels in her grandmother's closet, where they were secretly hidden. Convinced that books that were hidden must be better than those that weren't, Nicole greedily read them. It was only natural for her to start writing them—but now not so secretly!

HER LEGENDARY HIGHLANDER

Nicole Locke

MILLS & BOON

First Published in Great Britain 2021
by Mills & Boon, an imprint of HarperCollins*Publishers* Ltd,
1 London Bridge Street, London, SE1 9GF

www.harpercollins.co.uk

HarperCollins*Publishers*
1st Floor, Watermarque Building,
Ringsend Road, Dublin 4, Ireland

To the princes at the Kingdom of Café
in the faraway land of Finchley.

Thank you for slaying my deadline dragons
with your vats of tea and carts of toast.

Thank you, especially, for your friendship.
It was, and will always be, cherished.

Chapter One

February 1299—Basque Country

'Riders approaching!' Uracca yelled over the pounding rain as she ran up the tower's winding staircase.

'How far?' Andreona turned as her friend crawled through the narrow stone entrance at the staircase landing.

Their safety depended on the distance and purpose of any travellers through this part of Gorka of Ipuscoa's territories. They didn't have much else to protect them out here except the tower they'd built and their wits.

That this particular border defence was almost a full day's ride away from the protection of the central keep was on her father's orders. The way it was built into a mountain, with winding staircases and small crawl throughs, was her own creation and a necessary defence for the banished women and children.

Uracca wrung out her hair. 'Difficult to tell. There's two of them and they're about a mile or two out.'

Could be anyone. Hardly enough information to notify her father of any dangerous approach.

'Horses are fine legged,' Uracca added.

Outsiders, then, since Basque horses were stout. Grinning, Andreona went to the hutch and pulled out a silver tube and held it up to the window. If she were going to prove her worth to her father, Gorka, an overlord, she'd have to keep and maintain this area and she couldn't do it without surprising and giving him something worthwhile. Outsiders provided that possibility.

It didn't do to think of the fact her father hated surprises and those who'd tried before were usually killed. It only meant Andreona had to be cleverer than the rest.

Shaking the tube for its ineffectiveness, she went to the dioptra already set at the window. The surveying tool had proven useful beyond the building of the tower from an abandoned home... and she liked looking at it every day.

'You and your tools,' Uracca huffed. 'What are you going to do, build those men closer to here?'

If she could, she would. Closing one eye and then the other and looking down the thin line, she still couldn't see anything. It wasn't only the rain; it was the terrain. This part of her country was blessed with trees and boulders as large as mountains as well as actual mountains. To see any distance, they needed to be at the coast, but that wasn't their terrain.

'You could simply look out of the window like the rest of us,' Uracca said. 'Or wear shoes.'

'What do shoes have to do with anything?'

'Other than it makes it easier to escape if we need to?'

She wasn't escaping. 'I never bother with clothes.'

'As if your constant tripping over untied laces is something new to me.'

Her shoes weren't a concern. Where were—? There. Two riders. Male, if their size to their mounts was any indication. As suspected, the horses were struggling with the terrain. Fools. They didn't deserve any horseflesh if they were to...

Ah.

'They're dismounting, but still coming this way. What do we have?'

Uracca sneezed and drew her sleeve over her nose. 'If it remains the two of them, the nets with weights will work well. If that's what you want.'

'If that's what I want? I thought this was what we wanted?'

'Do you think it'll make a difference?' Uracca tugged at her cloak's laces. 'Do you think capturing some outsiders and presenting them to your father will change his opinion of us?'

Andreona straightened and turned to her friend, who was avoiding her gaze. It wasn't the words that alarmed Andreona, it was her tone. Uracca wasn't only weary, but defiant.

She swatted her friend's frozen hands away and untied the cloak herself. The laces were soaked and knotting. 'Why are you questioning this now?'

'There's two of them and the rain has been relentless—they could be simply lost.'

They could be, but Andreona didn't want them to be. 'You, me, the other women, we fixed this home, built this tower. We constructed those nets and set other traps. We've been working on this for a year. Why else did we do it, if not to help Gorka?'

'Gorka!'

'By helping him, we help ourselves. That's the way of life.'

'He's your father, not mine, and us sitting in trees doesn't seem to be much of a life.'

Whipping the cloak off her friend's shoulders, Andreona gripped the dripping wool in her fist. 'I'm not doing it because he's my father.' At her friend's expression, she added, '*I'm* doing it for my father, but we're doing it to quell unrest.'

'Unrest created by your father.'

Unrest was her father's kingdom. Gorka was no acknowledged *señorio*. He held no true Basque lordship, but that didn't matter to thieves, murderers and politicians. No, her father's territory wasn't as narrow as to be simply feudal like the lordships of Alava, Biscay or Onate. Her father ruled not over everyone, but under.

While the lordships were restricted to rules and laws, her father lived to break them. And sometimes the feudal lords wanted that, too.

In the simplest of ways, her father was a thief, a prosperous one. In an ideal world, his way of life wouldn't exist at all. But they didn't have the luxury of an ideal life and they didn't have the luxury of being hypocrites. It wasn't only she who allowed men like her father, but those in official seats like the lords and magistrates. If laws or negotiations couldn't get matters accomplished, they employed Gorka and his followers to do the task for him.

And Gorka kept the peace within his iron fists. Thieves, murderers, they were his domain and he let them know it by 'contributions' or rather regular payments.

'Peace brought about because of him.' Stepping back, Andreona shook out the cloak to get out the worst of the water and hung it by the fire. 'Before he contained and controlled the thieves, chaos reigned and no one was safe to walk the streets. You know this as well as I do.'

'We know nothing,' Uracca said. 'All those tales were told to us by Gorka and were before our time. And now that we're banished here, we can't ask Lord Alava or Biscay or any of them the truth. Not that they would talk to us.'

Not until they proved themselves. That's all it would take. Except, it was getting difficult the more time passed.

How long had they been in the outer territories of the Basque Country? A little over a year? When the lords of the Basque Country decided to become more united against Spain and France, Andreona, Gorka's bastard child from a French woman who'd died in childbirth, became a liability. Though she wanted to be near her father, and her half-brothers, Ander and Ximeno, her father didn't want her. Uracca and the other women had similar backgrounds with the other lords. None of them were desired before, but once new rules were adopted…some of the women worried for their lives.

On behalf of herself and these women, Andreona pleaded with her brother Ximeno, was granted funds, workers, craftsman and they'd built this tower in the outer territories.

Andreona's hope was to provide some use to the Basque lords and to Gorka. To prove to them that though they were of half-blood, they were loyal to the Basque Country. That they didn't need to banish them.

It hadn't been easy. Once the tower's foundation was built, the workers suddenly abandoned them, then most of the women who'd joined them had taken coin and travelled either to France or Spain.

With each hardship, Uracca had pleaded with Andreona to abandon her idea that they could be of worth to Gorka and the others. Andreona knew they just needed a little more time. And now, with these men, perhaps that time had come.

'Gorka and the lords won't talk to us now, just as they wouldn't when they ordered us away. This is nothing new, but can't you see with these men, our fates might change! Uracca, what is wrong?'

Her closest childhood friend flung herself in front of the fire. 'I'm cold, that's all, and the rest of the women are, too.'

This wasn't because she was cold. For months now, Andreona had seen Uracca's weariness in her shoulders and ignored it. After all, all of them had suffered bouts of hardship. However, since they'd been through far worse and Uracca had always bounded back before, what was weighing on her friend was significant.

The exhilaration of spying the men coming towards them dimmed. She'd need to truly talk to her friend, but she feared any heartfelt argument she could make was exactly because Gorka was her father who shunned her. All her life, she'd tried to gain his approval.

She couldn't remember a time she didn't feel her father's indifference to her and comprehend the cruel words of his followers that she was a halfer. He never forgave her for being born, but it only got worse after that council meeting. Now her intent was to remind him she was half-Basque in blood and all Basque in heart.

Uracca, on the other hand, had never been embraced by her own father and her mother was a woman best left unknown. She was here because the alternative was to be with a woman who was cruel and broken. They, and the other women in similar situations, built a life in the outer territories for different reasons. But none of what they built and wanted would have been possible if they hadn't gained Gorka's permission through Ximeno, her brother, since Gorka refused to talk to them.

'We have this tower because Gorka gave us the resources to be able to make it—don't we owe him some loyalty?'

Uracca looked at her knowingly. 'We wouldn't

need this tower that Gorka created if he hadn't banished us.'

'It wasn't only him. It was a mutual decision.'

Uracca exhaled roughly.

'We all sat down,' Andreona continued. 'We discussed what we could contribute and at least he gave us some funds to help provide.'

'Funds given so we could leave completely! Not stay here and—' Uracca waved her arm. 'I should know better than to argue anything about Gorka with you.'

That...hurt.

Uracca shook her head. 'After all this time, do you truly think anything we do would help change our banishment? Maybe we should let these men pass by.'

'These are the first outsiders we've had since everything has been set up. This is our chance. Where are these doubts? Is it the other women?'

'It's the sitting for hours in the trees, the cold, and Dionora is still not well and letting everyone know it.'

Andreona was certain these daily hardships weren't Uracca's issue. Still, some of them could be addressed. 'If she and Mencia are together, none of us get any peace.'

'They are as far apart in the trees as we could put them.'

That didn't bode well. A few criticisms could

be addressed and resolved, but if complaints were made with no resolution, the good they did here would fall apart.

No time for this now!

'What are the positions of Bita and Gaieta?'

'Dry.' Uracca rubbed her arms. 'Behind and under the big rocks.'

That was good. The natural valley created by the stones was another reason they'd chosen this area to build. Anyone coming this way would travel the valley as the easier route. Anyone except these men who kept to the rocks.

'And not seen?'

'No one is looking up on a day like today.'

Didn't mean they weren't spotted. 'What were the men like when you were out there?'

'I couldn't hear what was said, but it looked as if there was an easy banter between them. They won't see the tower in this weather and, even if they do, they won't know the way in. That way—' Uracca pointed to the small tunnel opening '—wouldn't fit either one of them and that one—' Uracca pointed up at the large opening in the back '—can't be seen by any usual observer.'

'Unless they know it's here. Unless we've been compromised.'

'Why would they...?' Uracca shook her head. 'Your level of mistrust matches that of your father's.'

Half her blood and all her heart—some day she'd make him believe in her. 'I studied him well.'

'If we…' Uracca began to say. 'When we catch them in the nets, then what do we do?'

'I'll stay here and you'll ride to Ximeno to bring his forces here. We could keep them tied and travel to Gorka, but, alive, they'll be too much risk to us.'

Uracca averted her troubled gaze. Andreona knew it wasn't because they talked of Gorka or of the women. As long as Andreona had known her, Uracca had worshipped Gorka's second son, Ximeno. Over time, the worship had turned to something more dangerous, for feelings of love and affection would never be returned. Uracca wasn't even the bastard child of someone important. Despite Uracca's obvious beauty, Ximeno never looked her way.

Her brothers, raised at Gorka's knee, barely looked at her. Her mother wasn't supposed to have become pregnant, or given birth, or apparently survived her capture. She was French—or so her father told her—and now dead from childbirthing. Her father had told her this as well. He had also told her it was for the best. She wouldn't know about best.

Her living was a reminder he'd once lain with a woman of a people he now detested. While

Andreona was a mere child, she'd been shuffled from one or another property. Under his protection, but not his regard until the lords and Gorka made their decision to tighten their ranks. Then she'd had to make a solution for her and others like her.

Which became clear when she overheard her brothers converse on the outer region's vulnerabilities. Why not have her and anyone else build something that could alert them to travellers? Through Ximeno she'd earned the funds and one year later they had a tower that housed them.

With the odd construction, their vulnerabilities were lessened. The other part of her plan, to earn her father's admiration, rested solely on the outsiders walking towards them.

'Now what do they do?' Uracca said.

Andreona squinted through the silver tube again. 'Now they've stopped and are talking.'

'How near the net traps?'

'Near enough.' And too far away.

'Any way around them?'

'None.' Or there shouldn't be.

'What happens if they don't go in the nets?'

Andreona couldn't let them pass. That would be failing. What would two men riding possibly French horses fetch for her father? A ring or two. Perhaps some information or coin.

'So certain they are deserving of your father?'

Uracca said. 'With the rain they could have simply got lost.'

'Lost people take the easier path. They can't be so lost as not to smell the sea and head that way.'

'What do you think they do here?' Uracca said.

'What they always do here.'

If they were here for women or food, they'd be at the beach. If they were on their way from France to Spain…they would have travelled further south. No one came this way. The Basque Country had held its own against enemies far longer than any of the countries surrounding it and would far into the future. People who were intelligent avoided this area altogether. The Basque Country was fierce in its autonomy. Her father was ruthless.

These two men were either fools or about to be extremely unfortunate. A couple of steps into the traps and they and their horses would be swallowed up.

Those types of horses were useless in the mountains and terrain, but they sold for coin. As for the men, they had weapons, coin…perhaps information. Because of her bad blood, she couldn't be the daughter her father wanted, so she could give him loyalty and priceless gifts.

A bellow of a horse. Uracca pointed at the tube in Andreona's hands. 'Is that thing working?'

Andreona shrugged. 'A bit better than gazing out of the window.'

Uracca snatched it. 'What was it meant for?'

'It was in a healer's bag.'

'And you're using it to look out of the window?'

'I'm not a healer, am I? So what use would it be to me?'

'You and your collections. Did Txaran or Zilar steal it?'

'Txaran stole it. It's an original. You know Zilar likes to make replicas.'

As a ruler of thieves, her father had some of the best craftsmen. Ignored she might be by her father, but Andreona loved collecting the 'found' or replicated treasures.

Uracca held up the tube, lowered it and raised it again. Huffed. 'Movement in the trees. One of them seems to be caught.'

Andreona leaned out of the window and the rain fell heavy on her head. 'A horse?'

Uracca pointed the tube in a different direction. 'Two horses on the ground.'

'How many men in the net?'

'I can't tell from here.' Uracca handed the tube to Andreona.

The rain was relentless and she willed her eyes to see distances no eyes could. 'I think there's only one. Where'd the other one go?' She turned around. 'I'm sorry.'

Uracca's shoulders slumped. 'You're going to make me go back out, aren't you?'

Andreona watched at night and took more risks. She was inside because she was meant to be sleeping. 'It's not me.'

Uracca grabbed her cloak and swung it over her shoulders. 'It's not you. It's us.'

'It's for us,' Andreona said, willing her childhood friend to agree. They'd been inseparable since they were infants. Because they were bastards, both had always lived on the fringes of their fathers' worlds. This tower, this bounty they would bring, could mean they wouldn't be ignored anymore. 'It *is* for us, isn't it?'

Uracca struggled to tie the laces. 'No matter what I say, or how many times I say it, you keep insisting it has to be.'

It would be. A year was simply a long time to wait for such a reward and everyone was tired. But this was their chance.

And even if Uracca was right, even if these men were lost, simply taking them to her father would prove their loyalty. The lords and Gorka had been…hasty in their decision to banish them.

'Here, let me do that,' Andreona said. She tied the laces down the cloak. The cloak wasn't dripping anymore, but it was still soaked. Unfortunately, it was one they shared and would have to do.

Uracca knelt on the ground and backed out of the tunnel.

'Good death to you,' Andreona called out, using the familiar phrase when they wished good fortune on another.

'And to you.'

Hearing the small tunnel hatch open and close, Andreona lifted the silver tube once more and carefully scanned the horizon. Nothing. She went to the dioptre, crouching to see down the thin line. That was better and she patted one of the three legs holding it up to the window. One man. Two horses. One man was still missing.

'Now where could you be?' she muttered.

'Here.'

Chapter Two

Malcolm of Clan Colquhoun wrenched the woman against his body and slammed his hand over her mouth. She kicked and squirmed, tried to break free. He would have none of it. Finding this Basque woman in this misshapen wooden and stone structure built on to a hill wasn't what he searched for, but she was here, while his friend Finlay was trapped in some net outside.

Miserable because of the terrain, they'd dismounted and let their horses follow the best they could. Malcolm's only thought was one foot in front of the other. Finlay must have been the same. They'd both spotted the ropes far too late.

He'd been first to pull his dagger, ready for the attack, but nothing could be seen in the relentless rain. It was one more insult he'd suffered in the cursed journey he'd vowed to complete and poor Finlay had volunteered to do.

'Settle, dammit.'

She drew up her legs. He stumbled to stay upright. When she jammed her feet back to hit his knees, he swerved and cursed.

Finlay was the one who'd yelled for him to get away from the trap. A wise decision since they'd unthinkingly walked in some culvert for an ambush. He'd only meant to get to high ground to defend, but he'd seen some movement he thought was in the trees. Up close he'd realised it wasn't the trees, but something man built. There was a window where he could see two figures and no entrance, so he'd climbed more.

Getting inside wasn't easy. No door, no rampart. A tower, with no entrance until his foot caught on a hatch like on a ship. Two women inside when he climbed the tower, but only one when he dropped in.

Only one. Fear gripped him. Finlay wasn't out of the net and the escaped woman could do anything.

The woman he'd caught dug her fingernails into his arms, drawing blood, and the hairs on the back of his neck stood on end. He shook her. 'Stop! I mean you no harm.'

A lie. Through the window, he had clear sight of Finlay in the net. About to break free? Little matter. This woman could see what had happened and was therefore responsible.

She kicked again, this time perilously higher, and he swung her. Her free leg swiped at some contraption by the window and she screamed words at him.

He didn't care that she was a woman far from Gorka of Ipuscoa, where it was rumoured the cursed hollowed jewelled dagger he'd been searching for for years was now kept. How that thief had got the dagger he didn't know—all he and Finlay intended was to study the keep and steal it back. Barring that, to wrench it from the man and fight his entire guards.

They were so close to completing their mission.

And this woman? He didn't care that she was in some forsaken forest and he couldn't understand any of the obscenities she was screeching against his palm. What he cared about was that she was in this drystone tower with a roaring fire, while his friend Finlay was hoisted up in some net like a floundering fish.

After years of travel from Scotland across England and France, Malcolm had learnt to search for thieves and murderers in every corner. To fight or avoid, to evade traps, or negotiate. Maybe it was the rain and rocks, maybe they were tired, but they'd never been caught like this before. He refused to believe they could be now.

'Are you settled now?' he demanded. The

woman shoved her elbow into his stomach and stomped her foot on to his instep. He lost his hold on her. Malcolm grabbed for her again and she dived for a crawl-through! He grabbed her ankle and yanked.

Twisting on her back, she threw a dagger at him, he ducked, she threw another, which cut through his breeches. 'Enough!'

She spat out words. From the narrowness of her eyes and the pure rage on her face, it couldn't be good. Whatever language she was speaking, it was nothing he'd heard before.

He tried French. 'Why are you trying to capture us?'

She swiped out with her fist. They wouldn't get anywhere like this. Not that he intended to reason with her, but he was left with little choice. He'd never hit a woman, didn't intend to, but with his friend at risk, he was tempted to hold a dagger at her throat.

He tugged on her ankle again; her fist connected with his cheek. Momentarily blinded, he grabbed for the other ankle, and yanked her free from the tunnel. Straddling her form, he pinned her to the stone floor.

'My God, I may not understand you, but you will understand me.' Grasping her wrists in his hand, he pounded them above her head.

She narrowed her eyes and seeing the rhythmic movement in her throat, he averted his head just in time to avoid her spit, but he didn't let go. Never again.

Finlay had his dagger and was now cutting himself out of the net. He didn't need this woman to break his friend free, he needed to know if that other woman meant him harm or if there were others.

These two women couldn't be all there was. This tower might look like nothing much from the outside, but that was its purpose. Inside showed how they'd used the tiny cliff here for part of the structure. There were cubbies carved into the hill that held odd-shaped items. Other contraptions littered the floor like the one they'd kicked over.

He might not know what half of them were, but there was wealth here of a sort, that silver tube that spun out of her belt being one of them. So, who was she?

Rough-hewn clothes, heavily layered, one sleeve unlaced and in a style he didn't recognise. Callused hands, but finely tapered fingers. A spilling of dark hair that reminded him of the rocks he'd climbed. She was strong and determined. He could demand, but she'd fought him the moment he caught her; this wasn't a female he could frighten. Now that she was pinned, should he try reason?

'Look, lass, we'll not get anywhere unless we can speak to each other.'

She jerked, then held still. He swore she held her breath.

Her stillness was so startling, it held something with him, too. She was tiny, her harsh breaths doing nothing to make her look any more than an angry kitten. But this sudden stillness wasn't him holding her; it was something else and sharpened his attention to her and his surroundings.

Slashing rain and the scrape of tree branches against the stone. The fireplace blazing with a promising crackle and its light cocooning them within oddly stacked stone walls. Her brows drawn in and an odd curiosity in those eyes that were still spitting anger at him.

Listening hard, he looked around. Nothing different and his position didn't allow him to see out of the window. Yet, this woman now...waited. 'Why are you so still?'

She growled, struggling, but he wouldn't let go. When she stopped, she was angrier than before and the curiosity was gone. Had it even been there?

He couldn't think over the roar of the wind and the unusual scent of this country. Part-ocean, part-forest, but not like a forest he'd ever seen.

The trees were different, the rocky lush terrain unfamiliar and the woman…who was she?

Plush lips, a sharp chin. Eyes the colours of grey, blue, green and volatile with her emotions.

'Ack, you've got eyes the colour of herrings, lass, and are reminding me of home.'

The woman stilled again.

'You're listening to me?' He spoke English, French; he knew no Spanish. She hadn't reacted…ah.

'It's Gaelic you're hearing. You ken?'

If that was all it took for this reasoning… 'Your friend, is she going to hurt mine?' He wanted to get up to check, but she was still now and he didn't want to fight her.

'Are you harming my friend?' he repeated, but she stayed quiet…still.

He had to look! Holding her hands, he lifted off her body. She immediately brought her knees up and he dropped back.

The woman spit out words, telling him in every way she was not co-operating. To drag her by her hands or feet? Why couldn't there be rope to bind her? Nothing was easy about this!

That wasn't anything new. This entire journey he and Finlay travelled on was cursed. He knew it to his very bones because it all began with Clan Buchanan. That hated clan had dragged his family into the mess he'd found himself in when they'd accidentally stolen the Jewell of Kings.

It was a gem hidden inside a hollow dagger. In stories, it was much like tales of Excalibur and the Holy Grail. The Jewell of Kings legend held that whosoever held the Jewell held the heart of Scotland.

It had been a favourite tale for King Edward given his war on Scotland. Although, in truth, King Edward loved any tales of King Arthur and all those useless romantic tales of valour, honour and quests.

Those happy tales were for children, while for him they were nothing but a nightmare. Especially since he'd discovered the jewel was real, it had surfaced and *his* clan was involved.

More than involved. Hidden away in Scotland, his clan had the gem, the Jewell of Kings, and some of the parchments that hinted at a great treasure. His only duty was to bring the missing piece, the hollowed dagger, back to them. It was all he was to do. Not fight some woman in the middle of nowhere.

'Why have you gone quiet?' he said.

He felt the strain in her wrists as she tried to free her arms. She was all anger and defiance even though he'd bested her. She might not be afraid, but he was. Risking his position, he yanked her up along with him and dragged her to the window.

A string of words left her mouth again and she almost got free.

'Why aren't you calling for help?' he said. The only time she'd shouted was when that item hit the floor.

He caught her staring out as he did. But her eyes weren't going to the net that was slowly falling as was Finlay; her eyes were scanning the trees. There were others!

Her arm jerked and he saw the whiteness of his knuckles—he was holding her too tightly. Loosening, but not letting her go, he leaned out of the tower. Was Finlay on his way here?

Who were these people? The Basque Country wasn't a large country and there should have been no one in this area; it was why they'd travelled this way.

These two women, though small, were besting them. How to explain to his brothers—?

Why was he thinking of his family when he'd purposefully kept away from them, purposefully stopped sending messages? Yearned, when he finally found the lost dagger that had hidden the Jewell of Kings and brought it back to them, to put them and this foolish quest behind him.

As he'd wanted to do ever since his family forced him on the quest. And it was force…for three years now. Oh, certainly they'd softened their words by begging for forgiveness from him by not telling him to stay out of the Battle of Dunbar—he'd gone and had the scars to prove it. Nor did they trust him with the truth about the Jewell of Kings and how they'd acquired it by their enemy Clan Buchanan.

He was the youngest brother, whom they protected and never trusted with the truth no matter his years, no matter his skills or deeds. He was never thought of as an equal. All because when he was twelve, he couldn't defend himself and his friend from three grown Buchanan warriors. Shannon had died, horribly.

He held immeasurable pain, agony, darkness and guilt because of that one fateful day. But ever since, his family had never let it go, constant with reminders that he'd never be good enough. That he'd needed to be rescued. That he couldn't save anyone, ever, and wasn't worthy to.

So he knew what this quest to find the hollow-handled dagger truly was: a way to get him gone from them as he wanted to be gone. To wait until his anger and acute betrayal abated. As if that would ever happen.

There might have been a chance to forgive his family for not explaining the reasons not to go to the Battle of Dunbar. Bram, his eldest brother and the Laird, had simply ordered him not to.

Without knowing the true reasons, Malcolm had gone. As far as he knew, his clan should have been at Dunbar and all of his brothers should have been by his side when his fellow Scotsmen fled to Ettrick Forest.

But they hadn't because his Laird and brother Bram received a private message from King John Balliol of Scotland telling him to stay at home and wait for a package. At the time, Bram hadn't known why the mysterious message told him to remain at home, he just did. Though he wanted to ignore the message, though he knew his fellow Scotsmen would turn on him, Bram couldn't take the risk. Death might come to him, but open defiance would harm the clan.

But Malcolm didn't know those facts and defied his brother. He went alone to Dunbar and almost died. Taking a slice from a sword from his gut to temple, he'd fallen and nearly bled out on the field, saved perhaps because other bodies fell on him.

Saved definitely because his brother Caird had found him and got him to a healer.

But it wasn't only his body that was broken that day, it was his family. They hadn't trusted him with the truth, still protected him as they'd always done since he was twelve years old.

No, it wouldn't do to think of Shannon and

that childhood tragedy now, or the moment Caird had taken a Buchanan as a wife. Or—

Malcolm felt a sharp pain in his arm. His hands released before he realised the woman had bitten him again.

She darted free. Malcolm lunged, but she jumped out of his reach. Arms out, he circled around the side and saw her goal, the small crawl through that was little more than a child could enter...or this tiny woman.

He swiped to the right and the woman danced to the left. He missed her, but he didn't care, she was out of the way of the escape. Her eyes darted to the corner, then back to him. Ah, she knew he intended to bar her. He grinned. She narrowed her eyes.

Sliding one way, then the other. She jerked and he watched her feet, her eyes widened, and he—

Oof!

A weight hit him on the shoulders. Clung there. A body! He staggered back, but they had wrapped a linen around his throat and wrenched it, cutting off his air. He grabbed the thin forearms and dug his thumbs into the wrists.

A harder yank and he saw stars. The woman in front of him shouted, the creature on his shoulders yelled. The other woman had returned. He grabbed the woman on top and flipped her over.

She didn't let go of his neck. The woman

he fought dived for his legs. No! He was going down. His size or theirs. He reached up to cage the woman as the blackness around the edges of his vision eclipsed everything. As he fell his head took the brunt of impact.

Then nothing.

Chapter Three

Uracca scrambled out from under the fallen man.

'He's out,' Andreona said, looking for signs of movement. Like this, he looked unnatural, but no less formidable. She could hardly believe they'd captured him. 'We need to tie him up.'

Uracca dashed for the closed barrel in the corner and pulled out two ropes. Andreona hefted the man's hands behind his back while her friend completed the tight and intricate knot. Grabbing the other rope, Andreona wrapped a similar knot around his ankles. The stranger let out a groan, but his eyes remained closed, his body slack.

'What of the other man?'

'He cut some of the rope and dangled right over Dionora and Mencia, who were waiting for him. When they could, they wrapped it around him again. I think he was injured when the net caught him. He's not moving very fast.'

Andreona sat back, a certain thrill of victory coursing through her. With one man trapped in the nets and held by the other women and this man here, plus the addition of two horses, this was a fine catch for her father's collection.

'What of Bita and her daughter, Gaieta?'

'They're still hidden.'

Good. When they started the tower there were many, now it was just five women and a child, but it was enough. They made for an odd look out, but they did watch each other. And maybe soon it would be better...

Could it be she'd finally earned her position in Gorka's household? She could hardly believe it. A full year of toil and heartache. Of broken fingers and cracked hands. Of far too many nights fighting the elements and the women for one more layer of rock to be done, one more rope to be made. All the time wondering whether she'd ever be good enough to—

'I'm fine, by the by, because of him,' Uracca said.

Andreona blinked. 'Because of him?'

'You saw what he did.' Uracca indicated with her chin. 'I'd have smashed my head on the floor or walls when you tackled his legs and upset his balance. What were you thinking?'

Where were these questions coming from?

They were under attack! 'I was helping to bring him down.'

'I would have done that soon enough.'

It wasn't soon enough for her. 'He wanted to flip you over, which would certainly have broken if not your head, then your stubbornness.'

'Stubborn?'

Why was she fighting with her friend? They'd always had each other and watched each other's backs. 'You've been cut…are you hurt elsewhere?'

Uracca snorted. 'You look worse than I feel.'

After pulling and punching with all her strength, her body both hurt and felt weak. The man was…strong, capable. Too capable. Oddly, she knew she'd have bruises from where he'd restrained her, but she didn't seem to have anything worse than that. It was like he wasn't truly fighting… No. Uracca's words had muddled her thoughts. Of course he'd meant to harm her! 'How did he get in?'

Uracca looked up. 'The same way I did, through the hatch.'

The hatch was open, rain coming in at a slant. The floors would soon be wet. Foolish to leave it open so long, they had enough leaks as it was. Carrying the ladder over, she climbed and slammed the cover closed. 'He shouldn't have known it was there to leave it open.'

'Would it be odd to say I'm glad since it allowed me to surprise him?' Uracca smirked. 'You should have let me close it—you're now as wet as I.'

How did he get here so fast and know that the hatch was there? If he was fumbling accidentally on the roof, certainly she would have heard.

'It must have been the rain covering his sounds above when we talked.' She shivered from cold and from the knowledge he had listened in on the conversation, their argument, about Gorka and Ximeno. Had he understood it? He spoke several languages and that one she'd never heard before. Who was he and where was he from? He didn't seem Spanish or French.

'I can't believe a man like that let us overpower him.' Uracca frowned.

'Let us!' He hadn't done anything but swoop in and fight.

Uracca continued. 'Don't think he expected to hit his head so hard when he fell, but that's what he got when he protected me.'

'This man is an enemy.'

'How do we know that? Did you ask him?'

'He came on foreign land and spoke a foreign language. He…travelled not by road,' Andreona said.

'Many come on this land and travel through,' Uracca said.

'Yes, but they use the road.'

At Uracca's still stubborn expression she added, 'And he was trying to rip you from his body and fling you against the stone wall.'

Uracca huffed. 'When he couldn't because of your interference, he kept his arms up protecting my head from the fall and not his own.'

'I was on the ground—I saw what I saw.'

'You think I didn't see?' Uracca shook her head. 'You're usually not this blind.'

Was she blind? No. Uracca wasn't here when this man attacked. He wasn't trying to talk to her. If he had, he would have spoken French or Basque. Instead, he'd yelled out words that could have been French, but his accent! And the rest was completely unintelligible. Probably a code for other men they hadn't yet spotted.

What was troubling her friend? Questioning their reasons for being out here, uttering words disloyal to Gorka, a man who funded and supported their building a community of sorts together. If Uracca's words were heard by any others, she'd be dead or banished for good.

No matter what disagreement they were having now, that couldn't happen. Andreona would do anything to prevent that from happening.

'You came for me.'

Uracca looked surprised. 'Of course.' She

looked to the man. 'Maybe we should keep our voices down or leave?''

'He doesn't understand our language.' She didn't think he understood Basque, but he'd said a word just when she asked a question. Had he been answering her?

'How would you know this? Were you having some sort of conversation about the weather before I showed up?'

'Hardly. He speaks a language I've never heard before.'

'The other man shouted odd words when hanging from the tree.' At Andreona's expression, Uracca continued. 'He kept yelling different words and languages, but one word was repeated—Malcolm.'

'What kind of name is that?' Was he waking? She thought…perhaps.

Uracca shrugged. 'It's the strangest one I've heard. But the man in the net repeats it louder than the others as if he is calling out.'

Andreona looked at the man whose eyes were closed. Could be awake; could be asleep. They were taking a chance by speaking this way in front of him, but only Basque knew the language.

And he was no Basque. He was taller than the men she knew, wider in the shoulders, his skin, browned from the sun, held hints of something much softer and delicate underneath. There were spots across his nose. He was almost…beautiful. The only indication that he wasn't all innocent was a long scar down his left cheek. From the depth of it on his chin, she wondered if it went further along his body than that.

No, he wasn't Basque, but he looked too raw to be French. English? Perhaps, but what did she know of that faraway place? But there were some who'd travelled from there and their boots didn't match his. What was his accent?

'Did the other man speak French or Spanish?'

'There were some words that sounded like French, but it was difficult to understand.'

Andreona had also heard a few words that sounded like French. Those she understood if she listened hard enough, but it was the other language that intrigued her in an accent, very thick, deep, with a cadence that was far too pleasing. So pleasing, in fact, she had requested he repeat his words. Whether he understood her or not, he had. And it was enough of a distraction for Uracca to surprise him.

'Mine spoke French.'

Uracca's eyes narrowed. 'Thus you believe this is proof they are enemies and men your father would want to harm? We speak French.'

'They came from that direction, too.'

'There are countries beyond. They could have come from there.'

She had thought so, too, but Uracca was arguing for arguing's sake. She thought they were one with this, that they thought the same. Andreona felt some sense of loss and yet… 'We've been preparing for this for a year!'

'I know,' Uracca said, 'but something seems off with this. Had he done anything else but grab you?'

They had these men trapped and secured. When would they have an opportunity like this again? And if these men weren't useful, if they were innocent, her father would let them go. He never harmed good Basque citizens—why would he outsiders?

Although the lords and Gorka had met and banished them because they were half-blood, but surely this would be different? It must. Moreover, bringing them in would prove her—their—worth. If only Uracca wasn't fighting this!

'You only deny this because you don't want to see Ximeno.'

At her friend's flush, she immediately regretted her words. 'I'm sorry—'

The man shifted and both women looked his way.

Green eyes locked with hers.

As he stood in the shadows, his words hurled like daggers, and his body a weapon of force, she hadn't taken in his appearance. He was an enemy and meant to be fought against. He only mattered by what harm he could do to her.

Now he lay at her feet, lying on his side and shackled. Dark wet hair containing streaks of another colour that made no sense, but she wondered none the less what colour it would be when it dried. Broad shoulders tapering to a narrow waist. She didn't know the size of him, but she knew the strength as he wrenched his shoulders one way, his bound legs the other.

'You won't break those knots. You're tied fast,' she informed him.

He wrenched one last heave and panted one rough exhale before he narrowed his eyes on her.

He was…breathtaking. His eyes were the colour of grass in the summer sun and spring foliage on trees. But nothing so still or tranquil. Certainly, nothing of celebration or renewal. Unrest roiled and retribution turned. That colour was never meant for such wrath and determination. But it was all that was there and none of it felt new.

Which was foolish, she knew, for how could any man hold rage for long? No, such vehemence was only because he was caught and his friend trapped.

That colour green wasn't created to be turbulent like the bay crashing against the shore. It was unnerving. Fascinating. Never in her life had she seen eyes like that. Never mind the strange rumble of words he used or the ones she did recognise in a cadence that made no sense. His eyes were the foreign entity.

'Did you have a nice rest?' Uracca said in French.

He darted his gaze to her friend and broke whatever hold he had on her, but she saw no comprehension. But then, if he were a true enemy, he'd be clever enough to hide that wouldn't he?

'He's an enemy, not Basque, and certainly not family.'

'I'm not family.' Uracca pointed to the man. 'What makes me any different than him?'

Whatever was disturbing Uracca was significant, but could not be addressed in front of the stranger.

'You're as good as blood,' Andreona said. 'Will you notify Ximeno to get his help or not?'

'You're making a mistake. This man isn't an enemy, your father is. The fact you can't...' Uracca shook her head, then looked away. 'Not everyone is like him.'

Andreona looked to the man who was following their conversation. It was in Basque and he might not understand, but there were no certainties. Her friend didn't want to do this and she didn't want to talk of her father when words could be understood.

'What if we tie them to the cart and get them there? It's a half-day's ride.'

'I think that's a worse idea.'

'Catching them can't be for nothing.' Andreona was loyal to Gorka and to his cause, she'd do it alone, but she preferred to reap the rewards with her lifelong friend.

Uracca's shoulders slumped. 'Let's get the other man in here, then we'll go in the morning when it's light again.'

'And not raining,' Andreona said.

Giving her a small smile, Uracca went to the crawl-through. Andreona turned to the man, who was staring at them intently.

'We'll get your friend,' she said in French. 'He's been hurt.'

The man struggled to get up.

'You understood me.'

'You've harmed him, you've harmed yourselves,' he uttered. His French was absolutely, chillingly clear.

'I guess we understand each other.'

He looked to the window, then back to her. 'Rain.'

'Yes, it's raining…' She froze. He'd said that… in Basque.

Chapter Four

~~~~~

Malcolm took a certain thrill at seeing the surprise and wariness on the woman's face when he repeated one of her words. He didn't understand anything of the words they had said, so he took a chance on repeating one, not knowing which one it was until she looked out of the window and waved at the rain.

He should have regretted revealing he was listening and understanding because they most likely wouldn't be as free with their conversation. However, he had enough regrets in life and he seized his pleasures when he could.

What he wasn't pleased about was watching two women drag Finlay, still wrapped in some net, as if he was a fish. It didn't matter they dragged him because there were no suitable entrances to this tower and the hatch he had fallen through was large enough to lower his friend in.

What mattered was that Finlay was hurt. Pale, with his breath hitching, and they took him to another room so he couldn't talk to him. Instead, he had this woman who stared at him.

'Will you co-operate?' she said. 'Malcolm.'

She knew his name. How? He looked to Finlay, who muttered words he couldn't quite hear. Ah.

The smile on her face was knowing. He almost wanted to smile, he also wanted to fight her, and she must have guessed because she looked to his tied hands. Did he want to co-operate? Not with Finlay injured, not without knowing why these women captured them.

'What are you doing with us?' He'd speak in French as long as she did. With Finlay hurt, it was best to co-operate.

'You don't need to know that. You're captured and, with your hands tied, you and your friend can't climb the ladder to the outside. But it doesn't matter. No harm will come your way... if you co-operate.'

'No one builds nets to trap people if they mean them no harm.'

'If you're as innocent as you say, then you will be set on your way, Traveller.'

She believed her words. He could see it in the way she stood evenly, just like her steady gaze on him. She believed there would be no harm if he were innocent. The only trouble was he wasn't innocent.

Not only because of his mission for the Jewell of Kings and finding the dagger, or his past deeds, but because the lace on her sleeve still wasn't tied and she wasn't wearing shoes. He was noticing her toes, the arch of her foot. She was distracting in a way that a woman is to a man. That lace…he wanted to untie the other one. He knew she was this way without purpose. There was no flirtatious glint in her eye or a dip to her chin with eyelashes fluttering. He feared she truly was that direct.

Did this mean he could trust her? He trusted no one. He didn't need anyone, yet his fate was tied to her, at least for now. Which meant he needed to understand her motivation. 'How many others have you trapped?'

'What?'

'You have this odd tower, you have those nets—how many other travellers have you caught?'

'What does it matter to you?'

'You seem so certain of my future health. I need to know why,' he said. This went beyond merely wanting coin. It would have been easier to knock them unconscious and steal their items, and not trap two men, who carried weapons, inside. She might have his sword, but she didn't have the blade in his boots. Which was useless unless his hands were untied, but the moment he and Finlay were together he was intending to free the ties.

She was frustratingly quiet. 'You have our horses, our coin, weaponry—do you mean to sell it all and then release us? What if I told you if you release us now, you'd have double what you took?'

Crossing her arms, she said, 'I am not a thief. You can't buy me.'

Loyal, then, but to whom? These few women or someone else? He wondered what it would mean to have such loyalty. He'd lost his years ago. 'What are we to you?'

'You're everything.'

He'd had a lifetime of riddles and hidden answers! 'Say that again.'

When she shrugged, he reined in his impatience. What had he got into? Thus far he'd counted five women and a young girl here. Not a man in sight. This wasn't an abbey, there were no religious artifacts in all those notches in the stone walls except enamelled boxes that he'd only ever seen protected by the Church and locked behind cabinets.

That threw the odd items in the room into perspective. What wealth did a contraption consisting of a few sticks with dangling rope and rocks have that equated with enamel? Yet this woman treated them all with the same reverence. Wealth was here, hidden, protected. But how wealthy? Warstones or a king's wealth?

Could King Edward's reach be this far? He doubted it, since he was occupied with holding on to Stirling. As for the Warstones, who'd plagued the Colquhouns for the Jewell of Kings since the beginning, their influence over the last years was waning.

The Spanish monarchies were a possibility, but he hoped not. There were enough people chasing after the dagger and Jewell of Kings as it was.

But the dagger did come here. As far as he could tell, the dagger was switched and replaced some time when Caird and Mairead had it. They'd had several run-ins with Sir Richard Howe, The Englishman. A knight who swore fealty to King Edward, but earned his coin from his deeds with the Warstones. Sir Richard hired mercenaries from everywhere, and some were from Spain…possibly the Basque Country.

They were near it, he knew it. But this place, this woman was delaying him! 'What is your name?' He looked around. 'What is this place, why are you here and what do you want of us?'

'Does it matter?' she said. 'You are tied, your friend is…incapacitated. '

'Where did you send that other woman?'

'I sent her nowhere—she's merely getting matters prepared for when the rain stops. What are you doing here?' she said. 'What do you want with my country?'

Finlay, with his even demeanour and patience, would have been better to negotiate. Malcolm hated wasting this time and loathed that he couldn't see how badly his friend was harmed.

'We've done nothing. My name is Malcolm—his is Finlay. We're from Scotland. We mean you no harm. If this is your land, we'll go another way. Our quarrel is not with you.'

'You have a quarrel?'

Dammit.

That mercenary hired by Sir Richard Howe, The Englishman, wasn't Spanish at all. That's what Hugh of Shoebury and Alice, two friends of Clan Colquhoun, had reported within a message sealed by a half-thistle symbol.

The Half-Thistle Seal. Malcolm cursed it all over again. That seal had also plagued him. A secret symbol used between a few people to exchange information on the Jewell of Kings. It was used to keep his Clan safe, but it made them all spies against kings and countries.

He didn't want to be a spy; he didn't want anything to do with his Clan either or the Jewell of Kings, which they had now sworn to protect.

And this woman delayed him! She was tiny, but she stood while he was practically lying on the floor. The ropes around his ankles were a bit looser. Not around his hands, but his feet...he'd get them loose.

Though he had to do it slowly, with her unerring eyes constantly on him. They were so... unusual. Hypnotic with her skin and her abundance of hair. She looked like something mystical. Which irritated because he'd had enough of legends and stories!

'I have no quarrel with you,' he said.

'You have a scar caused by a sword,' she said. 'Nothing else would cut that deep and large. You're not innocent.'

This wasn't possible. 'Let us out!'

'No,' she said. 'It doesn't suit our purposes to let you go. Only murderers and thieves travel this way.'

'I'm not a murderer or a thief.'

No, he was a spy and soon to be a thief. Malcolm and Finlay had journeyed here based on Hugh's information. The dagger being in legitimate hands, such as any of the lords of the Basque Country, was highly unlikely. No, the likelihood was the dagger, which had been nefariously switched, was in the hands of Gorka, a man known not to be honourable.

That's why they were here, travelling where

no one could see them. They didn't know exactly where this Gorka lived, but knew they'd find him if they kept to the shadows and enquired from the fringes of polite society.

Could these women be part of Gorka's realm? Not likely. There was something too direct in this woman's gaze and both he and Finlay were alive. If rumours were correct, Gorka would have already ordered their deaths.

There shouldn't have been anyone out in this area. Too rocky for agriculture, too many trees for livestock. Yet here they were, five women and a child. And he didn't know what to do with any of them. More importantly, he didn't know what they were going to do to him.

But what to say to change her position? 'We won't harm you.'

She huffed. 'You keep saying that, though you lie about everything else. Just stay here and accept your fate.'

'What fate is that?'

'That's not up to me.'

This wasn't good. 'Whose fate are we under? Whatever he or they are paying you, whatever he has on you, the debt will be paid by me by twice the amount. Tell me. Who is our true captor?'

With him tied up, feet almost loose, but Finlay in the other room looking in pain. Hurt, but how badly? There might be no speedy escape from all this.

'What matters are there to prepare for tomorrow?'

'I am done with this conversation.'

'At least take me to my clansman.'

'Your clansman? What does that mean?'

He could lie, but he didn't. 'Family.'

Some vulnerability in her eyes, some softness he immediately wanted to take advantage of. 'He's your family.'

'Not by blood, but by bond,' he said. There were days he wished to denounce his kin. 'Some would say it was stronger.'

She scoffed. 'That is a lie. Blood is always stronger.'

That was telling and she seemed to realise it as she glowered and turned to leave.

He had to keep her here, no matter the cost. Finlay was still lying down—he looked far too pale. 'Take me to him.'

She looked behind her, worried her lip, but shook her head.

This was a fool's errand! Kicking off the ropes around his ankles, he stood. The woman in Finlay's room gasped. His woman glowered and looked as though she wanted to bodily force him to stay.

His woman… He was amused by her with her

hands on her hips and wide stance as if to block him from storming past her to Finlay. It was exactly what he wanted to do.

At the image of how he'd do it, at the sudden tightening interest of his body, he realised he'd like that, too. A little too much. Surprised at the unwelcome spike of desire, at the sheer magnitude that he couldn't tamp down, at least not fast enough she wouldn't notice with his short tunic and his hands behind him, he looked over her head.

'Finlay,' he called out in Gaelic.

'In here,' Finlay shouted. Coughed.

Did that cough sound wet? Were his lungs punctured? 'Are you hurt? Thump on the ground to let me know.'

Absolute silence. Which meant Finlay was hurt. That man didn't like to admit to any injury. He eyed the woman again and spoke in French. 'He's hurt.'

'Ribs are bruised or a bit more,' a woman from the other room called out.

Not good enough. 'Let me see him,' he said.

Chapter Five

Finlay. What an odd name and what was this Scotland? Andreona shouldn't have any weaknesses when it came to these two men, but she, too, was concerned about Finlay. He was moving too carefully. If they were innocent travellers, or if her father didn't want them, them being damaged wouldn't be in her favour.

But she wasn't a monster. Giving him the eye, but not expecting this Malcolm to stay where he was, she went to the other room.

Finlay was pale, but he sat at an incline and his eyes… He wasn't dying any time soon. In fact, he seemed expectant, amused, when she merely looked at him, so she frowned. She wished Uracca was here, but Bita was probably the best to tend him for now.

She could only think Bita's daughter, Gaieta, was with Dionora or Mencia. She hoped it was Dionora.

Turning around, she expected Malcolm to be at the ladder or right behind her, but he was still in the room she'd left him in. She wanted to ask... why?

This man didn't look as if he was peaceful or ever still. He seemed to her like a rolling storm. Dark hair drying with streaks matching the fire that lit half his features.

The scar was lighter than the rest of his face and outlined a strong jaw, the fullness of his lower lip. No man should look both dangerous and beautiful. No man should be here at all.

'He's bruised, nothing more,' she said. 'He's uncomfortable and it must have happened when he got caught in the net. We haven't purposefully harmed him.'

He frowned. 'The set nets weren't purposeful?'

She wouldn't argue words with this stranger. 'Sit down and be quiet.'

'No, my legs have fallen asleep. I'll sit when it's time to rest.'

His hands were tied, Andreona repeated to herself. He might be standing, his feet might be free, but he couldn't go anywhere except up a ladder, which would be impossible, especially since she wasn't going to move the ladder near the hatch when he was free like this.

Still, he was dangerous and there was no way

she'd fight him again even with his hands tied. They should have tied the ropes to a chair to impede his movement. Especially since he took the few steps to the cubbies she'd made for her artifacts.

'Where'd you get those?' He indicated the enamel boxes, their value far surpassing anything most would ever see. But that was not why she kept them. She did because they were useful and beautiful. Because boxes with nothing in them held possibilities.

Not anything she could explain to anyone, including this stranger. Nor could she explain that she'd stolen them from her father. 'They were given to me.'

'Why?'

That wasn't the question she'd expected. He spoke slowly enough so that she understood his words, or perhaps she was growing used to his accent. When he spoke his native language, the sounds shivered up her spine. The lower rumble…the rough edges. That language fitted this man.

He was beautiful, yet he had that scar that went across his cheek, down thicker around his chin. Was it his anger or impatience that caused that scar? Because she knew those traits were within this man as well. Oh, he kept some amusement on the surface, but she could see the turbulence in those green eyes.

'I keep the boxes because I like them,' she said.

'Why?' he asked again.

An almost-smile graced his lips. He shouldn't have been beautiful. He shouldn't have been anything at all except a means to an end. He was either innocent or useful to her father. That was all.

This man before her might or might not be dangerous to her, but he was up to something. And if his claim was just, then Gorka would simply release him to a Basque lord, or whomever it was he had a quarrel with. If this stranger meant ill will, then he was stepping on her father's territory and would pay the toll appropriately.

As such she should simply leave. But that curve to his lips and that glint to his eye...

It wasn't anything she'd seen before in a man, at least not pointed at her, and oddly it made her curious about him. Curious the same way she was about boxes. Why did he smile, why did he look at her with a sudden intensity as if he wanted to know why she kept these treasures? Nobody had asked her such questions before.

'Boxes are mysterious,' she said. 'They're built to hold things inside, but what? Does it depend on the size of the box? No, it depends on the craftsman.' She waved to the wall. 'These are all beautifully made, art in and of themselves, but when they were so carefully crafted, the artisan dreamed of what would grace the inside.'

'What's inside these?' he asked.

This would amuse him. 'Nothing. That's why it's a mystery.'

Instead of Malcolm laughing, his expression drew a bit dark, his eyes a bit more intense. 'And it makes you mad with curiosity what the craftsman wanted in them, doesn't it? That's why you have them…because you wanted to know what went inside. Have you written letters? Asked questions? Demanded answers?'

How did he know these things? He had guessed so correctly, those strange eyes that were green, but not tranquil, never leaving hers. Despite averting her gaze, she felt a blush begin on her neck.

Making some sound in his throat that could have been amusement, but didn't irritate, rather… it drew her eyes back to him. What did he mean by that sound and why was it appealing? Nothing about him should be appealing. A scar across his face, hands tied, but somehow his feet weren't tied anymore. He wasn't Basque, wasn't tame either. An enemy was how she should see him. It was beyond reason she told him things she'd told no one before.

'Let me tell you this,' he said. 'When it comes to empty spaces, it's better not to know. Simply let them stay hollow. Else you'd be plagued with some journey you didn't know would take years.'

What was he talking of?

He strode to the groma and stuck his chin out. 'What's this?'

It was sticks, rocks and string. It looked like nothing except it was so perfectly balanced a great amount of time and effort was made in creating it.

'Nothing that would concern you.' At his raised brow, she huffed, 'It's for surveying… building. This tower didn't simply build itself.'

He stilled then. 'You built this.'

With everything in her being. But it didn't mean anything unless she could prove to her father the coin he'd given her to pay for the workers and the supplies wasn't wasted. She was so close to doing that and the man who appealed and confused her was integral to proving herself, but she knew better than to tell him that.

'Did you build with this, too?' Malcolm stepped towards the dioptra, except the rope was still dangling from one of his boots and he stumbled.

'No!' Andreona dashed across the room. Malcolm bumped the delicate instrument, but she caught it in time. What she also caught was one giant man, who sidestepped the contraption, but not her. Her leg skidded between his two, the front of her body slamming into his. Somehow one hand reached through the hole his made tied behind his back, while the other tried to break her impact by bracing in front of her.

A seemingly reasonable gesture, but with their height difference, with the angle her body was forced into when her arm skidded through his, her hand rested not on his chest, not on his stomach, not on either of his thighs, but right in between, right...*there*.

Then something instinctual, something far more than curiosity, something that she didn't even know to stop or else she would have, but her hand, her fingers curled.

He didn't make a gasp of surprise, like she did, but a new sound. Something low and rumbly. A sound similar to the language he spoke.

And the goose pimples she'd had, the startling awareness of what she touched and held, turned to something flooding her body fast, hot and sudden, from her toes to the roots of her hair.

And that right there was what alarmed her, what set her in motion. Not the heat of his torso pressed to hers, or the gust of his breath against her cheek. Not the way he smelled of steel and evergreen. Like something controlled and untamed. Not the way the thickness of his legs encased her much smaller ones. Or the way her breasts were flattened against his side and her hand, which had gone through his arms, had clutched his tunic.

She scrambled away. It wasn't easy, because something in him reacted, too, and the pulling away, which should have been nothing but a seamless glide with no contact at all, somehow became more.

All because she went left while he went left, which pressed and trapped his hip to hers, slid her hand hard against him until she felt *him* jerk against her palm. It startled any reasonable hold she may have had and shoved her completely against him. By then her breasts, the very core of her was nothing but tightened points, and her body let out a sound so similar to his, like an echo, like…an answer.

What was this?

'Don't move,' he rasped, the two words holding an order and a plea.

She understood that. On a rough breath, she bowed her head against his chest and gave up. Just surrendered and leaned into him. Which didn't help at all, apparently, because he shuddered and his heart hammered harder. 'Let go of my tunic.'

Mortified, she willed her arm wrapped around him to release and she pulled it back enough to almost get it through his arms.

'I meant your other hand.' His voice held a

bit of consternation and a lot of something that lowered it even more, made it husky... What was wrong with her?

She knew curse words, and if she could possibly say them now she would, but she couldn't get air past the tightness in her throat. It wasn't the only thing that was tight. Everything about her felt tight and startling.

'You need to let go, lass...now. I can't hold you and I've been glimpsing your ankles, that swing to your lace, and any moment I'm going to forget there's my friend and yours around the corner and—'

That did it. Horrified, she jumped back. This time, he remained still. Yet that bit of distance did nothing except put a bit of cold air between them. Cold air didn't help, it only reminded her of the warmth...the heat.

'Why did you do that?' His words were more of an accusation than a question.

He was looking at her as if she was some perplexing phenomenon. But not a good one. More like something clinging to the bottom of his boot and he wondered how it had got there.

Malcolm was raised in a large clan where secrets were impossible. He had played hide and seek, chase and all the other childhood games. Most of those games would inadvertently have him seeing or hearing conversations only adults were meant to hear. Run around a corner too fast and he'd bump into a man pressing a woman against the back side of a hut. Think the barn a fine place to hide and realise it was already occupied.

When it was his turn, a kiss, a touch, those lost hours were his escape from what had happened when he turned twelve years of age and couldn't defend his friend Shannon from Buchanan riders. Couldn't fight them off, protect her virtue, protect her *life*.

At twelve he understood the loss. A few years later he understood that ale and women were ways of forgetting that loss and he used both with a vengeance.

But his reaction to this woman, how they became entangled, her scent, the way her soft breasts gave against him with a hitch in her breath—that wasn't anything he'd experienced before.

He was half mesmerised, half angry at it. 'What game do you play?'

'I didn't do anything.' She wiped her hands down her legs. Nervous or because her touching him was distasteful? He didn't like it, didn't want her wiping away what had happened between them. What had happened?

He'd never been held and not held before,

never been touched the way she touched him. And it wasn't anything he could explain.

She stood strong, didn't flee and yet everything about her shouted she was embarrassed, humiliated...and aroused.

She crossed her arms, which did nothing to cover her chest and everything to do with accentuating the curve of her hips, the indentation of her waist. He needed his hands free of these ropes!

His time with Shannon had been nothing but friendship with the promise of more. Since her death, guilt was his constant companion. He and Shannon had been lifelong childhood friends, hand holding, her talking of kissing him some day, but her death made any relationship afterwards not as carefree.

No, that wasn't true, they were entirely carefree. He didn't care. When he'd found sex could be a distraction from the way he was, he used it. After Dunbar, and knowing his brother Bram's mistrust of him, of not telling him why the clan didn't go to the war, he had more need for distraction.

His very nature was impulsive, and he seized every challenge or fight around him. More nights spent brawling and waking up with a black eye and three women in his bed, none of whom he could name. The more it irritated his family, irritated his other brother Caird, the more he did it.

They didn't trust him, thought him irresponsible and so that was what he became. Sex was an amusement, a distraction from what was always taken from him: innocence, trust, loyalty.

That time he could have had with Shannon… That innocent handholding, that first kiss with the promise of more…he'd never felt that. Never.

Until this woman's body got tangled up against his and stuck. Rationally he knew it was as accident. Logically, he knew it meant nothing. He could even brush away the instant tightening and hardening of his body because she was a woman and was rubbing back and forth, pressing side to side and…

He exhaled roughly, pulled himself in, but it was no use. His body was drawn tight, and it had nothing to do with an accident and everything to do with the *way* she had touched him.

He was hard because her body felt right in a way he couldn't say, his balls drew up swift and tight because of her breaths of startled surprise. He was this close, this fast because her hand had acted purely on instinct and she didn't know what to do about any of it.

How depraved did that make him? No, not depraved. He hadn't acted like a man against a woman. He'd reacted because he had never felt touched that way. Not once, not ever. Because everything she did was an innocent promise of *more*.

Not realising his body was even hungry or thirsty for it, he revelled in that promise like a starving man. It was hunger, not depravity, making him surge forward before forgetting he couldn't yank her against him. He was thirsty and she was the only source to quench it. And then her words sank in. Not doing anything? She did…everything.

'What is your name?' he begged. He'd plead if he had to.

'Andreona.' She glanced in the other room, but he couldn't see anything and apparently neither could she.

Andreona. The exotic name fit her. 'What do you mean to do with us?'

'Nothing. When the rain stops, we'll go.'

'Go where? To your family?' At her startled gaze he added, 'You said blood is thicker than loyalty, isn't that what you meant? If your family is important, then it's nothing for me to guess that's where you're taking us.'

She scowled again. 'We'll be taking you to my father. He'll determine your innocence or not.'

No worries, not truly—once it was night, once he could talk to Finlay, they'd escape and leave this place. Yes, his hands were tied, but his feet were already loose. It wouldn't take much to simply escape even if Finlay was hurt.

These women had simply taken them by surprise. This woman had distracted him with her treasures and the flutter of her heart against his. The rain was heavy and he was exhausted from the years of carrying the burden, that was all.

It didn't matter what she wanted to do with him, he had his mission to fulfil. It didn't matter that she wasn't looking him in the eye or that he wanted to stare at her a bit longer.

He wanted…something more.

For distraction, for curiosity, he asked, 'And your father is?'

'Gorka of Ipuscoa.'

Malcolm couldn't help it, couldn't do anything to stop it: he laughed.

Chapter Six

'This, out of all your schemes, wasn't the brightest,' Finlay whispered. His voice so low it was barely audible. If they hadn't been tied almost together and strapped down to the back of the cart where their ears were practically kissing, Malcolm wouldn't have heard him.

The leather cover over the top of the flat cart provided some privacy for conversation, but it wouldn't do for anyone to overhear them.

The disadvantage was they couldn't see where they were going. At least the trip was meant to be short. A day's ride, if Uracca had told them the truth.

'The scheme was flawless, my execution of it may leave something to be desired.'

Finlay snorted. 'What isn't desired is the surface they have pinned us to. What is absolutely foolish is the execution of this. How could you have thought this sound?'

That admission pained Malcolm. Not that he was foolish, but Finlay had let slip he was in pain. Malcolm's own back ached with the bumps in the road and the hard wooden surface he was strapped to. Finlay's ribs were bruised or worse—it had to be agony.

Uracca and Andreona walked the two horses in front and they didn't check on their well-being. Just as well—with Finlay hurting, he didn't know how he'd react.

After he'd laughed yesterday, Andreona had looked mutinous. The other woman, Uracca, had come through the tunnel behind her and, with some spewed words, Andreona had disappeared for the day.

Uracca stared at him as if he had done something startling before she ordered him in the same room as Finlay, who was propped up with blankets. The net was piled in the corner. No other guards, simply an open room with no door.

Apparently, the ropes around their wrists were meant to keep them trapped. That level of security was laughable. With their daggers still in their boots, they stayed because Malcolm intended to stay. Because they intended to take them to Gorka, but also…he wasn't certain Finlay could make an escape.

'How are you feeling today?'

'About the same,' Finlay answered, which meant he was worse. 'It's my own fault,' he said.

'How can a net falling on you be your fault?'

'I didn't let go of the reins, the spooked horse bolted as I should have and the rope hit me at an odd angle. Would have been fine, but I broke myself out and hit the dirt too hard.' Finlay laughed. 'Years of this danger, but there's always something new out there to keep matters interesting.'

This wasn't interesting. He was a fool. He was filled with regret because Finlay wouldn't be here if not for him, but also ire because his friend wouldn't be harmed but for these women who'd set up the nets. Yet try as he might, he couldn't hate them and it appeared that Finlay didn't blame them either. He could be blamed for this trip, however.

He should have planned more, talked to Finlay further. Without any doubt, and as Finlay had demanded in the late hours, he should have simply broken free and waited for an opportunity to release his friend.

But he hadn't done that. He hadn't been doing anything this morning except watching one particular woman who was more than capable of cinching his hands and ignoring him.

If he hadn't had the training he had, or the years of fighting and spying, or if he were simply a traveller, everything Andreona and Uracca, who travelled with them, had done would have kept him secured with no way out. But he had seen several ways, least of all simply overcoming any of them, to break free.

Instead, he watched this woman who wore simple clothes go about doing her simple tasks, finding every task she did, every swing of her arms as she walked away from the cart, utterly fascinating.

She might have ignored him, but he didn't ignore her. There should have been nothing about her that caught his eye. No curve of the hips, no tight bodice encasing voluptuous breasts. No pout of her plush lips or a lowering of her lids as she cast a side glance his way. Nothing overt, nothing he had counted on his entire adult life as a sign from a woman that she wanted him.

But the moment she'd said her father was Gorka, the very man he and Finlay were meant to find... It was Fate. So, yes, he was fascinated by her, but it didn't mean he didn't have a plan.

'What's truly interesting is when we have to relieve ourselves.' Finlay said.

'Truth,' Malcolm said. 'I'm grateful it was the one with the child who took care of matters yesterday and the nicer one today.'

'Uracca.' Finlay smirked. 'Not the one who is avoiding you.'

She was especially avoiding him since he'd

begun his one-sided conversation on not arriving at her father's pinned to a cart.

It wasn't ideal, but it shouldn't matter. That could be negotiated or sorted later. It also didn't matter Andreona thought if he was innocent, her father would set them free.

Either he'd been hit in the head when they fought, or this woman was naive. But if she was his daughter, if this was an outpost for Gorka's territory, then shouldn't she be in a better position to know what her father was like? His information came from rumours.

His actions were reckless, but if fortune stayed with them, there was a chance this whole nightmare could be over without fighting their way into Gorka's keep.

'What were the chances she'd be the daughter of the very man whom we need to steal the dagger from? The way she talked of Gorka it was obvious they shared a bond.'

'But tied like this?'

Tied and causing Finlay more pain, no doubt. He was reckless, foolish. He'd risked both their lives simply because he wanted it over with.

'I apologise. I meant no offen—' Finlay started to say.

'It is I who should apologise,' Malcolm interrupted and, at Finlay's sudden silence, he wondered if he'd ever apologised for anything before.

Most likely not since it didn't feel comfortable now. 'What if we don't think of our…vulnerabilities and simply revel in it being nice for someone else to be carrying us on our adventure?'

Finlay chuckled.

Their talk was light, but the weight of the dagger and obtaining it was getting heavier the closer they got.

He might jest with Finlay, but the importance of what they did was never far from his mind. The Jewell of Kings was on Colquhoun land and now, soon, he'd obtain the dagger that had concealed it for years. Those two items represented a legend. Those together—with a few scraps of parchment and the scrollwork on the dagger— when interpreted, led to a treasure.

And that, right there, was the heart of the Legend. The true story. Not some tale like Excalibur about honour or valour, but great wealth. Of course an ugly gem could hold the heart of Scotland, the power over any country, if the damn thing held a king's ransom in gold and gems. Or whatever else would be there once they discovered where it went.

Yet another secret; yet another tale.

And he and Finlay were the ones to make it finally come true. Because he hadn't been trusted by his brothers with the truth of Dunbar or the Jewell until too late, they gave him an apology, not with words, but an action, giving him the sole responsibility of bringing the missing dagger back to the clan.

This was an apology he resented because it had proven near insurmountable until now. All of his family had a hand in retrieving the Jewell of Kings and its secrets. He was no exception and he couldn't fail.

It was his eldest brother, Bram, who was first involved. Several years before, Bram received King John Balliol's message to wait for a 'parcel' that never arrived. Then Caird, his second-eldest brother, fell in love with Mairead Buchanan, who accidentally stole that package, which was the Jewell of Kings and the dagger.

But Caird, for sound reasons, had separated the Jewell and the dagger. Little did he know that when he'd done so, the dagger with the hollowed handle had already been switched in an earlier battle.

It was Malcolm who had spied the fake. The gems weren't the same, the scrollwork different enough to be noticeable. Depositing the Jewell of Kings on Colquhoun land, Malcolm and Finlay set out to find the true dagger. In the years since, and with secret messages sealed with a half-thistle being passed from Clans Colquhoun to Fergusson to Warstone and Buchanan, it had led them here, tied to a cart.

'I did you wrong,' Malcolm said.

'Are you apologising twice in one day?' Finlay said. 'I'm not dying.'

The relief he felt was foolish, but it was there none the less. He'd never wanted Finlay to go with him, had wanted to do this mission on his own, to prove to his brothers he was worthy of truth and deeds. To return the dagger and then be done with the lot of them.

However, Finlay had insisted, demanded and, no matter what Malcolm said or did, Finlay was there. Now, after all this time, he was almost glad of it. Almost.

'You may not be dying, but you're hurt,' Malcolm said. 'And you wouldn't be if you had stayed in Scotland.'

'Who is to say that this wasn't what Fate designed for me?' Finlay's gaze went to the two women who were slow enough they were almost visible through some gaps in the cover.

If he hadn't seen Finlay's eyes stray more to Uracca than Andreona, he would have growled a warning. Possessiveness? Jealousy? He'd heard of those emotions, but had never had need of them.

As if Finlay guessed at his sudden tenseness, he chuckled. 'I suspect I know why you didn't. You have been watching her all morning. Will you never tell me what happened in the other room while I was being wrapped up?'

Never. It made no sense to indulge Finlay's curiosity. He was no entertainment.

'If they don't let us out of this cart, I'm one more bump away from pissing myself,' he said instead.

Finlay's eyes widened. 'This cart has a tilt—it's likely to trickle towards me.'

'Trickle? It'll be a river.'

Finlay chuckled low and then let out a groan. He didn't make that sound because his bladder was full.

'You're in worse pain than you told me.'

'Of course I am.'

'Can you ride at all?'

'I thought that was what we were doing,' Finlay said. 'But if you're asking if we could make a quick escape, I'd make a nice distraction for you to get to safety.'

'I am sorry,' Malcolm said, because it needed to be said.

'About me being with you all these years though you told me to not to, or because you didn't listen to me and escape last night?'

'Both.'

'It wouldn't be you without bad decisions and impulses.'

'That's true.'

Finlay chuffed. 'You're getting soft. At least you warned—'

They were slowing. Were they close to their destination? How would he ever know since they were pinned and under a cover?

'What I wouldn't give to see anything!' Malcolm adjusted. 'Here, get the dagger out of my boot. You need to stay here, but I'll be damned if I can't see what enemy approaches.'

Chapter Seven

'Stop! Go no further!'

Andreona jumped and startled the horse pulling the cart. She whipped around to see the cart steady itself, the heavy leather cover hooked over the sides remaining intact. The men inside were staying quiet.

It'd been over a year since she had been this close to her father's keep and Andreona still hated this part of the road. The dips from hills and the trees blocked views of the keep from any travellers…which was the point. But with heavy clouds settled on the ground, it was more difficult to see ahead.

One lone man, brandishing a long dagger, emerged from the treeline. She sidled next to Uracca, who didn't look concerned but merely patted the neck of one of the finer-legged beasts.

'What is the meaning—?'

In the dimming afternoon light, her brother Ximeno registered her presence at the same time she did his. But whereas her concern fled, Ximeno's eyes widened with a frantic worry.

'It's only me, Andreona,' she said as way of comfort. 'I come bearing gifts.'

Out of her two half-brothers, Ander and Ximeno, Ximeno was the better brother. Since her father wanted nothing to do with her, Ximeno was the one she pleaded to for funds and help, and he'd gone to her father and gained those funds. If she'd gone to Ander, the eldest, she would have been banished without means or something worse.

'What are you doing here?' Ximeno looked to the cart, to the horses behind, released his hold and stepped back. 'What have you done? All of you, turn around now and go back!'

'I tried to stop her,' Uracca said. 'I did what you said…it didn't work.'

Ximeno looked to her friend, a sneer in his expression that made Uracca wince. 'I can see it didn't work, but you let her get this close?'

A pebble of dread expanded in Andreona's chest. Her friend and brother acted as if they'd conversed. 'What's happening here?'

'You're not supposed to be here,' Ximeno retorted. 'She was to keep you safe.'

'Safe?' A scraping sound beside her, but the

cart stayed still, and the men inside the cart remained quiet. She oddly didn't take comfort in that. Not when Uracca was making distress sounds.

'What is he talking about?'

'Andreona, I'm sorry. I—' Uracca's expression sagged, tears welled. Andreona didn't care for the regret, she cared that she was betrayed by the only person she never thought could.

'What did you talk to Ximeno about? What did you agree about behind my back? Why was I not supposed to be here?' Was this why her friend had been increasingly disgruntled on the tower and on what they'd accomplished?

'Yes, we talked,' Ximeno said. 'I gave you that coin to keep you away from here, to—'

'*You* gave me that coin?' she said. 'You told me you went to Father for his approval and he granted workers and coin to accomplish the tower.'

'I have no time for this,' Ximeno scoffed. 'What's this cart doing here? What have you brought to Gorka's house?'

Something was wrong and her friend had been lying to her, but the cart, or more accurately, what was in the cart, mattered. Whatever else could wait for a few more moments.

'It's wealth for our father, coin!' she said. 'It's finally happened, Ximeno. Just like I said it would. To build the tower, to keep an eye on those cliffs we never could before. I even have something better— Oh!'

Ximeno grabbed her arm. 'Why are you and Uracca speaking French?'

Had they been? 'Practising... I was—'

'Don't talk. You weren't to bring anything.' Ximeno's vehemence shook her. 'You weren't to be here at all.'

'You're hurting me!'

'Leave her!' A low rumble of a voice broke through her pain and Ximeno's furious expression. A very male voice in a very low rumble that shouldn't have made any sound at all.

Andreona spun out of Ximeno's hold. Malcolm was straightening away from the cart. No sign of Finlay. Was he still under the leather cover? Didn't matter. 'No, go back!'

Ximeno pulled a dagger, and shoved Uracca behind him. Possibly he reached for her too, but she wasn't having it. She waved her arms like a madwoman. 'Stay in the cart, you'll ruin it all.'

Malcolm approached slowly, deadly. He, too, had a dagger, small, but the way he held it, Andreona knew he could be deadly.

'Step away from them,' Malcolm said.

'This is why you speak French! For this stranger in your cart who has a weapon!' Ximeno spat. 'What did you think to do, bring him inside to murder our father?'

Horror slashed her heart.

Ximeno charged forward. Malcolm sidestepped Ximeno's dagger and elbowed her brother low in his back. Her brother went down, gasping.

'No, wait! Stop,' Andreona said. 'You don't understand.'

Uracca crouched beside Ximeno, but he was already rising, wincing. 'Still speaking French, traitor.'

Malcolm grabbed Ximeno's dagger, held it to his neck and her brother stilled.

Over a year ago, she'd told her brother her dream of building the tower for an outpost to protect her father's territory and gain his approval. Now Ximeno called her a traitor. But who had betrayed whom? Ximeno and Uracca conspired to…what? To discourage her somehow…and Ximeno gave her the coin for the workers, *not* her father? Did her father know of the tower?

'Who is this?' Malcolm said.

'Her brother,' Uracca said.

'Which one?' Malcolm said.

'The second one,' Andreona said. 'How do you know of my family? Who are you?'

Malcolm smirked. 'Now that's a question you should have already asked.'

'Let me up!' Ximeno demanded.

'Not a chance,' Malcolm said. That rumble affected her, but now in a different way. It was decisive. Menacing.

Ximeno glared at Andreona. 'This is your fault. If you'd only listened.'

'I'm not a traitor. I did exactly what I said I'd do.' Unlike Uracca, Ximeno, and who knew who else. 'Even when the workers abandoned us, I increased my work to get it done.'

'She wouldn't listen to any of us, Ximeno,' Uracca said. 'Even when most of the women left, she didn't listen.'

'She's stubborn? That I can believe, but that's not my concern,' Malcolm said. 'If you're the brother and she's the sister, there's something I want you to do for me.'

'There's no time for this,' Ximeno growled. 'I'm keeping watch, but so are two others. You're fortunate I was here and not any other or else you'd be dead or brought inside for entertainment. Return to the tower and I'll get a message to you about this. Or better yet, Uracca will explain it to you, as she should have already done. Whatever scheme you intended today is forfeit. Make the most of it and leave while you can.'

'Are we forgetting who is holding the dagger to your throat?' Malcolm said. 'You're not in charge here.'

Something was terribly wrong. Uracca was

looking at her with pity, Ximeno with derision and frustration.

'I'm not a traitor,' was all Andreona could repeat. 'I'm—'

There was the sound of voices just on the other side of the hill.

Swallowing hard, Ximeno looked to Malcolm. 'Let me up.'

'No,' Malcolm said. 'Your being held hostage has an advantage for me. I need something from you.'

'Whatever it is, I'll get it, just get her behind the trees. I beg you.'

Whatever was in her brother's eyes, Malcolm stepped back. Standing, Ximeno pointed to Uracca. 'Stand behind the cart. I can't explain its presence without someone else being here, but maybe he won't recognise you if you're in the shadows.'

'Who won't recognise her?' Malcolm said.

'Gorka.'

Andreona's heart soared. She had weaponry and horses and these men weren't innocent. Not with the way Malcolm held the dagger to her brother's throat.

'I can make this all right, Brother,' she said. 'I've brought him value he'll appreciate. Gorka will know it's from me and we'll end the banishment.'

'Banishment? You innocent fool,' Ximeno cursed. 'You still believe? This strange man who held a knife to my throat wasn't revenge?'

'I've told her nothing, Ximeno,' Uracca said.

'Then you've harmed her terribly,' he said.

Uracca paled.

Andreona stepped forward. 'Ximeno, let me talk to him in Basque. I'll explain everything.'

Ximeno shoved her towards Malcolm, who grabbed her shoulders. 'I don't know what you want, but you won't get it unless you protect her now!'

Pivoting, Ximeno ran towards the hill where three figures were cresting.

Her father was just there, she could run to him, but Malcolm was quicker. One hand snaked around her shoulders and pressed her against him, the other slammed on her mouth to silence her.

When he dragged her, she fought him. None of her words were audible, but Uracca's were.

'Protect her well since I did not.'

Chapter Eight

~~~~~~~~~~~~~~~

'**W**hat do we have here, my son?' Gorka's voice boomed across the road.

At her father's warning tone, Andreona stopped struggling against Malcolm. He braced against her before he eased his arm across her collarbone and released his hand against her mouth. He dropped his head, a wayward curl brushing against her cheek, his breath brushing the side of her neck. She waited for his warning words, but he said nothing. Another breath from him, while hers seemed to stop. His lips were close to the shell of her ear causing goose pimples to rise, more so when he took his free hand and rested it on her hip.

Her father barked out an order to the two men guarding him and they stopped walking, while Gorka came closer. A strange tension slithered across from her father to Ximeno, to the two men behind him with their hands hovering over daggers…to Uracca who stood so still, she truly was one of shadows.

Andreona felt this tension wrap around her ankles and slither upwards, but Malcolm secured her back against his front and her front she braced against a large tree. She felt warmth and protection. She needed it.

It'd been over a year since she last seen her father from afar. Gorka had changed somewhat. She remembered him as larger than life, a worthy foe for his enemies. But not any longer. Wealth, privilege and the luxurious life he had fought for had taken its toll on him. Large, rotund, heavy jowls and a red complexion. Too much food, too much wine and he limped, which meant those habits had eaten at his body.

The disloyal thoughts surprised her, but were quickly extinguished as Gorka's gaze swept from his son to the cart and he suddenly stopped. He'd spied Uracca and recognised her. Andreona wanted to halt all of this. Despite Uracca talking to Ximeno of matters she didn't know, and of Ximeno's anger at her presence, Andreona wanted to wrap everyone up and take them away.

'Sir,' Uracca said.

Gorka rounded on Ximeno. 'What is she doing here?'

'I brought gifts,' Uracca called out.

Andreona's heart stuttered. Had Uracca and Ximeno played her for the fool? Told her to hide so they could get praise for the gifts? As if he knew her thoughts, Malcolm's hand tightened on her shoulder. He shouldn't worry. She'd stay quiet and still to find the truth of whether she was betrayed.

'Addressing him directly?' Ximeno said coldly. 'You have been banished for too long and have lost your way.'

'I don't know what you mean,' Gorka replied, his eyes only on his son. 'I see and hear nothing but you. Except you're speaking French. Explain yourself.'

'If there are…calculated words we need share,' Ximeno said slowly, carefully, 'French is the better language. After all, that one doesn't know it as well and your guards can't know it at all.'

Gorka chuckled. 'Clever—by all means we'll speak this language I hate because I hate her more. What is happening here?'

'I am on watch and heard her approach.' Ximeno clasped his hands behind his back.

'She's alone?'

Ximeno nodded her way. 'Except for three horses and a simple cart. I did a quick sweep and saw no one else.'

'I'm alone,' Uracca said though both men ignored her. 'These horses and weapons are yours.'

Gorka straightened, opening his mouth as if to address her, but didn't. 'Weapons.'

'A few gifts for you,' Ximeno said.

Uracca looked towards the forest where they hid. Could they be seen? Andreona shook her head, trying to tell Uracca to be quiet, wanting to tell her to run. Moments before she was begging to present her case to Gorka, but something was terribly wrong.

Gorka looked at the two horses tied to the cart, and the thick-legged one who pulled it. 'Useless horses. Useless offspring. At least the other one is gone, yes? I never liked this one who has brought me gifts, but the other one has been a grain of sand too long in my shoe.'

'The other one is gone,' Ximeno said. 'Just as you ordered.'

'Banishment wasn't enough for her, killing was the best way. I don't know why I tolerated her life as long as I did. Born of a French whore, living under my roof, good coin wasted on clothing and food all because she was half mine? Foolish waste. Yes, I was wise that day when I ordered you to kill her.'

Ximeno shifted his feet, his hands behind his back. 'She was only half my sister, hardly a loss.'

'Rightly so.' Gorka clapped.

'She would have only been a weakness of yours since she came of age and could no longer be hidden or ignored,' Ximeno continued. 'Best she is gone beyond all who could reach her.'

Gorka smacked his lips. 'I thought her beauty might be an asset, but the way the lords united against outsiders, her living risked too much.' Gorka approached the new horses, slapped one on the neck and it skittered. 'Useless horseflesh, but we may get some coin for it. And yet...how did she come by it and why bring a cart? What's inside?'

'A sword!' Uracca swallowed several times, her body swaying. 'Too heavy for me to carry.'

'She's talking to us again. I banished her, but maybe I should do more this time.' Gorka flitted his fat fingers. 'Kill her, too.'

'Of course.' Ximeno pulled his dagger.

Andreona couldn't make a sound if she tried. Malcolm's arm held her hard, his grip at her hip sank in. But it wasn't Malcolm who prevented her from rushing forward, it was her shaking.

'Except...' Ximeno said, 'Ander wanted this one. If he finds I killed her, he wouldn't appreciate it.'

'Your brother would get over it.'

Ximeno sheathed his dagger. 'He is the eldest and deserves my respect since he will get my fealty.'

'Are you weak as well? Should I order my

guards to do it? I feel like it since you talk of my death so easily.'

A pause. Ximeno laughed. It was forced and ugly, but he was making an effort. Gorka looked surprised, but then he chuckled as well.

'Very well then,' Gorka said, still laughing. 'Bring her along with the cart to the keep, inspect my gifts and ensure there's no poison spread on them before they're given to me…then banish her again. Gifts or not, she reminds me too much of the other one.'

Gorka pivoted, his corpulent body swaying as he returned to the guards.

Ximeno looked to them in the trees. Would he call out now? Gorka was still too close and Andreona wasn't certain she could move after hearing Gorka's words.

Malcolm didn't move either as Ximeno grabbed the horse's reins and motioned to Uracca to follow behind her father and the guards.

Andreona didn't know where to look. At Ximeno, who purposefully didn't look her way, or to Uracca, who couldn't keep her eyes from looking back despite the fact it might make Gorka suspicious. She didn't know what to make of her brother or her friend—were they trying protect her or themselves?

Uracca knew her father had ordered her killed. Why hadn't she said anything? Why would Xi-

meno have given her coin, but then have thought
she wouldn't use it for the purposes she said she
would? Why didn't he tell her he was ordered to
kill her and instruct her to run instead?

This went beyond betrayal or talking behind
her back. This wasn't even about usurping power
and taking something from her. They both knew
her father wanted her dead and didn't tell her.

Her body felt strangely not her own, her legs
heavy. If she had been forced to describe it, it
felt as though she was falling. As if someone had
kicked her off a cliff and she was spiralling into
the deepest, darkest cavern where there was no
sound, no light, nothing but a heavy ache.

Through eyes that only could see pinpoints of
light and shapes, she looked to her father whose
frame was large, but somehow frail with age and
cruelty. If possible, his walk looked poisonous.
As if his cruelty shaped his body and everything
about him.

Had he always been this way? She wondered
if she'd imagined him to have ever been great.
Her eyes swung to the rattling cart and to Uracca
walking beside it. Uracca, who'd warned her over
and over again and she hadn't listened. The family to whom she'd dedicated hours of gruelling
hard work, and rallied others around, wanted her
dead.

She was falling, she didn't know whether she'd

ever hit the bottom or if there was one. Maybe her life would be this falling into darkness forever.

Malcolm shook along with the minute tremors racking Andreona. But when he turned her away from the tree hiding them to see tears along her cheeks…his heart, which he'd thought was long lost, ripped. The betrayal on her face was something Malcolm had never seen before.

Oh, he could say his family didn't trust him and controlled him for their own agendas. But they'd never wanted him dead. And each mistrust they gave him was one blow after another until it built to this feeling of betrayal he could never shake. One he wanted over with, as much as he wanted the search of the hollowed dagger over with.

Andreona's family, her own father, had ordered her dead and that merciless blow came all at once. She shook against him, but he was surprised she could stand at all.

What did she do to deserve such betrayal? For if he understood completely, her brother knew of Gorka's order to kill Andreona. This wasn't a familial slight bit by bit, but by one cruel rendering.

Did she deserve such a betrayal? He'd seen her loyalty to her friends, he knew her loyalty to the family, for he was her gift to them. And he'd felt her stumble against him when her father declared himself pleased at her death.

Two entirely unwanted and opposite emotions swept through Malcolm at this realisation. One was the need to protect her from this pain, the other was protection, preservation, for himself.

He could not act on both. He had allowed himself to be captured, believing Andreona was an acknowledged daughter of Gorka. Her grand talk of her father, her loyalty and the risks she took—she'd acted as if they held some strong bond.

Yet she was talked of as if she were always hated. Everything in him wanted to leap around the tree and gut the man across his fleshy folds. Simultaneously, to save his and Finlay's necks, to achieve the dagger, he needed to betray her as well. Use her. Because no matter what, that dagger was still inside Gorka's keep and that was where he needed to be.

'My father…thinks I'm dead,' Andreona whispered. Her voice was faint and broken. 'Because he ordered me killed.'

She needed to separate herself from that family as soon as possible, and that would begin by her stopping referencing that man as her father. Malcolm cupped her face. 'Gorka ordered you killed. *Gorka.*'

'My father wanted me dead,' she repeated,

stepping back, but she stumbled into the tree. 'He—Uracca's not safe.'

'Finlay isn't safe,' he reminded her. He wanted to grab her back, to touch that soft skin and stop her trembling.

She gasped. 'What have I done?'

This was his fault! Her ways of trapping him hadn't been what had kept him tied up as a gift and he'd told Finlay, because of his injuries, to stay in the cart, to stay hidden. Now his clansman was being led into the keep without a means to protect himself!

A crunching of leaves and Malcolm yanked Andreona behind him, her back to a tree, him in front. It was poor protection, but it was the last one he had. She eased around him when they saw it was Ximeno.

'They're on their way. I came back. Run now, don't come back here, it isn't safe.'

'Has it ever been?' Malcolm snarled. 'What kind of mess have you made here?'

'Who the hell are you?'

'I'm the one who protected your sister as you should have done.'

'What of Uracca?' Andreona said.

Ximeno gave a warning glare to Malcolm, which he ignored. Armed with Gorka's men at his disposal and this brother was still no threat.

'I'll find a way to get her back before she's

harmed. You heard Gorka, he wants her banished again, but it may take some time. Wait at the tower.' He looked resigned. 'He thinks you're dead. You can't show yourself.'

Andreona's body jerked and Malcolm hated this brother who appeared to care, but was too much of a coward to tell her himself. 'No need to repeat. But there's something you should know. There're more than my weapons in that cart. There's a man…a friend. He's injured.'

Cursing, Ximeno looked wildly around as if it were he who wanted to escape. 'I'll get the cart to the blacksmith and we'll keep him there. Do you understand?'

'How can a blacksmith keep him safe?' Malcolm said when Andreona didn't answer. 'And I'm going to want those weapons back.'

A grin slashed Ximeno's face. 'I need payment.'

As expected. 'One of the swords at least. To protect your sister.'

'Swords?' Ximeno looked to Andreona. 'You brought more than a gift to Gorka. You would have made him proud of your thieving had he known—'

'Don't talk of him in front of her,' Malcolm growled. Why was he defending her when he shouldn't care! All he knew was it was wrong and he wouldn't stand for it.

Ximeno stared as if gaining his measure before he bit out, 'To the blacksmith, then, and I'll try to keep Uracca there as well. My sister will know what to do.'

'Will he be safe?' Malcolm said.

'You should have thought of that before you got caught by her in those nets she talked about. Because that's what happened, isn't it?' He shook his head, and laughed low. 'You did it, Andreona. You were supposed to take that coin and run to Spain, build a new life for yourself. Not construct a tower to nothing.'

Malcolm expected Andreona to retort in that resilient way she had. This was a woman whom he'd surprised, but she'd fought, taken him down and was determined to bring them, their horses and weaponry to her father for his favour since she knew she was banished. He might not have known her long, but he knew her strength far outweighed that of this brother of hers.

Ximeno must have been expecting a remark as well because his brows drew in. 'I can't apologise. I warned you and Uracca knew the terms. She told me what was happening. I did what I could to stop it, even encouraging those other women to return to the keep and they did. I thought… If you weren't so stubborn, this could have all been avoided.'

This was Andreona's battle, but Malcolm

wanted to pummel Ximeno until there was nothing left. The fault was entirely his because he'd lied to his sister. He should have told her what her father had ordered. It would have hurt, but it would be over. The sacrifices she must have made to build that tower and now to understand it was for nothing, that they'd thrown obstacles in her way...but she'd prevailed over nothing.

He wanted to shut up this conceited, privileged bastard, who from his clothes to his demeanour made it clear he hadn't suffered like his sister had.

He waited. Still, nothing from the woman whose back remained to him, but whatever was in her expression caused her brother's face to fall. 'You should have listened.'

Malcolm growled.

'You should go,' she whispered, her voice barely perceptible. 'We'll get to the blacksmith's.'

Clearly torn, which only marginally improved him in Malcolm's mind, Ximeno jogged away.

Malcolm didn't force anything, though his first instinct was to charge towards the keep and rescue Finlay. But rescuing Finlay wasn't the point of getting this close to Gorka's keep. They needed that dagger and, even if Finlay were grateful for the rescue, he wouldn't be pleased if they didn't have what they had come for.

And Andreona needed time...years of it. Kind

words, comfort and understanding. The fact he'd known her for hours, but watched her take blow after blow, wasn't any comfort. She probably was angry he'd witnessed any of it since he was her prize for her father. An atonement for mistakes he knew nothing about. If he'd known that, truly understood, he'd would have told her he wasn't anyone's gift, only a burden. A moment in his family's presence would have shown her that. But they didn't have years, or even moments.

'Andreona, you have to listen to me. Can you?'

Her eyes focused on him, but then just as quickly dismissed him. He wanted to beat her brother again, but then she spoke.

'The blacksmith's section is against the wall,' she said. 'Behind him is a little gate with a crawl through so he can have more air, but large enough for supplies. If Ximeno takes Finlay there, we can wait outside while they slip through the gate.'

And just like that they'd be back where they started except one sword short. 'I can't go anywhere. I've got to get into that keep.'

She looked over her shoulder at him. 'What are you talking about?'

'I have a mission. It's why Finlay and I were headed to Gorka's. I need something from inside.'

'What?'

'I can't tell you.'

She turned fully to him. The tears she'd cried were still tracked on her cheeks; her wild tumbling hair lay flat. There was some light to those herring-coloured eyes where before there'd been nothing but devastation. Unfortunately, that light was stubbornness, or perhaps hatred.

'I should have known,' she said. 'You're not innocent, you're as bad as my fa—Gorka.'

The familiar hot flare of his temper flashed inside, but he let it pass. He was angry, but at Gorka and Ximeno, and at the ridiculous circumstances barring him from completing this mission. He knew he should be angry at her, too, for setting up those nets and hurting his friend, for trapping them when they could have merely ridden by that misshapen tower. But part of the folly was his own and so he held it in.

All of it would come out later on more deserving foes. 'Don't compare me to him.'

She didn't back down. 'I can compare you when you don't tell me what you should.'

'You built nets to bring unsuspecting travellers to your father to judge whether they were innocent or not. Interestingly enough, you thought he'd judge them fairly.'

She paled and he cursed himself for his cruelty.

'I'm falling,' she whispered her eyes looking distant.

'What?' he said.

She regained focus, her eyes on fire. 'You...
lied to me!'

'I didn't mean that...those words.'

'I think you did and I deserved it. We need to
get your friend out. I'll...do that for you.'

With her soul wounded, Andreona was offering to help when he'd done nothing to deserve it.
By keeping his secrets, he lied to her.

'I have to get a dagger that was stolen from
me.'

'You're here for some ornament?' Andreona
said.

Malcolm looked over her shoulder and exhaled
roughly. He'd have to give her something, but
what would she believe? 'Not a mere ornament.
It has interesting features. And it's...sentimental.
You may have taken us, but you took us where
we wanted to go.'

Andreona shook her head. 'If you go inside
there, you'll be killed.'

'My only concern was finding a way to get
into the keep.'

She gasped. 'And I just gave it to you.'

He cursed. 'Your brother did.'

'I have no—' she said.

Oh, he'd been there before, wanting to deny
he had a family. 'You have a family and they're

bastards. It doesn't change that I have to get Finlay and that dagger out at the same time.'

Her features were pale, her body shook. From his words? From the fact her father said he'd ordered her death? How did she get the strength to stand there and fight him?

Why was he arguing with her when he could simply force his way, but...she was so strong and he didn't want to hurt her again. He'd do anything not to hurt her again.

'That dagger has meaning for my family and it's...unusual.'

Andreona blinked and Malcolm took in her darting gaze, her slight nervous pulling in on her lower lip. Elation rippled through him. He had to be certain it was the true dagger; it'd been switched before.

'Is it large with some jewels on it?' Andreona said. 'Hollowed handle?'

This was not...believable. 'How do you know it?'

'How many daggers with hollowed handles do you come across? It was brought in to my father by—' She stopped.

'You don't owe them your loyalty.'

'I don't owe you any either!'

Too true. 'I know it was stolen. It's been stolen many times. It's also been replicated. You know something of that.'

'Maybe,' she said.

He wanted to grab her, to demand she answer with all truths, but she was right, she didn't owe him any loyalty. What burned was that she owed him less than her family and they, at least her father, wanted her dead.

'Tell me what it looks like before we go any further. This could all be for naught, this trip a waste because the dagger has been switched again. If so, I could simply find Finlay and leave.'

She clenched her eyes, her body holding together by something he couldn't guess. She was so strong, but he had to insist, had to know.

'The handle is large, the silver blade and handle decorated with scrolls and odd patterns that don't make sense because it's not a picture or a scene, but all so carefully decorated. Then there's two red gems...' She stopped, gauging his reaction. 'It's the right one, isn't it?'

'I was told your father may have it and you've described it perfectly.'

'When no one was around, I held and studied it. It's beautiful and I wanted it for myself because—'

'You wondered what the craftsman built it for,' he answered for her. Those boxes in the tower all carefully placed and protected in a cliffside, held not for their wealth, but because she was curious of the emptiness inside them.

'You know what was in it?' she said.

Relief coursing through him, foolishly he answered her, 'I do know why.' When he realised his mistake, because he could never tell her, because he was now lying to her and this woman didn't need another betrayal, he continued, 'But I need it first before I explain anything.'

Chapter Nine

The knot of anguish and the heavy weight against her limbs altered Andreona's every thought and movement. She knew if she gave in to it, gave in to what she'd heard, it would take over everything. It was Uracca, her brother, her father's words. Too much anguish and there was no way to understand it, not now. Now she was desperate to ignore it, to do something and not think.

And Malcolm wanted to rescue Finlay and retrieve this dagger. She needed to ensure Uracca escaped. She could do that. There didn't need to be trust, or loyalty or betrayal between them... no emotions pounding her from the inside.

She'd do these little tasks, then she'd cry a thousand oceans because her brother and closest friend had lied to her. She'd run like she should have done long ago because her father wanted her dead.

She didn't know this man and hadn't asked. She knew he was lying that the dagger was sentimental, or it was his, but should she care?

The only certainty she knew was that it wasn't theirs. It had come into her father's possession when she'd been allowed within the keep's gates. One of Gorka's mercenaries who was hired out to some Englishmen. A foolish man, who thought a Basque mercenary was Spanish, when, in fact, he was one of Gorka's spies, and had switched the dagger.

Of course she'd noticed the dagger. The intricate scrollwork was enough to dazzle, but the hollowed handle intrigued her more. There was only one reason for that: secrets. But then she was banished as were other women and she let the dagger with its mystery free.

Now it was back.

As for Malcolm, she didn't know who he was, hadn't cared to ask because he was supposed to be a means to an end. A gift to her father to end her banishment. Now she was supposed to be dead and her friend, her brother, knew of it. There wasn't any of them she trusted. That was fine, she didn't need trust. She merely needed to end this.

'Where are you going?' Malcolm said from behind her, but was soon in front of her, stopping her from leaving the little copse of trees.

She waved towards the keep. 'I'm getting your dagger.'

'You're getting it?'

'Isn't that what we agreed to?'

'No, you can't go in there.'

She pointed to herself. 'It's my home...*was* my home. I know where the dagger is, you don't.'

He blocked her again when she tried to go around him.

'Wait!'

She spun on him. 'No, every delay means leaving Uracca or Finlay in danger.'

'You're not going in there.'

'Like hell I'm not.'

He stopped and so did she. 'What are you expecting of me, wanting of me? You tell me you need a dagger, so I'll get the dagger and you can tell me the story of why it's hollowed, then be on your way. What is there to argue about?'

If they went on like this, they truly would argue. Too many emotions, ones she was barely holding back, would be involved.

'You are stubborn and—' He looked away and huffed.

And what? Andreona was no longer falling or clutching at branches as she fell into the dark cavern that her father, brother, that Uracca had pushed her into by their betrayal. Her feet felt firm on some precarious ledge. Why? Because this man, whom she didn't know just days ago, didn't truly know now, needed a dagger from her father's keep and she intended to get it for him.

There was no reason she should other than it was something to do to keep the pain away a bit longer when she could think about it slowly. Like thorns she could pull out one by one.

So, protecting Finlay, grabbing this dagger, was simple.

'Why would you do this?' Malcolm said.

'Why not? I'm certain you have reasons to want it, none of which you mean to give me. So I won't ask because I'm tired of being lied to.'

'I don't want to lie to you.'

'But you have, haven't you?' she said. When he went quiet, she almost appreciated it, because that was a truth.

'I can't, shouldn't, tell you everything about the dagger, or why we're here,' he said.

'I'm certain you can appreciate how my not being told about matters grates?' she said.

He gave a curt nod.

She believed him and not because he'd heard every painful word from her brother and father, but because of those churning green eyes of his. Had he felt what she did now?

The pain. She desperately wanted to stop clutching at the branches. Once she did these two deeds, she'd let go, fall down the cavern.

She almost didn't care what happened to her. Afterwards, she could break apart at the bottom.

She turned, but he grabbed her wrist. 'If you're caught, you'll be killed.'

'Don't talk, don't touch me!' She batted his hand away. 'If *you're* caught, you'll be killed.'

'If you're caught, you're not only dead, so is Uracca and Ximeno who lied.'

'You bastard,' she said.

It was dark now, she shouldn't see all of his features, but he almost looked as though he hated what he said. Too late.

'We both get to the blacksmith,' she said, her voice firm. 'I'll tell you where to go, I'll wait for you to return, then we leave immediately. No more arguments.'

When he grinned, she should have been warned, but she wasn't. He grabbed her hand, pulled her towards him and wrapped his arms around her small frame. He was so large, so monumentally there she felt tiny against him. There was warmth from his body, but a tenderness to his touch. Relaxed arms, his hands linked behind her. It was a hold she could easily break away from, but didn't want to. Not when he pulled her in a little more, leaned into her frame as if he was resolved and relieved at what they'd agreed to.

'Thank you, Andreona,' he whispered, his

words rumbling though they weren't in that language of his.

She was stunned, not by his cheek rubbing against the top of her head, though she somehow felt that movement everywhere. Not by his hold, or his words, but by her reaction to his arms around her. Like this there wasn't a precarious ledge or falling into a cavern, but safety, warmth, sincerity. Something she only recognised because, with certainty, she'd never had them before.

Following Andreona, Malcolm almost crawled through the small door cut into the wood fence. This was Gorka's keep? If this was his gate, where was a tower or the guards? There was a simple latch, but no lock. Anyone could simply breach this so-called fortress. If he and Finlay hadn't been caught, if Finlay wasn't hurt, they would have had the dagger and been done with all of this already. Straightening, he wondered at the possibility. It would have been easy and he wouldn't have met Andreona.

A gasp to his left and Andreona grabbed his hands and yanked him to the side. They were in shadows and he couldn't see a thing, but she knew where she was going. 'What were you thinking, standing like that? You would have ruined everything. Just stay low and follow me.'

She pushed on something, perhaps a door, but it was heavy. Inside was a small room lit by a single candle. Then as he moved further into the room, he saw Uracca standing in a corner, her face mottled from tears and Finlay laying on a pallet. His friend was hurt…again.

'Shut the door,' she ordered. He did, but then he was by Finlay's side.

'Jesu,' he cursed when he saw his friend more battered than before. 'You were laying in a cart, now a pallet. What happened?'

'Stop hovering over me,' Finlay asked.

'If you stop gasping, I would. Can you even breathe? No, don't reply to that, just save your breath,' Malcolm said.

Finlay gave a weak smile.

'How much can you move?' Malcolm said, realising he was being contradictory, not strong like Andreona who was staring at him floundering about.

'The blacksmith tore the leather cover down on top of me. The iron hooks didn't care if I was cart or man. Since they hit me in the chest, how do you think I'm doing?'

'You need to get them wrapped. We need to get you wrapped. They could be broken.'

'They feel like it.'

'If your ribs are broken—' Malcolm said.

'I won't make it,' Finlay said. Not enough light

in this storage room, but even so, he could see the pallor of his skin, the fact he fought for breath. 'It's not your fault.'

'Not my fault!' Malcolm seethed. 'This entire journey is my fault.'

'You told me to…stay away. I didn't.'

'I should have punched you unconscious and left immediately before you woke.'

Andreona made some sound and he looked to her. But though she sounded distressed, her eyes held something like a curious surprise. What that meant he didn't know and, again, there was no time to wonder.

'Now I know you better—' Finlay clenched his eyes '—I'm surprised you didn't knock me out.'

Yanking his tunic over his head, Malcolm ripped the fabric, which failed to give very easily. He grabbed the knife in his boot and made quick work of it.

'What are you doing!' Andreona said.

'I'm saving my friend,' he answered.

'How are you to get the dagger if you have no clothes?' she said.

'I don't intend to get caught, so my clothing doesn't matter, only my hands and eyes.'

'Dagger?' Finlay said. 'You told her?'

'She's going to help us get it. You can't yell at me any more than I'm shouting at myself.'

'Thanks for sparing me...the trouble.'

When the strips were the best he could make them, Malcolm asked, 'Ready?'

'As much as I can be,' Finlay answered.

Hooking his arms under Finlay's arm, he pulled his friend to standing. He moved his friend as little as he could, but knew that it hurt like hell. 'Tomorrow I'll make it up to you.'

'How will you do that?'

'I'll sort out a way.' Malcolm tied one knot and began on the other wrapping.

'I still think that was foolish,' Andreona said.

He looked over his shoulder. 'Tell me how to get to the dagger.'

'How much does she know?' Finlay said. 'I wasn't gone that long.'

'Stop talking and breathe,' Malcolm said. 'It will be fine.'

'I need to find my brother first,' Andreona said.

'He said he'd fetch a new cart and he'd be right back,' Uracca said. 'We're supposed to leave.'

'How long ago was that?' Andreona said.

When there was a telling silence, Malcolm wanted to throw something across the room. Ximeno had proven he wasn't loyal and they waited there like prey.

'We get him out of here through that door,' Malcolm said. 'I don't care if there's a cart or not.'

'And leave the dagger behind?' Finlay said.

'I'll come back in and get it.' Malcolm wasn't intimidated by Finlay's frown. If Malcolm had been injured, Finlay would be doing the same thing.

'What is this dagger?' Uracca said. 'We're not to do anything except leave.'

'It's better you don't know,' Malcolm said. 'How did you escape unscathed?'

'Gorka doesn't want me, he wanted the cart and the horses,' Uracca said.

'He shoved and hit her first, until she hit the ground,' Finlay said.

Uracca gasped. 'You didn't need to tell them that!'

'You limp now, you think they wouldn't notice?' Finlay said. 'Or the fact I couldn't protect you from it?'

'I twisted my ankle was all,' Uracca said.

At the mention of her father, Malcolm watched Andreona. The determined look was still there in her eyes. Good. He worried when bleakness seemed to overtake her. When he'd told her of the dagger, she'd drawn some strength to fight him on it. Unwise to mention the dagger, but he was learning he'd break rules to ensure she didn't give that abusive man any more thoughts. He'd wonder about the reasons for that later.

'Let's not speak of him,' Malcolm said. 'Where is the dagger?'

'The last I knew it was adjacent to the coin room,' Andreona said.

'So we get it and go to Hugh and Alice's,' Finlay said.

He'd have to tell Finlay later what Andreona knew, which wasn't much, and now she knew of Hugh and Alice. 'We're not going there. When we have the dagger, speed will be our course.'

Finlay didn't blink. 'I gave you leave when we didn't stop at their home on the way here. I'm the one who retrieved that message from Hugh reporting the dagger was likely in Gorka's hands. I, too, was eager to be here.'

'This is not your fault,' Malcolm said.

'I know it's not.' Finlay's brows drew in. 'Can you, for once, stop being rash and think this through? We must stop through there.'

For three years he'd done nothing but think. He switched to Gaelic. 'I'll be dead before I stop by there. You know what that means. I stop there, a Half-Thistle Seal message goes to my clan to report the disaster of us getting caught and you injured. I'll never hear the end of it.'

'They're going to find out anyway,' Finlay said in French.

Stubborn man. He'd put it off as long as he could.

'Are we done? I'm not standing around here any longer,' Andreona said. 'And no more talking that language around me. I've had enough of that.'

Malcolm scowled. How he wished he could tell her all he knew, or that he understood what it meant when family and friends plotted behind your back. But she knew of Hugh and Alice—he didn't want her knowing of the secret messages sealed with the Half-Thistle Seal that allowed the plots to continue.

Narrowing her eyes, Andreona pointed at him. 'I can't tell you where the dagger is because it might not be near the coin room anymore, so then you wouldn't know where else to go and you have no clothing.'

One lone candle, one small secure room. Malcolm didn't know the layout of this keep, but Andreona did. It was foolish to think he could go, but he didn't like the idea of her risking herself and Uracca appeared not to know of it at all.

If this was all about the retrieving the dagger, Malcolm would send her out. What did he owe her? She was the one who'd trapped them and injured his friend.

Yet…he had absorbed her trembles as she heard her father wanting her dead, and her eyes had lit up when she told him of her fascination with boxes.

Between those nets and now, he didn't want Andreona to make sacrifices as he had done. But what choice did he have?

Chapter Ten

Andreona didn't like Malcolm's expression. Was he going to deny her?

'This is—'

The door burst open and Ximeno stepped in. 'Hurry, gather him up, there's a cart with provisions outside the gate.'

Andreona stared at her brother, whom she wasn't certain she knew anymore.

'Why are you all standing around?' Ximeno cursed. 'And where is your tunic?'

'Around me,' Finlay said.

Ximeno's eyes grew wide. 'You look worse than before—can you even crawl through the gate?'

'I can crawl.'

'We'll get him through,' Uracca said.

'Good,' Ximeno said. 'I've preoccupied the guards, but I can't hold them indefinitely from their duties and, even if I did, everything would be ruined.'

Andreona had had enough of secrets. 'What's everything and why would it be ruined? Are these more hidden secrets you were to tell me?'

Ximeno looked at her, but didn't hold her gaze. 'This comes from me, not Gorka, and it's better you don't know.'

She'd heard that before. Crossing her arms, she said, 'I think I need to know.'

Ximeno still wouldn't look at her. 'What we need to do is get you out of here.'

They couldn't stay here forever without getting caught. Trapped in here with no weapons, they wouldn't survive. But... Why would Ximeno care to save her after he'd lied to her?

Just a few tasks, then she could think of all the heartbreak, just retrieve the dagger and get Finlay and Uracca out. But Ximeno was here and she had to know.

'Why did you give me coin, but not tell me?' she said.

'To save you!' he said. 'Maybe I should have told you and not Uracca.'

'Maybe?'

'If I spent any time talking to you, explaining, answering questions...it would have been suspicious. I'm to hate you as our father does.'

'Careful,' Malcolm called out.

Andreona didn't turn to Malcolm and his word of caution made little sense. What was he warning Ximeno of? But Ximeno's words...

Why had he been saving her? Because that's what he had done: given her coin, workers, didn't inform Gorka she lived. She wished, fervently, he hadn't done it so wrongly.

All her life, she'd wished to be a true and worthy sister to him. Ander frightened her, but Ximeno, with his unkempt dark wavy hair, and blue-green eyes, was someone she wanted to laugh with. His manners were brusque; clearly he was agitated about their presence. In her thoughts she'd revered him, now she realised he was as flawed as anyone else.

'Tell me something,' Andreona said. 'Could I have done anything different?'

Ximeno looked over her shoulder. 'No, now let's go.'

Andreona knew Ximeno spoke a mixture of French and Basque, and perhaps that was the reason Malcolm and Finlay just stared. For her, it wasn't the words, it was the meaning. He'd sided with Gorka. He now acted as if he were there to help them.

'It was all a ruse, wasn't it?' Uracca said. 'All this time you've been playing a game against Gorka.'

'Not again,' Finlay groaned.

'Don't say another word when someone could overhear. There is no time to discuss this now,' Ximeno said. 'It's rumoured Ander is on his way home.'

'Ander's not near, is he?' Malcolm said.

'How do you know my family?' Andreona said. 'Is this from another message from Hugh and Alice?'

'You told her of them?' Finlay said.

'You told her!' Malcolm said. 'You want to mention something else she isn't to know?'

At Malcolm's words, Andreona wanted to throw the candle at him. Her life was a lie and everyone had secrets. All this time, she'd simply told Ximeno and Uracca all her hopes for their future, but they'd never been interested in her wants. Even now she demanded answers and they weren't giving her any. Emotionally, she swung from falling into an abyss to burning with determination. She was owed *something*. Rounding on her brother, she poked him in his chest.

He staggered back, not because of how she pushed him, but more, she knew, because she'd startled him. Good. 'We need something and you're going to get it.'

Ximeno stared at her. 'I'm doing enough. Our father doesn't know you're alive and you've been building this tower like a beacon for him to find.'

A wave of sorrow swept over her.

'She's had enough,' Malcolm growled.

Why did Malcolm keep warning her brother? That man didn't know her and he was hiding his own secrets.

'There's a hollow-handled dagger somewhere inside the keep, decorated with two gems—you know of it? It used to be next to the coin room in the cellars.'

Ximeno nodded.

'We need it. You're going to get it and bring it back.'

'You'll be here too long. The guards may not look here, but the blacksmith may return.'

'Then be quick and grab an enamel box for me, too.'

'Why?'

'Because I want a box,' she said. 'As to the other? It's none of your concern.'

'If I get them both, Gorka might notice.'

Ximeno didn't call Gorka his father...perhaps Uracca was right and Ximeno had other motivations. 'I think he'll care more if I'm found than if two items are missing.'

'You won't leave until I get them, will you?' Ximeno said. When she shook her head, he retorted, 'Stubborn.'

'Strong,' Malcolm growled.

They all swung their heads at Malcolm when he said that word. Something passed between her brother and this strange man from Scotland. Something that made Ximeno back down.

Ximeno glared at everyone. 'You will all have to stay here.'

'Give me your weapon, then,' Malcolm said.

'If I walk out of here without this dagger, it'll be noticed.'

'You left it at the blacksmiths.' Malcolm held out his hand. 'It's getting honed.'

Ximeno handed him the long dagger.

'Over the years, you've said things in front of your guards, in front of Father.' Andreona hated to talk of this in front of others, so she switched to Basque. Uracca already knew her pain and how she was trying to prove herself to her father… and to her brothers. 'You acted as though I was nothing.'

Her brother closed his eyes. 'You were right to call for me, but there are matters I can't discuss. Ander is in Spain. He's got some new mercenary as large as a mountain to use for certain tasks. I have this freedom right now to help you because he's not here and our father sleeps. You can either trust me or not, but either way I'm here to help.'

'But all these years!' Her father appeared so different, or perhaps he'd always been that cruel and weak. She wasn't his true daughter; she wasn't anything but blood and hurt. All she felt was pain. She needed this to be done, so she could let go of this branch and fall.

'To say what I think in front of Gorka's guards? I could never tell you. Which is why I talked to Uracca.'

'That didn't work.'

'Andreona—' Uracca said.

'Can we speak French again?' Malcolm interrupted, his gaze staying rapt on her, as if he understood she was in pain. Why did she keep feeling this way with him when he was a stranger?

Scowling, Ximeno turned to him. 'I'm going and when I return with this dagger, and a box, I expect you all to go immediately.'

'Ximeno,' Andreona said in Basque. This felt like the last time she'd see him and maybe it would be. Maybe he'd get caught, questioned and killed. Maybe he'd bring back the items, but they'd still say goodbye. She'd never had him as a brother and now it felt like she'd never be given the chance. Something unquestionably sad churned within her.

How much more did she have to take?

'I know which box will be for you,' he said gruffly.

Ximeno was not simply grabbing any box, he was choosing one for her?

'Thank you,' she said in French, then again

in Basque, and one more time in Spanish. She didn't know why she did it, perhaps to show the depth and breadth of her gratefulness.

'Is that all it takes? I should have done better by you.' Ximeno closed the door gently behind him.

'One of us should have gone with him,' Malcolm said. 'We don't know if it will be the right dagger.'

Andreona turned to Uracca, then to the man who laid quietly on the pallet. Finlay's eyes were steady on hers.

Then she looked at Malcolm. The room was small, but how could this man take up so much more presence than the other two, or, for that matter, her own brother whom she'd worshipped all her life?

'How could it not be the right dagger?' she said. 'I described it.'

'It was switched—'

'By us, there wouldn't be any others who would do it as well,' she said. 'Gorka sends out men to act as mercenaries, they're truly spies for him, we… Gorka has one man, Zilar, who is given a great amount of coin to make such replicas.' Andreona felt the twinges of guilt for confessing all these secrets, but they weren't hers to protect anymore. 'Gorka is a ruler of thieves. He finds…amusement…in switching priceless artifacts with fakes.

'I am not certain it's your dagger, only you would know. But I will tell you this—out of the thousands of baubles Gorka has stolen, this one gave me goose pimples.'

'That's the one,' Finlay said.

'You've never seen it,' Malcolm said.

'People get goose pimples when they're afraid,' Finlay said. 'And I have a healthy fear of that item.'

Andreona had never felt fear with the mysterious dagger, but she felt wariness with these men, and the longer they waited for her brother the more her unease grew. Because there was another truth that would arise when Ximeno returned. Just a few tasks and then she could fall apart. But she had nowhere to go.

'So we get the dagger and leave,' Andreona said. 'Then what happens to us?'

Andreona watched Finlay look to Malcolm, then to her. 'There can't be an *us*.'

'We leave here and you return to where we found you,' Malcolm said slowly as if he was only now realising the truth.

She wanted to hate him for that sentence, but she, too, was coming to the same conclusion.

'That's the intention—that's all we have?' she said.

'Andreona, what else can we do?' Uracca

said. 'There's coin there and your boxes. There's means to flee to Spain or France.'

She didn't want to return to the tower and face the women or her broken hopes that the tower would be approved by her father. She didn't want to talk to Uracca at all about…anything, let alone flee to another country with her. Her closest friend and she couldn't trust her. Yet, she couldn't stay here either.

Just a few tasks and then she could fall apart, could simply scream and cry because her family wanted her dead. But she couldn't because she had nowhere to go. Heavy weight and darkness pressing on her, she…might fall apart now.

Eyes sheening, heart pounding, she looked to the man who was a stranger, and pleaded. 'Malcolm?'

Malcolm ran his hand through his hair. 'Let's get the dagger and make certain we escape, then we'll talk. Just hold on.'

Chapter Eleven

The cart they were provided with was small and fully padded. Even so, Finlay paled when they lowered him into it and hissed out a breath when he had to adjust himself. Despite the warnings of not staying in the blacksmith's storage cupboard, they'd had to wait. Now they travelled in the dead of night when traps could be laid out for any of them.

There was nowhere else to go except towards the tower, which was a half-day's ride. Malcolm tried to count the benefits to this journey. They were alive and not being pursued by any of the guards. He suspected if Ximeno wasn't a favoured son, there would be torches and outrage.

And Ximeno had left them with one of their swords, as well as a long dagger and half the content of their purses. Given what was in there, it was enough for a bounty for Ximeno, but it left them short for any full journey to Scotland. That could be remedied in England since he knew there was coin hidden on one of the estates for the purposes of protecting the dagger.

If they made it to England, or even France. He'd thought once he had the dagger, all these uncertainties wouldn't matter...he'd simply fight through them. Did that make him rash and impatient? Yes, all of that and always.

Years of disappointments, of never acquiring the dagger, had taught him little in patience and apparently having the dagger didn't help.

And they had the dagger. The true one, which was too astonishing to believe, but also... believable. When had the dagger last been in Colquhoun hands? Two...three years ago. How many countries had he been roving in all that time, how many inns and caves had he slept in?

How much darkness had saturated his thoughts in all those years? Then it all came to this: he and Finlay wandering an unknown Basque forest having a general sense of what direction in which they went, only to get caught by a woman who knew where the dagger was all these years.

This woman, whom he'd known for just a few days, had changed everything, which had nothing and everything to do with the day he'd tripped on those ropes in the tower and... Her touch!

How could a simple, accidental touch have affected him so?

Because it hadn't been simple. The flush of her body against his, the way her hand curved, that hitch to her breath. The fact their bodies moved together. Then she had brought him to her father's home and within moments everything changed again. Ximeno's confession, Gorka's cruelty and Andreona's world fell apart.

He had witnessed, felt, *understood*, all that she struggled with. The only part he didn't understand was his response when she'd turned to him with those eyes reminding him of Scotland, of a place he hadn't thought of as home in years and said his name.

Ximeno had gone off to get the dagger, Finlay was barely breathing, Uracca was clenching her hands because she worried. But she wasn't as frightened as Andreona as she came to some conclusion he didn't understand.

She'd looked to him for help, and he'd told her to hold on. How could he help?

He, like Finlay, intended to leave her in the Basque Country. He could defend her on the way back to the tower, but after that, she'd be on her own. He and Finlay were on a mission. The dagger, once out in the open, brought danger.

Half a day's ride and it took twice as long in the dark. What if Gorka became suspicious and sent men this way? What if the Warstones discovered he carried the hollowed dagger? How, with one sword, could he defend his friend and two women? Especially with Finlay injured, Andreona unnaturally quiet and Uracca flitting from Finlay's side, then to Andreona's to whisper frantic words in her ear, but Andreona not saying anything back.

Malcolm was concerned over Finlay's injuries, but his worry was with Andreona. She was physically well, but the woman who'd fearlessly fought him grieved for the life she'd lost—he could see her retreating to a place where her friend couldn't save her.

Where he couldn't save her. *Hold on.* To what? He had this sense of absolute dread. A warring inside him that he didn't want to leave her behind ever. A flash of arriving with her in Scotland, introducing her to his clan as—

He couldn't think like this!

Mere hours he'd known her. Simply because he felt some unreasonable connection to her meant nothing and it was truly foolish to even argue with himself. He didn't intend to stay in Scotland. It was simply that he hated to see the flatness in her mesmerising eyes.

There was also this certainty they weren't going to make it, even if Gorka or the Warstones never found them. Every bump along the road brought a grey pallor to Finlay's skin. Every word from Uracca's lips increased in volume and urgency and was ignored. They weren't going to make it. Not like this. Finlay now stood, but sweat beaded along his brow. His friend was in pain.

Malcolm needed to leave them behind. He carried the Jewell of Kings' hollowed dagger. The mission was to get it securely to his clan. That must be done. He'd argued he wanted to be finished with it all because he was tired of this game, but abandoning Finlay and stranding Uracca and Andreona simply to ensure the dagger arrived with his family didn't sit right in his thoughts or his heart.

As the cart's wheels silently turned, the more his thoughts were plagued with what could be done. If he left them now in the Basque Country, there was no certainty they'd be safe. The tower wasn't secure or far enough away from Gorka if he realised, or if Ximeno was forced to confess, the dagger or that enamel box were missing.

But if he travelled with them, he'd be too exposed and could be caught with the dagger. There was one location, however, he could leave them all well protected from Gorka, from Warstones... and a place Finlay could get care.

He simply needed to convince them. Stopping

off to the side of the road, Malcolm announced, 'It's time to talk.'

He looked to Finlay, then to Uracca. When he looked to Andreona, she didn't look back.

'Shouldn't we get to the tower first?' Standing, Finlay gripped the side of the cart and stretched his shoulders.

'We need to come to an agreement before we go further.'

Malcolm watched his friend look to Uracca who was gripping Andreona's hand. Over the last few hours, Finlay had shared many a conversation with Uracca. He wondered if there was something between them. 'The tower won't work, and you know it,' Malcolm said. 'We bring more danger there now than before—those other women need to be considered as well. We know now Ximeno is plotting something. Gorka could become suspicious, or someone else could trace the dagger's location.'

'Where else—?' Finlay looked north and cursed. 'They won't make it there by themselves.'

'You'll go with them.'

'Where are we to go?' Uracca said.

Finlay's expression softened. 'There's a stronghold for us...in France.'

Andreona's head whipped up and her eyes narrowed on Malcolm's. 'For *us*, in France?'

'We're not partial to France,' Uracca said.

'You can't stay in the Basque Country and travelling further risks all of us,' Malcolm said. 'You know we can't take a ship to make it easier, we'd be too out in the open. The journey must be by land.'

'Separating isn't an option,' Finlay said. 'We should all go to Hugh and Alice's. We'll make informed decisions there on what is to become of us, the dagger and the women.'

'You won't make it that far—already you risk your life with your ribs. And if we're pursued, they gain.'

Finlay huffed out. 'There's not enough coin for two journeys.'

'I'll give you the share, and I can make it to Nicholas's.'

'Nicholas?' Uracca said.

'Nicholas and Matilda of Mei Solis in England. A man named Reynold left funds I'll steal to make the rest of the journey. Since it's there to defend the dagger, he can hardly complain.'

'He'll complain anyway,' Finlay said.

'That Warstone doesn't need as much as he has.'

Finlay laughed, then held his ribs, his expression quickly turning sombre. 'You've thought this through too thoroughly.'

He had and he could feel Andreona's eyes on him this whole time.

Is this what he meant when he'd told her to hold on? He didn't know. There were flaws in all this reasoning. There were no certainties Andreona and Uracca would face any danger from Gorka or Warstones if he left them at the tower. But the thought there could be was enough to risk keeping her. Not just her, all of them, a bit longer.

He could get them to the Warstone fortress and then be on his way to Scotland. Or they could separate once in France, and they could travel to the fortress.

'Who are these people you talk of and who would pursue us?' Andreona said. 'My father thinks I'm dead and he banished Uracca.'

Malcolm wasn't prepared to tell her all the stories, so to where the danger came from, he'd have to lie. 'Anyone from your father's employ could notice the dagger's absence. Maybe they'd want it.'

'Or maybe you're not telling the truth,' Uracca said, 'and are endangering us.'

'We're trying to avoid it,' Finlay said. 'And he's right, I do need to recover. The place he thinks of is shorter passage.'

'How far?' Uracca asked.

'South of Paris, but close enough.'

'What is this Paris? Why *France*?' Andreona said.

Uracca turned to Andreona. 'It's different for us now.'

Andreona blinked and looked away.

Malcolm held his tongue. He didn't understand why Andreona didn't like France, but he did like her arguing back and showing her strength. Now with Uracca's words, she went into herself again. It wasn't his place because soon he'd be gone, but it bothered him all the same.

'There's a village along the way, next to an abbey.' Malcolm said. 'You all can stop there first. There's a man named Evrart, he can both hide and defend if the time comes.'

'And when we get to the Warstone fortress—' Finlay began.

'Warstones?' Uracca said. 'Who are they for us to trust? We don't even know you.'

Malcolm looked to the sky, shook his head.

'What is it?' Andreona said. 'Are they trustworthy or not?'

Because she was looking at him again, he answered, 'No, never, but—'

'Then why are we staying at their fortress?' she said.

'Friends have control of it, the Warstones are barred.'

'Is it under siege?' Uracca said. 'How is that safe?'

'It's complicated, but it's better than being in

the Basque Country and the village cannot hide you forever,' he said.

'Why do I have to be hidden at all? No one wants us!' Andreona said.

She was breaking his heart, which was something he shouldn't feel at all. He had no patience or care for words. His immediate response was always to walk away or attack. Andreona needed...comfort. Something he couldn't give.

Except she'd looked to him and something in him had responded to her. What was this? A feeling of responsibility because of the dagger? Or understanding because he knew what it was like to be betrayed by family?

There was something deeper motivating him when it came to her. That innocent touch, his need to protect. Nothing of it held any reasoning. It just was.

'I need to ride to Scotland and quickly,' he said. 'The fortress would be better for you all. We'll go to the tower, tell the women, who can make their decision, and that will be it.'

'I don't like it,' Finlay said. 'But I know why you do it.'

Uracca released Andreona's hand. 'Then that's good enough for me. We'll go.'

Chapter Twelve

Andreona knew now when she was being lied to and betrayed. They didn't know these men, didn't know their plan, but it had something to do with that dagger and the danger that followed it. Why there was danger now and not when it was in her father's possession, she didn't know.

She shouldn't care. She only knew she couldn't, wouldn't, travel with Uracca to this Warstone fortress.

She wasn't ready to be locked up somewhere safe. For a year, she and others had helped build a tower with a leaking roof and too many holes that she thought were good to spy enemies approaching, but instead they let the wind in. There were stormy days she wondered if it would be better to be outside the tower than in. She wasn't prepared for whatever journey there would be with Uracca reminding her of the life she'd lost, apologising to her for having any part of it.

She refused to acknowledge the other reason. The one she could feel on the edges of her heart and all her thoughts. Black, dark thoughts, heavy with something she'd never felt before, but increasingly impossible to ignore. It was seeping a heavy weight into her very soul. She'd been able to ignore it while she'd ordered Ximeno to get the dagger and helped Finlay to the cart, and could almost avoid it while Uracca talked in her ear.

She knew she wouldn't be able to ignore it once she returned to the tower. To face those women, the humiliation... For a year she'd talked of how they'd one day return to Gorka's protection if they proved themselves.

She'd been telling them lies. And it didn't make her feel any less vulnerable knowing there were only a few of the women left.

'Do the others know?' Aware that Malcolm and Finlay watched, she rounded on Uracca. It was so late at night it was almost morning and there was some light from the moon breaking through the trees and the light mist. She was cold and exhausted, but Malcolm had stopped them here and she'd take advantage of it.

This whole conversation could be done somewhat in private...at least away from the tower.

'Who?' Uracca said.

'Dionara, Mencia, Bita...little Gaieta,' Andreona said. This mountain of weight was crushing her with how she'd failed, how she never should have tried, how she was never loved. 'Do they know of Gorka's intention to kill me? Or were they ordered to be killed, too?'

'It was only—' Uracca's voice broke '—only Ximeno and I who knew of Gorka's orders.'

'You lied to them, too?' Andreona didn't care that Uracca flinched. 'What else have you lied about?'

'Nothing,' Uracca cried. 'Nothing.'

Andreona couldn't trust her. There was nowhere else for her to go where she wouldn't be reminded of this time. No keep, no tower and she couldn't stay locked in some fortress somewhere with a friend who'd lied to her. Not a secret like this.

'We can go to the tower and tell the women of our intentions, but I won't travel to this keep and stay.' Andreona ignored Uracca's gasp and Finlay's look to Malcolm. 'I'll go with you.'

'You weren't invited,' Malcolm said. 'It's not safe to go where I'm going.'

'It's not safe to go where they go, either, and I can't return.'

'Why?' Uracca whispered.

She didn't want to say how humiliated she was that her friend and brother didn't tell her. Not in front of these men who'd witnessed enough. 'He's got the dagger. I'll go with it.'

'You're not going,' Malcolm said, his expression dark.

He couldn't intimidate her. 'I'm not going with them, so that leaves me standing here. Is that what you want?'

'Andreona—' Uracca said.

She glared at her friend. 'Don't.'

Andreona turned back to Malcolm, who studied her. What did he see? That she was barely holding on? That the weight of her family's betrayal and Uracca's lies were agony inside her? Malcolm had told Ximeno she was strong; she wanted to tell him she was trying. But her world was ripped apart and she needed time.

This man with his turbulent green eyes and scarred beauty...did he understand what she was going through? That she stood before him, trying to hold on for just a bit longer, and if he gave her the chance to be away from everyone who'd hurt her, everything that reminded her—Gorka, Ximeno, Uracca...that tower—she could do it?

'Malcolm?' she said.

He inhaled sharply. 'I accept. But we drop this dagger with my clan and I won't stop there. If there's a place along the way that's safer for you, or somewhere you wish to stay, you'll do it without more negotiations. Do you understand?'

He could have demanded harsher terms and she would have agreed to any of them. She needed to get away and he was the means to do it. This journey would give her time to come to terms with what happened and that's all she needed. 'I do.'

Malcolm turned to Uracca. 'And while we're travelling west, you go north, exactly where this man tells you to go. No questions and no intentional harm coming to him. Do you agree to this?'

Uracca's gaze locked with hers and Andreona's heart seized. After everything, would she deny her this? When Uracca nodded, Andreona let out a breath.

'Is this wise?' Finlay said.

'You think you can't get to Evrart's in a cart?'

'If I could walk, I'd punch you,' Finlay growled.

'I'm not leaving her here.'

Finlay's frustration morphed to laughter before he held his ribs. 'It's like that, is it? That's unexpected.'

Andreona didn't like Finlay's knowing, amused look.

'Andreona, can we talk?' Uracca said.

She didn't want to talk, she wanted to study the look Malcolm returned to Finlay. He now looked half-angry, half-surprised he'd agreed to take her. He also looked discomforted by his friend, which made little sense. She wasn't forcing him to take her—he chose to. And she had no intention to ask him his reasons, nor did she care.

As if sensing her watching him, Malcolm swung his gaze to her, then to Uracca and back. He was oddly quiet until she realised he was waiting for her to respond to Uracca.

He was giving her a *choice* to talk to her friend and something warmed in her chest. When she nodded, he said, 'We'll take the cart and horses and continue travelling to the tower. You can catch up.'

Andreona felt Uracca's eyes on her, but she kept her gaze on Malcolm, who was leading the horses away, and Finlay, who was holding the cart and walking slowly by his side.

After a moment, she sighed and turned to her friend. There wasn't a moment of her entire life that didn't have Uracca nearby. They'd gone from sharing wet nurses, to playing games in the different houses they, and other children like them, were shuffled to.

Over the years, they'd argued over skipping games, and the best bites of fish. They'd cried in each other's arms when Nabarra caught the cough and died and rolled their eyes when Emazteona bragged about her first kiss. Andreona had no more cherished friendship than Uracca's. She would have died for her friend if it came to that. Now she wondered if she even knew her.

If Uracca's mother had ordered her death, Andreona would have told her, they would have fled together. If Uracca had argued against it, she would have knocked her over the head, thrown her in a cart and got her to safety. She wouldn't, not once, have conspired behind Uracca's back as if she had no skill to determine her own life.

'I didn't make the right decision,' Uracca said. 'I cannot say how sorry I am.'

Those words hurt. She didn't know if Uracca had ever admitted to a mistake. The fact she did spoke to the wrongness of the offence.

'He wanted to kill me and you knew it. You conferred with Ximeno and intended not to tell me…for a *year*.'

'I know,' Uracca said in a small voice.

'I stayed up night and day building that tower. I cried when the workers didn't stay for the final stone and despaired when we lost the other women. That pain I went through was intentional?'

Uracca put her face in her hands, her shoulders shuddering, the sounds of sobs barely muffled. 'I don't know what I was thinking, or what I was doing. We kept thinking with every challenge you would let it go. Instead, you simply worked harder.'

'Was it Ximeno who ordered you not to tell me?' Andreona said.

Uracca shook her head and then wiped her face on her sleeve. 'Anything I say now would be wrong. If I tell you your brother suggested it, would that make you forgive me? No, because I still agreed and, in truth, I don't know who first suggested it. We met several times in private.'

And so her friend's infatuation with Ximeno grew. For the first time, Andreona felt something other than her own agony at the betrayal. Her friend longed for Ximeno and having private meetings would have only made it harder.

'Did he make you promises or return your feelings? Is that what happened?' Andreona said.

'Never, not by word or smile. When we left the blacksmith's, he kissed me on the forehead like a sister.'

Andreona's agony returned. Ximeno hadn't looked her in the eye. His betrayal was as severe and, despite him retrieving the dagger and releasing Finlay, she was hurt by his decision. He was supposed to be the good brother. Was he still? He'd said some things that hinted he went against Gorka's rule, but that didn't mean he was actively pursuing taking down their father.

'We'll be at the tower soon,' Andreona said. 'I think it's best the others know everything.'

'Everything? What of this dagger?'

'It's significant to these men; perhaps dangerous. They wouldn't want it so badly from my fa—from Gorka, unless it had meaning. The women need to know there's danger. But also... there could danger where we're going.'

'What do we do?'

Andreona noted Uracca looked to her for this decision. At one point all the women had looked to her for advice. Now it felt wrong somehow.

'We'll let them make the decision on whether to stay in the tower or to travel with you.'

'We don't know whether those men want Bita or the others to travel with us.'

'They don't get a choice. Mine was taken away and now we have little time for any sort of decisions. At least the others will know they can go or stay.'

'I didn't mean to hurt you,' Uracca cried out suddenly. 'I should have told you. Will you ever forgive me?'

She hoped to, but it wasn't a promise she could make. 'If the women stay at the tower, when you get to this fortress and find it good or safe, will you message and invite them?'

Uracca's eyes already welled with tears. When she clenched them, they broke down her cheek, but she nodded firmly. Resolutely. 'I won't leave them there.'

Andreona couldn't imagine them staying since

the tower leaked and was far too close to Gorka who could find them. No, they were strong and would most likely travel with Uracca despite what Uracca had done. They weren't as close to her friend as Andreona was.

And…if they did take the chance on the fortress, on France, Andreona would give them the enamel boxes for funds. That would give them the start they truly needed to make it all better. Not the false hope of a leaky tower and the lies she had previously given them.

Andreona looked over her shoulder at Malcolm and Finlay who were making slow progress.

'Finlay keeps looking back towards us, but not the other one,' Uracca said. 'Do we trust them?'

Despite everything, she still worried for her friend. 'Uracca, they are asking you to make this journey, in France, to a village you don't know, then to a fortress that sounds foreboding. Finlay's in no condition to protect you and he will be a burden for you.'

Uracca's expression grew pensive. 'Our differences with France were always Gorka's differences and I've changed over the last year to shrug off those thoughts.'

Andreona felt the barb that shouldn't have been there.

'Sorry,' Uracca said suddenly.

'No need to apologise, I never felt like those

were my views, I knew to keep quiet because—'
Andreona felt tears sting. 'Because I tried to
please a man who couldn't be pleased. I was
wrong to even pretend otherwise. Now we know
two men from Scotland. If anything, people are…
human, aren't they?'

'Is there any chance I could change your
heart?' Uracca said. 'Malcolm seems like us,
but he carries a darkness.'

It was an apt description of a man with dark
hair that held red and green eyes that roiled with
too many emotions.

'Would you take the thistles in my satchel and
pin them to your doors?' Uracca untied a pouch
around her waist and handed it to Andreona.

'You brought thistles?' Andreona eyed the
sack of silver dried flowers that looked like the
sun to protect homes against evil spirits.

'The blacksmith had a basket and I grabbed
several. It seemed wise since we're going on this
journey. If there's a door, I'm doing what I can.'

'I'd…like that,' Andreona said. It would be a
part of the Basque Country that wouldn't bring
terrible memories.

Uracca's worried expression eased. 'At least
Finlay's friendly and isn't likely to leave me on
the side of the road.'

Andreona knew Uracca meant to be humorous, but despite not knowing Malcolm long and

the danger he attracted, she knew he wouldn't leave her stranded either. He wasn't leaving her stranded *now*. But there was a wistfulness in her friend's expression and tone of voice that reminded Andreona of how Uracca was with Ximeno.

'Did this Scottish man make any promises to you?'

Uracca placed her hand on her mouth. 'No, but what does this say about me? He's kind, but my heart's bruised, and after this, I don't deserve him. They seem loyal, don't they? And I betrayed my only friend.'

'I do wish you a good death, my friend,' Andreona said as way of some comfort. Uracca had hurt her deeply and she couldn't stay with her. It was too soon and there were too many memories, but she could wish good fortune for her friend.

'And to you. Always,' Uracca linked her arm with hers and they hurried to catch up to the men who were walking slowly.

With a gentle smile on his face, Finlay looked to them both, but Malcolm took one look at her and her alone, his green eyes locking with hers, before he swung his gaze away.

Was he wondering if she'd changed her intentions to travel with them?

They didn't know these men at all, but they'd captured them, and now she and Uracca were left with the consequences. Something else Andreona felt the weight of. Soon, before she was ready, she feared all of these matters would simply crush her.

Chapter Thirteen

Three days since they made the decision to separate from Finlay, Uracca, and the other women, who frustratingly were told of the Warstone fortress and, despite being warned many times of the danger and the journey, had packed their meagre belongings. Meagre except they took Andreona's precious boxes. Since they were hers to give, Malcolm could not counsel otherwise, but what did she think to live on?

As for Finlay's dismay and concern over such travelling companions, Malcolm would have laughed, yet something about the way his friend looked at Uracca—he didn't think the man minded as much as he let on.

The troubling matter was Finlay only had the daggers to defend them and injuries far too grievous to make those blades worthy of a fair fight, but the women insisted they were not helpless.

What was it with stubborn Basque women? They were *strong*, his mind reminded him.

Now he and Andreona were in France and travelled some of the same roads he and Finlay had gone on. They stopped at the same spots, he saw the same trees, he ate the same food and drank the same drink. But this journey wasn't the same and it wasn't because of the position of the sun, or because his horse was pointed west instead of east, but entirely because this time a stranger was by his side, and he'd had to leave his friend behind.

And he resented it, he resented it all even though he was the one who'd helped to make the decision on Andreona coming with him and them leaving Finlay behind. Further, he was certain what prompted the decision wasn't sound reasoning.

He was impatient and often forged forward before thinking of any consequences. That's how, as a child, he'd lost Shannon. She'd suggested travelling to the lake, but if he had simply thought of the dangers, he might have argued they shouldn't. And when Bram ordered him to stay on Colquhoun land, if he had stopped to think about why his brother had ordered him, maybe he wouldn't have rushed to the Battle of Dunbar.

But rushing ahead was what he'd always done.

Sometimes it helped, but more often than not, tragedy occurred. Accepting Andreona's proposal, had he made a mistake?

He thought once he had the ridiculous dagger and was making the journey to Scotland, he'd feel some sort of relief from the constant anger he felt. Soon this ridiculous quest would be over and he could get on with his life.

Three years and three days of chasing after a dagger he didn't want. He felt the three days of being separated from Finlay most of all. Logically they'd made the correct choice of Finlay travelling with Uracca to the Warstone fortress. It was closer for his friend with possibly broken ribs and too many women to defend.

What wasn't logical was taking Andreona with him to Colquhoun land. He wanted this journey to be over with. He hated leaving Finlay behind. He raged that he now had to travel with the woman who'd not only trapped his friend, but harmed him, too.

He had no use for people, yet when Andreona had looked at him and demanded she travel with him...he'd let her. It was the desperate determination in her eyes, the words of Gorka, her father, still ringing in his ears. His need to have her with him went beyond pity and into protectiveness...possessiveness.

That he hated most of all. Hadn't he learnt his

lesson? Only once had he felt such emotions before, with his childhood friend Shannon. They'd been inseparable until she was killed in front of him. At age thirteen he couldn't have protected her against those three men, but it didn't mean he didn't feel it. Or that his memories wouldn't let him forget her cries and his grief.

Andreona wasn't like Shannon at all, yet those feelings were there.

It went beyond the golden hue of her skin or those eyes of hers. What was beautiful about eyes the colour of herrings swimming in water?

Her accent was distracting, too. The way he had to focus on the cadence of her words and the way she formed them by watching her lips. Watching those lips was…distracting.

And the way she moved…graceful, efficient, like a thief in a packed room. As though she didn't want to be seen, yet still took command of the space around her.

For three days, he didn't want to pay her any attention. He'd abandoned his friend, he was angry with her, with the circumstances. He wanted nothing to do with her and yet, even though he searched his surroundings, his gaze inevitably went to hers.

Three days he had raged with the injustice of being caught by women who were more victims than enemies, to Finlay being incapacitated to do anything except accept the help of some women who didn't seem much better off than street thieves.

He noticed Andreona, however, not as a captive, or as a thief, nor as an enemy, but as a man would a woman.

Which frustrated him all the more. He didn't want anyone by his side. Andreona was a reminder he shouldn't have allowed Finlay to get close to him because he'd got hurt and Andreona would be hurt as well.

Three days noticing her silence; her unnatural quietness since they'd left the tower. Worse, three days of her muffling the sound of her tears at night.

Malcolm combed his fingers through his hair. At night, it was all he could do to reason with himself to let her be, to come to turns regarding her family's betrayal and realise she was better off without them…without anyone. He hadn't had, hadn't wanted, anyone to talk to or see him when he was at his lowest. The least he could do was afford her the same courtesy.

But all that reasoning warred with his need to protect. To gather her in his arms and hold her. Or kiss her until she forgot all about her anguish for an hour, a day…a week.

And it would be a week at least to ease the primitive hunger building inside him when it

came to her. He fought it, himself, raged against
the circumstances and whatever emotion it was
prompting him to keep her close and take her
with him to Scotland.

Anger allowed him to ignore her the first day,
frustration and sheer determination the next…
but this was the third day, and he couldn't ignore
her any longer.

Because after three days, he had run out of
food and she had not.

'Explain yourself.'

Blinking, Andreona looked up at Malcolm
who loomed over her. The day was pleasant, and
they'd stopped to relieve themselves and to eat.
Stopping was tiring and she wished they could
simply continue riding, but she knew somewhere
inside her Malcolm needed to eat and rest and
so, whenever he stopped, she looked to him and
did the same.

That was easier than thinking, which she
didn't want to do or she feared she'd keep crying.
Cry as she had every night since telling Uracca
goodbye. At least she had the comfort of not disturbing Malcom when she did so because he was
never around the fire where she slept. He was always out somewhere in the shadows, walking or
resting or guarding. She didn't know.

During the day, she could remember facts and

try to come to terms with what her family had done, but at night she was only emotions that held little reason. Sometimes she threw rocks, other times she curled herself up under a blanket and cried until her hands, her hair, the very ground, was wet with her tears.

Now, however, that heavy darkness weighed on her and she wished for silence. Except she couldn't be quiet, couldn't stay numb because there was a man glowering down at her. She'd only sat in the grass as they had for days. Why wasn't he?

'Are we not stopping to eat?' she said.

His frown deepened. There was something behind that frown, not merely displeasure, but concern, but how was she to know when he looked at her with those turbulent green eyes that were far too startling when her life held only grey?

'No, we're not stopping to eat. We stopped to relieve ourselves and give the horses a reprieve.'

She looked up at the sun in the trees. 'But the sun is in the sky when we eat.'

'You observe the sun, but not me? Not your supplies?'

Why would she observe him? And as for her supplies, they were around her. She'd taken them out of her satchel as she had done every day. But if this wasn't the time… Andreona put her food back in the satchel that rested in her lap.

Malcolm made some sort of sound, but she ignored that. It was easy to ignore sounds and, if he moved and got back on his horse, she could ignore him too. He was disturbing the heavy silence that was comforting her, that felt like a thousand blankets she could bury herself under.

Standing, she hoisted the satchel over her shoulder. Malcolm did not move. Had she missed something? 'You are welcome to my food if you ate all of yours.'

'Why are you being so polite?' he said. 'Where is the woman who wrenched my arms behind my back, tied them, all to gift me to her father?'

That hurt. Andreona flinched and the abrupt movement shifted some of her numbness to an ache. She'd gone on this journey to get away from her family and reminders of their betrayal. She'd hoped, with time, she'd come to some understanding of why and how she felt, but not now. She didn't want to think; today she wanted to get away from him and herself. Why couldn't he leave her alone?

'I'm not polite. I'm—'

Malcolm clasped her upper arms. 'We had a supply of food for three days. You should have nothing left.'

He was looking at her too closely. Since they'd left Uracca, he'd hardly looked her way at all. Now he was studying her every feature, her every thought. There wasn't any darkness in his eyes; whatever fevered light was there was concentrated towards her.

'I don't eat as much as you,' she said.

'You have dark circles under your eyes and your lips are cracked. Are you even drinking?'

What was it to him if she ate or drank? His large hands felt warm, secure, his thumbs feathering up, then down. Fully clothed, she shouldn't have felt much of his touch at all, but she did. Too much.

She wrenched her arms to break his hold. It didn't work and that distressing internal ache she'd been ignoring between them bloomed. His questions, his questioning gaze, scraped across the heavy blanket she'd wrapped herself in. She didn't want to cry! 'Let me go.'

'Answer me.'

She pulled and stumbled back. He snaked an arm around her waist and held her steady. One breath, two...until her body caught up with how warm he felt against her, the uniqueness of his leather and steel scent, the heat of his breath against her neck as he bent his head to look down at her. The intimacy of their embrace and the gripping curve of his fingers as if he wanted to, but just restrained himself from, pulling her closer.

He...supported her, but she didn't want his help.

'I've eaten.' She pushed against his firm chest until he stepped back and released her. So strong, she knew he only reluctantly shifted away from her because she wanted it. 'Every day, we sat, ate and drank.'

Growling low in some response she didn't want to guess but was helpless to. Was it his displeasure from her words or because they no longer touched? Before she could react, he snatched her satchel, turned it upside down and dumped the contents to the ground.

She shrieked. 'What's the matter with you? That's perfectly good food.'

'It's perfectly good if you eat it,' he grounded out. His eyes pinged from hers, to her mouth, down her body and back up. When his eyes returned to hers, they were darker. 'Explain yourself.'

He heaved in a breath as if he'd run for miles. She suddenly felt the same, but underneath it all was pain she wanted to ignore. She hadn't felt like eating…hadn't been aware she wasn't eating. This journey wasn't for that anyway. It was to take her heart away from those who'd broken it. Food, sleep and that touch of his were to be inconsequential. Except right now, Malcolm was staring at her as if he wanted to force her to drink…eat. As if *he* was hungry and wanted to devour her.

'I don't have to explain myself to you.' She licked her lips.

His eyes tracked her movement, stayed there. The air they breathed stilled, clashed.

'What are you—?'

He kissed her. Hands on her arms, body straight, he half lifted her until his lips were on hers. Warm, softer than his words or deeds. The bite of his fingers a reminder he was frustrated with her, but his lips...

They coaxed, beckoned, and she answered. A touch, a taste, and his hands eased up her arms, releasing their grip so she could use her hands and lean towards him. In that touch there was a promise hinting at more, one he delivered as his arms went around her and he deepened the kiss.

One moment, two, until her heart pounded and her breaths were non-existent. Until whatever he was telling her with his lips, his breath, the way he held her, she almost understood. Until he utterly let her go and she stumbled back.

His shoulders rose and fell, while she couldn't move at all. 'No, you don't have to explain yourself to me, no matter if it's what I want. What we both want. Though—'

He blinked and looked over her shoulder. When his gaze returned to hers, it wasn't as heated or intense, but it retained an intimacy she couldn't quite shake.

'What we agreed upon was that your friend would care for mine,' he continued.

Why did he keep saying words, but looking at her as he did? She couldn't move, couldn't think past numbness to irritation to this…her first kiss. With this man, this stranger, who was beautiful and scarred. Who was angry and concerned. This man wasn't merely contradictory, he was a conflict and one she felt in her very blood.

'Will Uracca care for Finlay?' he said.

He talked of their friends. No, he talked of his own, because he cared for the soft-spoken Finlay. 'She'll do what is necessary, as will the other women.'

'I only made one promise.'

True. 'We Basque women aren't as calculating as my…as Gorka.'

His eyes, which had softened, turned cold. 'No, you're strong, aren't you? Building towers and nets, harming my friend in the first place.'

Any warmth or heat between them was gone. This man…did he kiss her or hate her? Touch her with softness or angrily dump her food on the ground? She couldn't, didn't want to, think. They could have kept to their silence, but he chose to break her from that.

'As you mean to harm me now?' she retorted.

Regret flashed across his features. 'Andreona—'

She turned her back on him. His regret was a

false emotion as was any warmth she felt from him. Malcolm was right, she had harmed his friend and it was good he reminded her, so she remembered that no one truly cared for her.

He could try to break her from her silence again, but she'd be better prepared. Already the heavy feeling weighed on her chest and shadows edged her vision. She grasped the blanket off the horse.

'I want to sleep,' she told him.

Chapter Fourteen

The moment Malcolm saw the lone house in the middle of a wide field, he held up his hand to Andreona. 'Stay here.'

She looked to the field and to the house, but didn't ask any questions. As it had been for the last two days, that dull light still marred the beauty in her eyes that was why they were here. A place he didn't want to come to. Something was wrong and he wasn't enough for her. She was more than tired or melancholy and all he'd done was yell at her and dump her food on the ground.

He'd always been impatient, but his pushing her was bordering on cruelty. He wanted to make it right. Why he felt as though he had to do something for her, he didn't know. It was more than concern, far more than responsibility. He feared it had something to do with caring. Though it did him no good, coming here was his only choice.

It was that or kiss her again. No, he wanted to do more than kiss her. It felt like forever since she'd looked at him, even more since she'd talked or yelled at him. He couldn't get the way of how she felt out of his thoughts, his body, which made all his feelings for her more confusing. Because now he knew and wanted more. And in his current state, he wasn't right for her!

Was being here, at this house in France, any better?

He and Finlay had avoided Hugh and Alice when they'd ridden through here last. Finlay had retrieved the Half-Thistle Seal message Hugh had left in the tree. The very message telling them that the dagger was possibly with Gorka in the Basque Country and they'd never altered his route.

He avoided Hugh as he avoided all of his family. Hugh was friends with Black Robert of Dent, who was married to his sister, Gaira, and they lived in hiding on Colquhoun land. Robert was an English soldier who had helped Gaira and four orphans travel the length of Scotland.

That English knight had earned his family's respect when he protected Gaira; he'd earned Gaira's love by protecting those children. Hugh, to protect his lifelong friend Robert, had agreed to travel distances to report on anything that might harm the Colquhoun clan by sending messages via the Half-Thistle Seal.

And so Hugh and his wife, Alice, lived here for now, in France near the border of English territory. Able to spy for any information that might harm the clan, but also might help the cause for the Jewell of Kings and the dagger.

Hugh and Alice were good people. That didn't mean Malcolm wanted anything to do with them. But he'd come here because Andreona barely ate, her father had ordered her death and her brother and friend had lied to her. She had been so uninterested the last few days, as if her fate and anything that might affect her were meaningless. He was reluctant to come here, but loathed the light being lost from those eyes of hers.

Glancing behind him, stealing one more gaze at her still figure atop the horse, Malcolm strode towards the home that looked inviting, but—

'You fool!' Out of the treeline to his left, Hugh of Shoebury charged towards him. Malcolm didn't have time to block the punch to his jaw.

Staggering, he didn't block the next jab into his side. That one doubled him over, but when Hugh came in for the third strike, Malcolm blocked it with his hand and struck out on his own.

When he connected with Hugh's chin, the deep feeling of satisfaction was all encompassing.

'You show up now?' Hugh circled, swung out,

Malcolm ducked. 'How many did you bring upon us? How many followed you?'

Malcolm swung, Hugh stepped away, but not enough to avoid the blow glancing across his cheek.

Malcolm grinned when Hugh hissed. 'No one!'

Hugh swung forward. 'There's no certainty! You came from Spain, from the Basque Country! You went to Gorka!'

Fists raised to block or to strike, Malcolm jogged back. 'I did and I have the dagger.'

Stunned, Hugh stilled, giving Malcolm the opportunity to strike again, splitting Hugh's lip. Hugh cursed.

The front door opened and the fire and candles inside illuminated more of the field. 'Hugh?'

Hugh held his split lip and warned Malcolm with his eyes. 'I was meant to keep you safe, protect you, but you took my messages and went there alone?'

Malcolm's fury overwhelmed him. He'd fought those exact words his entire life. He wasn't weak or a fool! Malcolm didn't care that Hugh's wife, Alice, or Andreona were watching, he swung again, hard. Hugh blocked with his arm, cursed hard and stepped away. Alice ran forward. 'What is going on?'

'Nothing I haven't handled before, Wife.'

'Nothing you haven't provoked before,' Malcolm said.

Hugh grinned. 'I got that message. You always did hold your reins a little too tight.'

Alice pulled Hugh's arm towards her and frowned. 'It'll have to be wrapped.' Then she turned her eye on Malcolm. 'I'm assuming since my husband didn't gut you with a sword, you're more friend than foe.'

'Alice, this is Malcolm.'

Her eyes widened. 'Colquhoun's Malcolm? Robert's brother-in-law?'

Malcolm hissed. 'She knows?'

'Everything.' Hugh said.

'And you came here to what? Take a swing at my husband?' Alice said. 'What is wrong with you?'

Not shame, but something close to it overcame him as he took in the petite woman's glare. 'I came here for help.'

Hugh laughed. Alice looked at him as if he'd lost his mind. Maybe he had.

'Help?' Hugh said. 'If you have brought danger to my family—'

'I didn't bring danger.' Hadn't he, though? Andreona was to be free of danger, too, but she wasn't well and he didn't know what to do for her.

He looked behind him. Two horses, one still

mounted. Finally he was getting to fight the man he'd wished to for years and he turned his back on her. What did she think of him leaving her vulnerable like that?

'You brought the Jewell of Kings' dagger here,' Hugh said. 'You could have been followed by Warstone spies!'

Alice gasped. 'You've got it. Are we finally done with all of this?'

Hugh took her hand. 'It's got to get to the clan and be decided.'

They needed to be quiet! Andreona spoke Basque, seemingly didn't understand his English and barely his French. But he had an accent and Hugh did not. She might understand Hugh better. Further, in the days they spent together, he was beginning to understand some Basque phrases, so what could she have learnt from him?

'It's tied to my chest, but I was careful,' he hissed. 'I brought nothing…but her.'

Hugh straightened. 'Her?'

'And you've left her out here while you punched each other?' Pivoting on her heel, Alice walked to Andreona. 'Both of you need to get cleaned up. Food's about ready.'

Hugh frowned, something else flitting across his features. 'That's not Finlay.'

'It's not. And she knows I carry the dagger,

but not what it means, although she heard all your words.'

'Where's Finlay?'

'He—'

'Dead? Did she have something to do with it?'

'Not last I checked,' Malcolm shifted his jaw from side to side. 'But he wasn't—'

'Then who is that woman?'

'If you'd let me get my words out, maybe I can let you know.'

Hugh spat on the ground and brushed the back of his hand over his lip. 'Is there blood on my tunic?'

'Your tunic?'

'It's been years since we saw you last. I have children inside.'

Malcolm looked to Alice, who was conversing with Andreona as she slowly dismounted. Then he swung his gaze, and at the open doorway where a fire flickered in the background. Children inside. Hugh's anger at him was justified.

'Now you hesitate?' Hugh clapped him on the shoulder and Malcolm winced. 'That one struck true?'

'The only one you'll get,' Malcolm said.

'Let's get cleaned up. I can't let the children see.'

'Your lip will give you away.'

'At least they'll know what happened to your chin.'

With his jaw throbbing, Malcolm looked to the women. Alice was talking, Andreona was not, but she was looking at him. She was *looking* at him. An unknown relief flooded through him. Maybe coming here was the right course.

But coming here presented its own problems, least of all how they were welcomed. Alice needed to know Andreona didn't speak English, but did Andreona need to know of the Jewell of Kings? She wasn't supposed to know and now he didn't know how to approach the subject or if it was safe.

Alice stopped and looked at them. 'Are we not eating?'

'She doesn't know anything,' Malcolm said.

Alice opened her mouth, closed it. 'I thought she was tied to you.'

What could have been said? 'She—'

Hugh cursed. 'Who are you?'

Andreona didn't say anything. It pained him to see her so distant. Not the woman who built towers or kissed him. He cared far too much than was good for either of them. He felt tied to her, but who was she to be to Hugh or Alice? He needed to stop these thoughts. She shouldn't be anything to any of them.

He'd agreed to take her, but only because…

only because she'd seemed lost, like she did now. Who could blame her? Not him, not when he blamed himself. Still, Hugh and Alice deserved the truth.

'Gorka's daughter,' Malcolm said.

'You son of a bastard!' Hugh slammed his fist against Malcolm's jaw, and he hit the ground.

Andreona cried out. Stunned by the sound of distress, and her look of concerned fury, it took him a moment to stand.

Hugh pointed. 'You said you didn't bring danger to my house—what do you call her?'

'Maybe we shouldn't shout. There is the baby,' Alice said.

Hugh rounded on Andreona. 'He says he has the dagger, but you're the one with it, aren't you?'

'*We* have the dagger, Hugh, and she helped me get it,' Malcolm said. 'And none of this matters because we are still speaking English!'

Malcolm took Andreona's hand. Her eyes widened at the contact and he felt the same in his own. It felt right to hold her hand. Something he'd either think on or try to ignore later.

'She is as lost as the dagger was, she can't return to the Basque Country.' Malcolm said in French.

Hugh looked torn, Alice resolved.

'She's not lost now,' Alice said. 'And you both have a roof over your head tonight.'

'Alice,' Hugh said. 'This risks you.'

'I'm risking myself.' Alice wove her arm through Andreona's and pulled her away from Malcolm. 'Let's get you inside. Hugh, you have blood on your tunic. Clean up, before you come inside.'

Watching his wife's retreating form, Hugh clapped his hand on Malcolm's throbbing shoulder.

Malcolm knew it for the warning it was, but it was too late to heed it. Though he'd fleetingly wondered if Hugh and Alice's might be a home where he could leave Andreona, that foolish thought was now tossed aside. Hugh wouldn't want to risk his family.

Perhaps somewhere else along the journey to Scotland would be safe and good for her. She needed that and he needed not to get any closer to her. Even if he was finished with this quest for the dagger and the Jewell of Kings, with too much darkness in his past, and no intentions of any settled future, he wasn't right for her.

Andreona wondered at Malcolm's sudden claiming of her in front of these strangers. Who were they, this Hugh and Alice? Finlay had mentioned the messages that they'd sent, but what were they doing here, at their house? Why did

Malcolm hold her hand and why did she squeeze his before Alice took her away?

She hadn't cared they'd shouted their foreign language in front of her or when Alice came to greet her. She had cared that, after she had heard her father's name, Malcolm was punched.

Then their words became a smattering of English and some French by Malcolm. None of it she understood, except the word dagger, which was repeated and seemed important. Especially the way Hugh and Alice stared at Malcolm's chest as if they wanted to see it.

That she knew wasn't usual. What also wasn't usual was wanting to protect Malcolm from Hugh's fist and feeling anything at all after days of nothing.

All this time, Malcolm had barely spoken to her, which suited her; she didn't want to speak. Her father had wanted, and had expected, her death. Ximeno was meant to be the kinder brother, but he'd lied to her. She'd taken his coin, thinking she had approval from her father for the tower. It would have been kinder to tell her of her father's opinion. Not to give her coin knowing she built the tower in a vain hope to gain some acknowledgment.

She would have... She didn't know what she would have done differently or where else she would have gone. Uracca had tried to tell her for months and she hadn't listened. Ximeno had given her the coin and told her to build a better life. She thought she was.

Now she had nothing. She *was* lost. Her father hadn't even put out a price to kill her, simply ordered someone to do him a favour, and she had revered him.

She travelled with a stranger for reasons she didn't fully understand. She had insisted on going with him. She'd surprised everyone, hurt Uracca, but she couldn't face her friend. There weren't enough apologies for ignoring Uracca's warnings and she was a coward. So, she travelled with a man she didn't know for the sole reason of running away to think.

She wasn't acting like herself. She'd always preferred deeds to inaction. Some workers taking her coin, but not finishing the build? A father banishing her? Simply go out and prove your worth by doing something...building a tower, tying some ropes for nets. But now she didn't feel like getting up.

She was relieved she didn't have to sort out a place to stay tonight. She wasn't worried if they were good people—how was she to judge? She hadn't even known her father wanted her dead. And Malcolm obviously didn't think it important to introduce them because he still hadn't.

Malcolm.

Days of quiet. Of getting up in the morning and stretching the aches from her limbs since the ground was hard. Of pretending to eat when Malcolm did, sleeping when he told her to, riding when he swung his leg over his horse. Days of… not doing what she had done for the past year. Of ordering people about, of not listening, of being so sure she was right—she'd never once questioned whether her decisions could be wrong.

Now she simply left her life up to strangers. Alice's grey eyes were kind, though she didn't understand what she was saying until she began to speak French, but she followed her into the warm home anyway.

At the table was a young man with unruly brown hair fingering with his left hand. In his right was an abacus, to the right of that was another…and another. All of different sizes, all well-worn.

When Alice cleared her throat, the young man jumped as if he hadn't heard them. Eyes widening, he quickly stood. More rattling of words she didn't know and these sounded expectant. When Alice pointed at her, she said, 'Andreona', hoping they were asking her name.

The woman clapped her hands and said some more words in rapid French, only some of which Andreona caught.

The room was large, but welcoming. Something steamed near the fireplace and several loaves of browned bread were piled on another table with other bits to eat.

Nearest to the door on a broad table, and sound asleep, was a swaddled baby in a basket. Alice went to it, her face softening immediately as she said some words in a singing voice. The young man smiled gently until he glanced up at her, flushed across his cheeks and quickly sat down.

'We'll need to talk,' Malcolm said, striding in. His hair and tunic were wet, as if he'd dunked his upper torso into a barrel of water.

It plastered his tunic against his body and she couldn't move her eyes away. It wasn't because the dagger was removed or that the scar was outlined through the fabric. It was the way the linen hitched on his hip and sagged wide around his neck, displaying a lone droplet of water trailing down his neck and pooling at his collarbone.

'Did you sort yourselves out?' Alice said.

'He's a fool as I've always thought,' Hugh said.

Andreona couldn't help it—she laughed.

Malcolm froze, his green eyes on her. His jaw was slightly swollen, but there was a curious light in his expression that broke through his usual grumpiness. It changed him and her laughter, which startled even her, didn't ease. In fact, she felt the smile stay on her lips...until Alice exchanged a look with Hugh.

Then she remembered where and what she was. She knew nothing because the one man who was looking at her as if he wanted her to laugh again kept his secrets.

Avoiding those eyes, she looked to the baby. 'Beautiful.'

Alice lifted the baby from the basket. White hair, blue eyes slowly opening. She looked like her father, but there was something else. 'A girl?'

Alice nodded. 'This is little Bertrice. We named her after a dear friend and that's William, who is staying with us for the year. Apparently, keeping ledgers isn't all he's interested in.'

'A boy turning to manhood may need to defend those ledgers, my dear,' Hugh said.

'I like the swords.' William gestured to abacus. 'These are torturous.'

'As much as being Boy Bishop?' Alice quipped.

William let out a groan at the same time as Hugh laughed. There was something comforting about the domestic scene and their shared memories.

'I'm Andreona,' she said, aware of eyes on her, but Malcolm's were the ones she felt. 'I like your abacus.'

William picked one up and handed it to her. 'You can have it.'

Andreona took it with no intention of keeping it, but she liked the distraction. It was a useful object to look at and play with when green eyes were too curious on her.

Turning to Andreona, Malcolm pointed. 'This is Hugh and Alice. They are family acquaintances and we need to talk.'

About that they were more than acquaintances? 'He hit you.'

Alice made some sound and Hugh coughed.

'True,' Malcolm said.

'Is this about the messages?' she added.

Malcolm turned to Hugh. 'Finlay's mouth.'

Hugh smirked.

They were all so familiar with each other, but none of this was familiar for her. She wasn't ready to talk to them. She liked this bit of life here, liked moving the wooden beads on the abacus, which was simply a contraption to make order out of chaos. She could play with this for a long time and slowly think of her father and her brothers.

She could avoid thinking about Malcolm holding her hand or kissing her. Not when Malcolm was looking at her...curiously. Not when the rest of them did as well.

'I don't want to know,' Andreona said.

Stepping towards her, Malcolm said, 'It can't be—'

She held up her hand. 'I have my own matters,

you know that. Whatever this is about, I don't need to know.'

'Until it comes after you,' Malcolm said.

'Will it come after me? Am I in a danger any more than I have ever been before?' she said. Her father had ordered her death. She was spared because her brother lied to him. Ximeno had protected her, but he'd lied to her as well. She wasn't grateful because she had played the fool in front of everyone she trusted.

Malcolm ran his hand through his curls. Without the sun, she could see none of the red.

Holding the baby in one arm, Alice steered Hugh towards the bowls. 'How about we eat first?'

Chapter Fifteen

The house was finally still and Malcolm took a long slow breath. There was no steady pounding of footsteps across wood floorboards. Alice and Hugh had taken Bertrice to bed and William had long gone to his own room. In order to avoid notice, Hugh and Alice's place wasn't large, which meant Andreona and he were sharing a room. All through the meal, he'd tortured himself with visions of her in his bed. Wondered about the texture of her hair against his palm, the softness of her skin, the way her lips would feel when he kissed her.

And it was wrong to wonder. They'd met because he'd jumped through a hatch. She'd fought and surprised him with her strength and determination. He had an agenda being there and so did she. He noticed the loose lace of her gown swinging, but their accidental touch, their entanglement, changed things.

The feeling didn't go away despite her resolve to gift him to her father and only escalated as he hid and protected her body, but not her vulnerability, as they heard her father's cruelty.

And she worried him. Riding across France, she'd become distant. He wanted to protect her. Which was likely reasonable, but he also felt possessive. There was a primitive part of him that felt she was his to protect, to guard.

What had she made of the fight between him and Hugh and the words they'd exchanged? Her eyes kept drifting to his chest, her brow drawing in. She knew the dagger was important or else he wouldn't have risked Gorka's claim to it. She was also no fool and knew he lied when he'd said it was sentimental to his family. Yet she'd reported she didn't want to know anymore. He could barely understand why he wanted to tell her the truth, or at least part of it. It must be her and those eyes of hers. They reminded him of Scotland, of home. And he hadn't thought of Scotland as home in years.

Danger everywhere and this mission was almost over, yet he could do nothing to stop his thoughts or the way his body tightened when Andreona was near.

When all the heated, whispered words between him and Hugh were spent, he went to the room, half hoping she was asleep, except she wasn't there. So swiftly, silently, Malcolm let himself out of the room, but after searching the house, he knew Andreona was out in the night, and he was compelled to go.

The night was cool, with a heavy mist blanketing everything. The full moon casting the field and the trees beyond in an otherworldly light. After a night of talking of legends and tales, the last thing Malcolm wanted to see was a field in France looking as though it was visited by faeries and pixies.

Out around the house, he searched through the barns in the back. Further yet, and he felt unease slither up his spine until he spotted her through some trees.

She wasn't dressed. Or rather, it was the white of her chemise fluttering behind her alerting him towards the direction she went, which was further from the house and him.

Lengthening his strides until he was almost upon her, Malcolm called out, 'Don't go any further.'

Gasping, Andreona pivoted. 'How did you find me?'

The angle of her body, the wrapping of the chemise, her arms around her waist defining every curve, slowed Malcolm's steps. He thought the night was a vision of faeries, but nothing compared to Andreona.

In his lifetime, he'd held the Jewell of Kings and the Jewell Dagger, he'd fought in battle and had sought and found many pleasures. But he'd never seen anything like Andreona in the moonlight with mist swirling around her. She was intangible to him like true legends were meant to be. Something beautiful to reach for, but never to actually hold.

And that thought made him crave.

'You weren't where you were meant to be.' Near him, by his side. In his bed.

'I couldn't sleep. It was too warm.'

'I can see that,' he said.

She rubbed her arms. 'You're not meant to see me like this. I didn't intend for anyone to. I thought I'd be back before you retired.'

He'd seen her feet bare, a lace or two loosely or not tied at all, but never had he seen her bared like this. Perhaps she hadn't meant for anyone to see her, but he couldn't stop looking at her now.

'You're too far away to protect. Even if I wanted to leave you alone, I couldn't.'

At her blush, he wondered what he said that could have… He'd given away that he didn't want to leave her alone. Hadn't he made that apparent when he'd kissed her? He was unexpectantly impulsive with her. Something startling to himself and his own sense of self-preservation.

'Why are you here? You look cold now,' he said.

'This part of France has a dampness in the air. It seems to seep into my clothes.'

'So you decided to come outside with few clothes to truly test the weather.'

'I like the outside.' She held out her hand and caught the rain. 'I like how this feels.'

The chemise covered her from neck to ground. It was large and thick. Nothing that should have felt revealing, except when she held her hand out, it pulled the fabric away and revealed her wrist.

He wanted to be that mist landing at her pulse. More, he wanted his mouth there to taste it.

'You'll like Scotland then. The mist there seeps into your bones.'

'You miss it.'

'Sometimes.' Now they were travelling that way, he felt a pull to return, but if she had asked that question a month or two ago, he would have answered no. He wondered if it was because his vow was almost complete or whether it was her. Was he thinking of home because she travelled with him, or because he wanted one with her?

'Is your Scotland where we'll go next?' she said.

Not intending to take her at all, he'd reasoned

he could leave her with Hugh and Alice, or perhaps Rhain and Helissent in England. He travelled with the dagger and could be set upon by any of his enemies. It would be safer to leave her along the way.

Hugh voiced his concerns with Andreona, but Alice had willingly agreed to take her in. Yet, though Malcolm was the one who talked to them about it, he also felt as if he couldn't leave her here. The way she looked in the mist, he wondered if he'd be able to leave her anywhere.

'You like the outside,' he said.

'I do.'

'Is that why the tower leaked?'

'We were constantly battling the rain.' Her expression tightened. 'You seem to have your battles.'

He wouldn't even pretend to not understand what she meant.

'You weren't meant to know any of this.'

'But I was involved the moment you wanted the dagger.'

'You knew their words?'

'I know that word dagger in several languages now.' She laughed. 'I know they stared at your chest all throughout the evening meal and that, right now, it's no longer across your chest as it has been these many days. Does Hugh have it?'

'Yes.'

'Why?'

He shouldn't answer her.

She huffed. 'Are you trying to protect me? I have no home. I have a friend who for over a year lied to me. I have you and apparently whatever that dagger represents.'

'This is your curiosity talking.'

'You stated you'd tell me who made it and why.' She took in his expression. 'Or did you lie to me, too?'

He didn't take that well. Everything inside him wanted to protest. Why did it matter? A few days in this woman's presence, she shouldn't matter to him.

And yet…he'd held her in his arms, felt her trembling at her father's words. He knew to his very soul what it was like to be betrayed by family.

He took her loss personally.

'I tell you this goes beyond curiosity. I could give you a purse of coin and we'd separate. Hugh and Alice agreed to take you in. You don't need to make the journey with me.'

'You talked to them of my future.'

'I shouldn't have taken you from Uracca.'

'That wasn't solely your decision. I didn't want to travel with her.'

'Why?' he said. A slight flinch was the only

indication his words were unexpected. 'She was sorry she'd lied.'

'She was, but that isn't enough right now.'

'What is?' he said. He told her she was curious, but he was afflicted with the same emotion.

Eyeing him before she turned away, Andreona raised her face to the mist. She wasn't going to answer his question. He knew it was too personal and he was too impatient. He let her walk, but when she hit the other treeline, something inside him rebelled. She was too far. 'Don't.'

Tapping her hand against the trunk, she said, 'I could keep walking. You wouldn't have to part with your coin and these friends of yours don't have to pretend hospitality.'

'They're not friends.'

She turned. 'I think you need to tell them because they acted as if they were.'

'Hugh is friends with the man who married my sister... Robert and Gaira.'

'So, more than friends—he's family.'

That irked him. He and Hugh had never got along, but the truth was they were family in a way. The pursuit of the Jewell of Kings, the treasure, the dagger, the taking down of the Warstones. The messages between the Half-Thistle Seal had made them strong.

He hated it, but it had been his life for years. This woman could simply walk away.

'What is it?' Andreona brushed her palm up the trunk and slid along the branch above her head.

'Do you truly not want to know?'

'About Hugh?' She shrugged.

'About the dagger,' he said. 'You said earlier you didn't want to know.'

She dropped her arm. 'Why do you want to tell me?'

'I could tell you because it might not mean anything more.' The Jewell, the books and parchments written in codes for the treasures were already in Scotland—there was just this dagger he had to get to his family. Already, Hugh would be writing messages, sealing them with the Half-Thistle Seal, sending them with mercenaries trained to hide, to fight and protect the messages. It wasn't the task for him since he carried the dagger.

But those messages would be ridden with haste to notify Reynold, Louve, Robert, Nicholas. He'd agreed with Hugh he would ride to Rhain and tell him of the dagger. Others would be told: Eldric, Balthus... Everyone who fought The Englishman, Sir Richard Howe, the Warstones. Anyone who kept the secrets and fought to protect the jewel would be notified, all to meet again on Colquhoun land.

This was almost over and that knowledge

rocked through Malcolm. It was as if the ground shifted under him. His balance—his world—was altered. And Andreona watched it all as he came to that realisation. All his toil and pain, he knew it was to come to this, but only now it sank in.

And all because he knew he could…tell this tale if Andreona wanted to hear it. Oh, there was still danger, they weren't in Scotland and surrounded by people who could help him. A thousand mistakes could be made between now and then.

But the possibility was there…no, it wasn't only because of the possibility. It was her.

She was here and he wanted to tell her. Why? Because she was looking at him, because unbeknown to her they shared a family knowledge of betrayal.

Because.

'The dagger is hollowed to hold what is known as the Jewell of Kings.'

She leaned her shoulder against the tree trunk, but her expression never changed. She didn't walk away either.

'It's a legend that whoever holds the gem, holds the heart of Scotland,' he continued.

'A story?' Her brows drew in. 'Why would you risk your life for a story? If you hadn't had me and gone straight to Gorka, you'd be dead.'

'Because some powerful people believe the story to be true.'

'Powerful people?'

'Kings and those who make them. Your father had the dagger that hid it.'

'My father wouldn't have wanted it. He works in shadows.'

'How did he get it?' When she hesitated, he added, 'We don't need to talk of him.'

In fact, he didn't want to talk of him. It seemed too soon, and they stood in the mists as if they didn't belong to the rest of the world. He wanted nothing to touch this moment.

'No, it's—I want to talk,' she said. 'I came out here to think and we have much to learn. My father has spies, men who pretend they are hired swords and then bring information back to him.'

Her father was clever, formidable, but it didn't mean he wouldn't gut him for treating his daughter the way he had. He was a stranger to her, and she didn't owe him anything. Everything he represented was a failure for her...and yet... She stood in the moonlight, her hair loose, the tumbles outlined against the linen of her chemise.

She was beautiful and brave. Not only talking to him, but sharing anything at all.

'And this mercenary knew to switch?' he said. 'How could he know what the dagger looked like?'

She pushed away from the trees, hugging her arms around her waist. Taking a few steps away and then even more back, she said, 'My father's *power* is from stealing. He is the king of thieves. Part of the art of stealing is making the switch.'

'But the scrollwork on the dagger, the gems, it's all very precise. To be a craftsman and a mercenary? To be in your father's employ and train enough to have any skill with both? It's not possible.'

She paced faster than before, his words agitating her. He wanted to stop talking of this, stop hurting her, but at the same time they were so close to the truth.

'There's only one man who could have done it.' She turned to the tree and back again. 'He was gone from my father's keep for many years. In truth, the task of doing so could have been done over a length of time and involved several of my father's thieves. I don't know. I haven't lived in the keep for years and I was never favoured, though I tried, and I—'

Two steps and his calloused hands cupped her cheeks. So *soft*.

'You don't have to say any more. You don't need to tell me. I understand.'

Stilling, she encircled his wrists and pulled his hands away. 'No, you don't.'

He did, so much, and he wanted and hated to

tell her why. How he wished his brothers treated him as they did themselves, that they thought him unequal to trust or bear their burdens.

She took a step back and he grabbed her hip, holding her still. She gasped. When she twisted to move away, his fingers flexed and she stilled.

'You don't know what it means when a father wants you dead.'

No, she was right, his parents were dead.

But he did understand what happened that day when they got tangled together. When her fingers simply curled into him. Because he was doing the same. *This* was the same.

As he gripped her closer, his mouth descended on hers.

Chapter Sixteen

Andreona's chest felt pummelled with emotion, her thoughts were a roiling dark chaos. Malcolm's kiss should have been nothing she wanted. But though his grip on her chemise was fierce, and some energy was roiling off him towards her, his lips were firm, soft. They coaxed and she answered.

Her hands on his chest, leaning in as she had the tree, finding support, strength in him as she did its roots while he murmured words she only half understood. When he trailed his tongue along the seam of her lips, she gasped. Lips parted, they both took in air and their need for each other.

His hand released her hip and moved to her throat, his thumb resting on her pulse there. Her heart beat that bit faster.

'Andreona?' he asked. His green eyes studied her, though it was difficult to know what was in his thoughts since the moonlight barely shone through the tree canopy. She was aware the house was out of sight and perhaps its occupants were asleep or not. Any of them could take the same walk she had and the trees didn't provide privacy or shelter from the elements.

She didn't want shelter from the elements. She wanted Malcolm to say her name like a question. One that only she knew the answer to.

Leaning into him again, she brushed her lips against his and his hand skimmed the column of her neck to cup her jaw, his lips pressing more, giving a longer taste of his kiss, of this man.

Sifting her fingers through his wayward curls, then drifting them along the back of his neck, she felt his body shiver at the small touch.

Liking that, she brushed more of her fingertips behind his ear; he shuddered, slid his hand along her waist and pulled her impossibly tighter.

His lips turned hot and demanding, slanting his head, his tongue finding hers, searching for the answers she hadn't given him yet. A breath of a moment—was she willing?

Yes, she was. The way he felt, the way he held her... She was willing to give him anything. Everything. Using his shoulders to pull herself up, she couldn't wait to increase their kisses and shuddering breaths.

He froze so suddenly she didn't know what

he was about until he pulled back. No green to his eyes, no questions, only a distance that was confusing with the heat of his hand against her cheek, the tight grip around her waist.

'It's late and cold,' he said. 'We're outside.'

Why was he talking of their surroundings? He shifted and she realised he wanted to leave her.

'No,' she blurted. Her hands clutched his shoulders. His expression was unreadable. Hers, she knew, was too tender and exposed in the swirling mists.

She wanted whatever this was. Kisses, the hint of more. Having never had a brush of a man's hand against hers, she was as untouched as could be, but she'd seen others in the corners of halls.

The want, the urgency. Stolen moments between two people broken apart because Gorka's child stumbled upon them. Did all those intimate embraces start like this?

'I want more,' she said.

His lips parted, the bottom one, slick from their kisses, caused her stomach to flip. 'You stiffened.'

Because despite him kissing her gently, he'd taken her by surprise. All of this touch was a surprise, but how to articulate it? 'I'm not used to this.'

His expression softened. 'I know.'

So those spied moments weren't enough to teach her how to kiss.

His mouth curved and he brushed his thumb across her upper lip, trailed his fingers down the vulnerable cords of her throat. 'You told me in those sounds you gave when I touched your pulse.'

Oh. 'No one's even looked at me—'

'I can't look away,' he said.

She could think of no verbal response, but something inside blossomed with an eagerness she barely contained. After her father...where did this hope come from? Malcolm had his secrets. He'd told her some, but there was no certainty he told her everything. Still, something in her trusted him, or else she wouldn't be out in the night mists with him.

She wasn't to be with anyone. Undressing for the night in the quietness of the room, she suddenly couldn't be inside and had run from the glow of the house to escape with her thoughts.

Now she felt caught by Malcolm, who hooked her tresses in the crook of his finger and separated a curl until it fell away. Then he clutched more, causing goose pimples to flush along her spine.

He seemed to not want to do anything else except play. Mimicking him, she captured one of his curls, felt him shiver when her fingertips touched his skin there. He'd done that before. Curious, she stretched to touch more while Malcolm's gaze roamed and took in her every feature, as if she fascinated him.

When her height and his precluded her from playing with more of him, Malcolm growled roughly and hoisted her up.

Everything about this was right: his weight, the press of his hips, his chest, the support of his thigh he inserted and rested her upon. She could touch and discover more of him now.

Her gaze searching his, she pressed her fingers along his jaw. Lips curving with mischief, eyes almost wary, he tilted his head to expose more of that vulnerable skin to her curiosity.

Rubbing her cheek against his to let him know she meant no more than this, she pressed kisses along his neck, her tongue tasting the tender lobe of his ear. His arms tightened around her; his breath hitched.

She liked that, too. Pushing up from his shoulders, she tasted more of this part of his body. Riding next to him for days, sitting next to him at dinner, this tender part of his neck was what she saw the most when he didn't look at her.

His skin was warm and soft. She felt everything from his breath to when he swallowed hard. It was vulnerable yet utterly masculine with the scruff of his stubble, the clean steel scent of him. He waited patiently while she explored under one ear and then under the other until her soft kisses and flickering tastes weren't enough for her or him.

Not when she felt the clasping of his fingers at her sides, the roughing up of the chemise, the way his breath became a force moving her, pressing her breasts against the heat of his torso, their hips locking and unlocking with each dip of her head, each push of her hands against his shoulders.

It wasn't enough, some instinct, some wanting need, and she bit against the strained cord across his shoulder.

Grunting, Malcolm wrenched his neck away from her, slammed his lips to hers, devoured her with short choppy kisses and uneven breaths. The apex of her thighs rubbed against the rough linen of his breeches, the sudden dampness of her core against the hard bar of his need.

'Oh,' she gasped.

He yanked impatiently at her chemise, his lips and teeth nipping her neck, her jawline. Doing to her what she had done to him, but in a hundred different ways she felt in a thousand different feelings. Heat racing, doused by shivers, only for warmth and sensual licks and tender kisses to start again with the tiny nips.

All the while Malcolm streamed a litany of words she didn't understand. He used that language of his, the one of growls and rumbles, searing her to huffs of breath and greedy moans. To desperate desire. Until Malcolm took even those weak broken utterances by kissing her again. Sucking in her bottom lip, stroking his tongue with hers. He was everywhere and not near enough.

Resting her forehead on his shoulder, she whispered her pleas as his words and touch became urgent. As he rocked against her, his calloused fingers and roughened hands swept across her bared skin. She felt the bark of the tree, the unwanted heavy fabric of her chemise bunched around her waist, one portion half hanging off the tips of her breasts until he pulled away and it collapsed between them.

Then it was cool air hitting the damp evidence of his kisses on her skin. His nostrils flared as he took in her pebbled skin and the tightening of her nipples.

'Ah, you're beautiful, Andreona. More than I could have guessed.'

His words were heated reverence. She'd never heard such praise between a man and woman. Those stolen moments she spied between others seemed to pale in comparison, but what did she know? Were his words for her alone, and if so, what did they mean?

'Were you guessing?' she said.

He gave her a wicked grin. 'Wishing, more like.'

Now she was the one with the questions. While her world was falling apart, was he merely wishing to lie with her? Was that all this was?

Malcolm took in her expression and whatever he saw there dimmed the heat in his eyes. Exhaling roughly, he looked away before he straightened her clothing.

He didn't release her. It would have been too sudden, too cold. Mist fell heavy on their skin. She wasn't certain she wanted this to end and yet somehow it did simply by a few words and a few doubts.

What had she done?

Malcolm watched Andreona's desire flicker out and cursed his wayward tongue for reminding her of anything prior to this moment. He was here with Hugh and Alice because her eyes had lost their light and she'd gone too quiet. Because he was worried about her. A few hours in their company and she was asking William to show her the intricacies of the abacus and wanting to know if she could help with Bertrice.

She wasn't that fierce woman who had defended the tower, but whatever sorrow was in her eased with the distractions of Hugh's family.

He'd been right to bring her here, but now he'd carelessly hurt her again.

'I didn't mean my words…the way they sounded,' he said. Could he be any more clumsy?

She licked her lips. 'How did you mean it? It sounded like… I'm grieving, Malcolm, and—'

He pulled her closer, feeling the needful heat they created, but also the warmth, her scent, the way she felt in his arms, the strength and softness that was all her.

'I know you are,' he said, aware she gave him much with that truth. He eased her down, but kept his arms around her, brushed his cheek against her head. 'I'm sorry, this isn't the time, I simply…'

'You what?' Andreona said. 'I don't understand any of this. I have never kissed a man before and then we're here.'

'I was wanting you before I knew of your father and only more after he said those words because I felt them, too. When I held you, when we hid behind that tree, I wanted to hold you much, much longer.'

She placed her hands on his chest and he felt the push, but he was loath to let her go.

'No, you can't know what I feel,' she said, her eyes darting around them. 'You're right, this is too soon. I don't know you. How can I trust you?'

He stepped away. 'Why did you go with me,

then? Why didn't you leave with Uracca, your childhood friend, or Finlay, who is far more agreeable than me?'

He wanted her to tell the truth, that there was something between them and, despite not knowing him long, she trusted him. He wanted some acknowledgment that what was between them mattered. Because she mattered to him.

'Why do you want to know?' she said. 'Days ago, we didn't know each other, and yet you've witnessed one of the most humiliating times of my life. My father ordering my death hardly factors when it comes to my brother and my friend lying to me. What they—'

She suddenly stopped, let out a gasp, began to run and he grabbed her wrist. When she wrenched it free, he let go. Waited, but she didn't run again.

He knew now why she'd left with him, not because of him, but because of them. That thought didn't sit well. It had made no sense to bring her with him, but he'd done it because he was relieved she'd got her spirit back. He didn't want to part with her, but she only wanted to avoid her family and friends. Perhaps he was the only one who felt something. Still, he'd do right by her if he could.

'We'll leave in another day. The journey where we must go will take some time and we'll cross water. It will be dangerous. I'll try to protect you as much as I can, but if you have doubts about travelling further with me, if your only intention was to get away from them, you can stay here. Hugh and Alice are good people. And in time, Hugh can take you to the Warstone fortress when you want to see Uracca again.'

Her tresses cascaded down the chemise, which was laden with the moist air. She looked part-faerie, part-street wench. She was so beautiful it hurt.

She turned away, placed her hand on a tree and, as she did before, felt along the roughened bark. His body tightened as he imagined those fingertips on him.

When she was done with that tree, she went to the next and the next, winding around the copse, not going too far out for him to call back, but enough, he was certain, to give them distance.

He'd never waited for much in his life, everything he'd done was because he was forced or jumped into it. But he waited now because he knew she needed him to wait, because he knew if he didn't, he'd lose her.

The wind had picked up and his hair was plastered to his cheeks by the time she turned to him. He couldn't see her expression at all, but he heard her.

'Can I put a thistle on Hugh and Alice's door?'

'A thistle?' It wasn't the request, but the object that startled him. A thistle meant so much at home and it brought too many poignant, bitter memories.

'It's so Lamiak—a bad spirit—won't enter the house and steal the children. Also, it'll protect Hugh and Alice.'

He wondered if he said yes, would she stay? But if she needed a thistle to protect her, he'd hang a thousand of them.

'Hand one over and I'll do it tonight.'

He could barely see her smile, but the hint was there, and it lightened and saddened him. She'd hang a thistle and then she'd be gone from his life.

'I want to continue on,' she blurted. 'I want to go with you.'

He'd rushed towards her before he even knew what he was doing, spanned his hands around her waist and spun her. She cried out before he set her down.

'What was that for?'

Because he wasn't ready to let her go. A mistake, maybe, and part of him warned he was rushing ahead with no thought of consequences, but it didn't feel like it. He already knew he didn't want to leave her here with Hugh and Alice. Maybe Rhain and Helissent's inn would be better, though his chest constricted at the mere thought.

What was he doing with her? He had no intention of having a friend, let alone a woman who rode beside him, a woman he wanted to kiss again.

When it came to her, he was conflicted. Because he had never cared before, these conflicts weren't anything he expected to have. Maybe they could make it to Scotland and keep travelling? He shared things with her he'd shared with no one else. They were both betrayed by those closest to them. Both had learnt they didn't need people.

He didn't know why he couldn't let her go when he knew he couldn't get closer else there was the chance she'd betray him, too. But she said she wanted to continue travelling with him and he was more than willing for her to do so. She'd also asked a question and he needed to answer it.

These were important words. Too important for English or French, only his own words would convey what he meant. 'I dinna ken, but now we have time to find out, do we not, lass?'

'You do know I didn't understand a word you said?'

He winked.

Chapter Seventeen

⟨⟨⟨⟩⟩⟩

Andreona missed the smell of Basque seafood and sea air, but she didn't miss much else as they travelled through France. It was hard to do so. The few days they'd spent with Hugh and Alice had eased her soul, given her some time to sift through her thoughts and bring out one painful memory after another.

It was easy to do when Bertrice would smile, or William would grumble. When Alice talked about sheep and the wool industry, she could let her mind be occupied or wander.

Her thoughts often caught on this Malcolm of Clan Colquhoun with his green eyes and dark hair she swore had red in it, but he insisted it didn't. That no one had ever seen it and therefore it didn't exist. There were no more shared kisses or touches, but lingering gazes and teasing comments. It had felt good.

However, getting back on the horse, and travelling west and closer to England wasn't all good.

It was the warnings Malcolm whispered. How he stayed off main roads and close to shadows. They travelled at odd times and sometimes would stay overnight in inns or out in the open air.

There seemed to be some political upheaval she'd known nothing about between England and Scotland. While they travelled in France, Malcolm was free with his speech with strangers. Once they came to the French border, he got quiet and changed his accent. All the way she was aware of his studying, pensive gaze.

He'd kissed her, held her! As Gorka's bastard child, she'd never expected a man to take any interest until her father did and even then...she'd never be certain it wasn't because they wanted to gain some boon from her father. No, her time, her thoughts and deeds had been only on her father acknowledging her as he did her two half-brothers.

Now her thoughts were on what she'd given up and what she'd gained by setting those nets. She travelled with this man who held her as if she mattered, but also a man with conflicting emotions in his eyes.

She rode with Malcolm to get away from the betrayal of her family and Uracca, to think about what they had done and how her life would be, but now she wanted to stay for the mystery of this man and the way he made her feel. Was it the danger he worried about?

Often he'd touch his chest, the outline of the dagger constantly visible. He'd told her some stories, but she'd never been to Scotland or England and they meant very little to her. All she knew was the dagger was fascinating and held possibilities for why it was created. Until she saw this gem they went on about, she could still imagine secret messages or dried flowers inside the dagger's hollowed handle.

Late at night, and in the cover of darkness, he'd take it off and let her play with it. She also played with the enamel box Ximeno had stolen for her. It was the smallest box in all their collection, but because she suspected Ximeno had chosen it because it had the oddest shape inside, as if the craftsman was storing something specific, it was more valuable to her than the dagger.

Knowing he'd stolen that, had probably looked inside, eased her heart a bit towards her brother. And as they hung silver thistles on every door they stayed at, she was reminded of happier times with Uracca.

Her heart was easing…mostly because of the man at her side. He told her stories of his family: Bram, the eldest, who was once Laird of Colquhoun, but now Laird of Fergusson, and the second brother, Caird, who was now Laird of Colquhoun, his younger sister, Gaira who was married to this Robert, and Irvette, the youngest, who was killed along with her husband in a Scottish village.

As he talked of family, every so often Malcolm would get this closed-off expression, as though he was remembering or not wanting to tell her something. Something about danger and Warstones and kings being after her if he did. It was too fantastical to be true, but she liked the stories of his family best.

'So Cressida was an archer,' she said. Cressida was apparently married to a man who was friends with Hugh. Though Malcolm denied any of them were friends or people he wanted to be close with, the connections of everyone intrigued her. She'd been cut off from her family and he had so much. Why did he deny them?

'*Is* an archer,' Malcolm replied. 'Her and Lioslath, that's Bram's wife, like to get into these competitions. I've never seen it, but it's reported no others dare participate. Except Bram. I think he cheats to give his wife a chance, but he swears he doesn't.'

Andreona liked the idea of a husband cheating in games for his wife. Did she have such stories to tell? No, but she had her own antics with

Uracca. Her stealing enamel boxes from her father being one of them.

'Are you certain you want to know of this?' he said.

She did, but mostly because he seemed reluctant to do so. She wanted to know what the mystery of Malcolm was.

He'd been away from this Scotland of his for many years. Given her own response to run from the Basque Country and her friend, she guessed his staying away had to do with his family, but he did talk more freely of other people in his life.

'And Cressida's husband's name is…'

'Eldric—he's Hugh's friend, but Cressida's enemy.' Malcolm huffed. 'They were enemies first, now they're married.'

The way her and Malcolm had been enemies. What were they now?

She'd liked the kiss they shared, but he had stopped it because she was grieving. It only seemed to attract her more to him. No, they weren't enemies any longer, but what they were she didn't know.

'Why were Cressida and Eldric enemies?' Maybe they were similar to them, maybe there were some clues here on how to understand what Malcolm was to her.

Malcolm's horse sidestepped suddenly as if

he held the reins too tightly and he quickly loosened them.

'Why do you want to know?' he said. 'Talking of families cannot be easy for you.'

If they talked of her own, that would be true, though…she was beginning to forgive Ximeno and Uracca. 'These are long rides you have me going on between food and sleep. It's too quiet otherwise.'

His gaze swung to hers and his frown deepened. 'Would it help?'

With her wondering if Eldric and Cressida were like she and Malcolm? 'Yes.'

'This tale isn't easy…there's much conflict. I think with you, and everything, perhaps we should talk of the differences in our food or drink.'

No, she wanted to know of his world. 'Please?'

His eyes roamed over her, and he sighed. 'Cressida's father is Sir Richard Howe, but for many years, we thought of him as "The Englishman". He was hired by the elder Warstones to find and bring back the Jewell of Kings and the dagger. In fact, he had them both at one point, but lost them to my family.'

'And Cressida?' she asked.

'Was raised by him to…' Malcolm stopped. 'I don't know if she'd want you to know.'

She was the bastard child of a father who'd wanted to kill her. 'Is it because I'm—?'

'No,' Malcolm interrupted. 'Cressida was born from a woman who was not loved and a father who ordered her death.'

Andreona's hand flew to her mouth, to keep in whatever sound she wanted to make.

'I'm sorry,' Malcolm said. 'My family has more than accepted Cressida. I was a fool to tell you, there are too many similarities.'

Andreona marvelled at the connections of Malcolm's family and now she wondered about her own. How was it possible for such cruelty?

'Tell me more.' She adjusted in her seat and the horse flicked his head.

'Why do you want to know? How can this be good for you?'

Because Cressida was married to Eldric. They fell in love though they started as enemies. Maybe something was there for her and Malcolm, too.

Was she falling in love with him? Malcolm was impatient, but kind. Surly, but loyal. He was direct in a way her family had never been. Though he didn't speak of them, he had emotions... She only wished to know more about them.

'Cressida, who is very good at fighting, was

ordered by her father to kill Eldric. Instead, they...co-operated.'

'The Englishman is dead?'

Malcolm's hand tightened on the reins he held before he loosened it again. 'No, he's still out there—he's who I worry about catching us with this dagger. He wants it very much, but his reason is slipping. He—had another child, Maisie, by my sister Irvette.'

Grief was etched tight around Malcolm's neck as he swallowed hard and looked away. Andreona understood why, but she wished he hadn't. She wished to show him, if not with words, with her own eyes that she knew what loss was like.

This story was difficult to understand and to hear. Eldric was Hugh's friend and therefore a friend of Malcolm's clan. Eldric loved his enemy, Cressida, and the way Malcolm talked of her, his clan cared for Cressida. Yet, Cressida's father had harmed Malcom's family terribly.

'The Englishman forced Irvette, didn't he?' she said.

'Yes,' Malcolm cleared his throat. 'It's only Bram, Caird, Gaira and I that know. The Englishman killed Irvette and the man she married.'

'Oh, Malcolm. How do you talk of this? I'm sorry, I shouldn't have pushed.'

'There's good to it,' he said. 'Gaira, my sister, saved Maisie when she was young and has been raising her with Robert, who is Hugh's friend. Maisie has a good home and is happy.'

She was a long way from gazing into pretty boxes and imagining other people's lives. Her life was not easy, but from what Malcolm said, no one's was. It shouldn't have, and she wished no harm on anyone, but knowing others lost, grieved and still found love gave her hope.

"It's all fine now and Cressida has us, she lives with the clan and her half-sister, Maisie, so they are very happy. Like…' Malcolm stopped.

'Like?' she said.

Malcolm shrugged one shoulder. 'Like you will be one day when this is all over and you're away from all this danger with daggers and travel with challenges.'

Was this to be over for her? She didn't want it. Her family had hurt her, but she couldn't imagine simply leaving behind Uracca or Ximeno. As for her father? Perhaps she'd never forgive or understand him.

But it wasn't like her to dwell on pain. If she had, she'd never have built a tower or tried to gain her brother's trust. Or any of the deeds she did after each challenge and each disappointment.

No, she didn't need to be away from this man and his stories about enemies and lovers. About mercenaries chasing daggers and terrible, tragic, heartbreaking losses.

'You sound like you admire most of these people…except Hugh.'

He grinned then. 'You caught that, did you?'

'Difficult not to when he swung a fist at you.'

'I have challenges liking him since the first time I met him years ago.'

'But we stayed with them for a few days and you trained with him and William.'

'Yes, and I left him with blackened eyes before I left.'

Andreona laughed. She heard the disgruntled respect Malcolm had for Hugh. She wondered if he'd be that way with Ximeno, but not Ander.

'I don't like my brother Ander,' she said, 'so perhaps we're the same?'

He sobered. 'If the rumours are true, it was good he wasn't around.'

'It's odd you know of my family, but I don't know yours.'

'I had to have some information else I'd be blind entering the keep to steal the dagger. It wasn't perfect. I didn't know of you…' Malcolm cursed. 'I seem to not know what to say around you.'

'I…ken,' she said on purpose, the Scottish word sounding not as pleasing in her accent as it did in his. But she tried to be lighter. 'You wouldn't know of me because my father…' She stopped. 'No, you're right, let's not talk of him.'

'Understandable. It's good to hold on to your anger.'

She didn't know if it was anger or pain. She hoped her emotions would ease, like her disappointment with her friend and brother.

'Ximeno says Ander has a mountain of a mercenary he trained. I'm glad Uracca and the women are no longer nearby.'

'The moment Finlay reaches Evrart's village a message will be sent to the fortress, and perhaps to Colquhoun land as well. Evrart is a strong mercenary, nothing much beats him.'

'A story for another day?' she said.

'Most assuredly,' Malcolm said, slowing his horse. Andreona slowed hers as well. 'Tomorrow we cross the water to Dover to an inn. Until then the less we talk the better. If I don't talk at all, you'll know I shouldn't. It would be best if you speak…only if speaking needs to be done.'

'Why?'

'My accent will give me away as a Scot. Matters aren't friendly between our countries. I doona need to add more challenges when it comes to the dagger. I will protect you, but I also have to protect the dagger, else everything I and Finlay have done will be for naught.'

'And for your family, too,' she said, worried he was slipping between languages, something Malcolm only did when he was concerned. 'They'd like this to be over.'

'My family made this mess for me. I need to clean it up,' Malcolm said. 'Of course, you'd know something of that, wouldn't you? I bet you can't wait to be free of all this, and not carry the burden anymore. Just as I don't want my burdens.'

She wasn't so certain her family was a burden, though the weight of what they did seemed unbearable some days. But Malcolm's words worried her for other reasons.

His certainty she'd leave once they'd delivered the dagger and the fact he wanted to leave as well.

But then, what hold did she have for him? A few kisses, his arms around her, but she was the bastard daughter of a man who wanted her dead. Perhaps she wasn't worthy of him. Though her heart, the one that accepted every challenge thrown at her, wouldn't stop wishing for it to be true.

Chapter Eighteen

If Malcolm could avoid Rhain and Helissent's inn near Dover, he would. Unfortunately, most if not all, of the messages sealed with a half-thistle went through the inn. It was essential for his and Andreona's continued safety across England and on to Scotland to exchange information with Rhain.

But by doing so, there were more delays, and though the journey across France and then the sea had been largely uneventful thanks to good horses and a strong wind, he kept looking over his shoulder at every opportunity.

He couldn't shake the feeling he was being watched…that danger waited for them. He'd protect Andreona with his life, but the dagger couldn't be risked. Not when they finally had it and they were this close.

Every time Andreona asked to look at it, he

studied it, too. The scrollwork meant nothing to him, neither did the gems or the craftsmanship. What mattered was what it represented: a place for the Jewell of Kings, a way to a treasure. The certainty that, once he ripped it off his neck and threw it at his brother's feet, he'd be done with it all. Free to roam, to leave behind the painful memories Scotland, his clan, his home, always pulled out of him. He resented all of it.

Except now he had Andreona. And nothing about her did he want to rip away from his life. Although, he would have to. Else *she* wouldn't be free. Yet what to do? She stayed with him and the elation he felt was unexpected. He knew he simply wanted to spend more time with her, but the closer they got to home, the more complicated it felt.

They'd deliver the dagger to his clan, he'd leave and then did he take her back to the Warstone fortress? That was the best option, which meant he'd spend more time with her and it would be even more difficult letting her go.

However, leaving her with his clan in Scotland seared a jealousy he'd never felt. Leaving her there meant, in some way, his clan would take something else away from him. Remembering his loss of Shannon was enough agony—to lose Andreona would be more.

Then there was the hard truth wherever he left

her some other man would see the joy she was. How could he suffer with that?

To keep her? To ask for her hand? To marry her...? Was that even a possibility? The fact he asked himself meant at least a small part of him wanted it to be. But that was overridden by the scars of his past, the fear of his loss, the fact he was far too cynical for her.

There were times he wished he were different, remembered a time he had taken pleasures in life. Perhaps he would have some resolution if his past only included the loss of Shannon and his family coming to rescue them, but then came Dunbar and Bram not divulging the truth, Caird marrying a Buchanan, the Jewell. He no more righted himself with the world, than the world came back and told him he'd always be mistrusted and betrayed.

Yet...didn't she hate her family, too, since they had betrayed her like his had done? Perhaps he and Andreona couldn't have love between them, since love meant trust, but maybe they had enough in common to be together?

Releasing a breath he'd held too tightly, Malcolm knew his thoughts weren't to be realised. However, maybes and possibilities weren't good enough for a life with her. Which simply proved he didn't deserve her and right now wasn't the time. They might not make it alive to his clan for any of these thoughts to become true. It didn't do to think about possibilities when the present needed his attention.

Yet surveying the landscape for danger meant his eyes fell to her, which was difficult, because, travelling with her, he realised she didn't like clothes. He'd thought her roaming in her chemise was an anomaly.

But the further they went, the more of her he discovered. Her feet were often bare. She'd wear a head covering if they neared a village, but the moment they weren't she'd yank it off. The laces of her gown were often loose as if they were too constricting.

Maybe she was this way because she'd lived in an isolated tower with only women, or maybe it was only her.

Whatever it was, it was driving him mad with desire, need, lust. He had kissed her, pressed himself against her core, felt the dampness— her need was enough. Seeing the arch of her foot, a glimpse of her ankle under her gown, the dip of her gown around her breasts as if she'd been thoroughly made love to was too much.

No, it was safer and more dangerous not to survey the beauty of their surroundings, but soon they'd be at Rhain and Helissent's. They could be themselves. Would she run around at night in only her chemise again? Would she look like some faerie or, now that they'd kissed, would she be a siren he couldn't resist?

He needed to resist. She was grieving and it was far too soon. Yet he knew she liked that tiny box Ximeno had given her and was pleased when they hung those dried thistles on doors. She even coaxed him into talking of his family, which Finlay wisely avoided. They knew each other more now and there was an ease to her. Perhaps her grief was only anger now and—

What was he thinking?

No, they'd arrive at Rhain's today. Rhain, though happily married, was blessed with looks that were more a curse than a blessing. Once she spied Rhain's beauty, maybe she'd realise a kiss from a carved-up surly Scotsman wasn't such a good choice. Hadn't his family pointed out to him often enough how inadequate and untrustworthy he was? Scars or not, he wasn't much of a choice at all.

Something was bothering Malcolm and it wasn't the usual caution he had, or the fact he was more protective as they crossed the sea to England.

Whatever was now troubling him caused him to scowl and glance her way. Was it because she was slowing him down, or revealing too much of herself? He'd stressed the importance of staying hidden.

She'd placed her head covering on when they were crossing on the boat and hadn't taken it off since. The populace was too dense, and Malcolm had said it'd be better not to be noticed. So that couldn't be it.

'Is the inn very far now?' She didn't like Dover. The docks were crowded and smelled of men's sweat more than sea air and fish, and it was far too chaotic, nothing at all like Basque docks. She was glad to have meandered their way through the bustle and back on to the open road with the occasional home, packs of dogs and flocks of geese. The road they travelled was clearly a main route and it showed with the riders who passed them, but the trees and the sun trying to shine through the oncoming rain clouds eased a bit of the worry from the passage over.

'The inn is up ahead. I can see it now,' Malcolm said.

Andreona craned her neck to the side. Up ahead was a sign that as they approached grew in size, as did the clearing around it.

This wasn't like the other inns they'd stayed in. Those were tiny places, more like barns on farms lent to them. This place could bed many and was the largest she'd ever seen.

'I thought you said it was best to stay hidden?' she said.

'Helissent's cooking and baking are renowned. If travellers don't stay overnight, they travel simply for the fare. It's far from the noise, yet close enough to Dover to get traffic.'

He knew the cook's name? So, this was an inn he and Finlay had stayed in before, but hadn't Malcolm said it was unwise to travel the same way twice?

Was it the food or this woman that brought him here again and why should it matter to her? He'd only kissed her, true, but since then they'd shared family stories. She felt closer to him, was fascinated by the way he watched her and the fact he got surly quickly, but just as soon could smile.

Green eyes, dark hair, that scar that ran deep across a flawless jawline and masculine strength. His contrasts were what made him beautiful. And now they were to see this woman Helissent.

Hungry, tired, but she was too disquieted to find any comfort that they had reached their destination. Four boys came up and Malcolm gave them coin, two took the horses, and the others helped them with their satchels.

They greeted Malcolm by name and he granted them a smile as well as placed his finger across his lips. A sign for them to keep a secret. So they knew him very well here, and his presence wasn't to be announced? Did he mean to surprise this Helissent who could cook and bake, something Andreona could never do? She wasn't upset she couldn't. Not everyone could use Roman surveying tools either the way that she could.

Her tools…she had had to leave them and her enamel boxes with the women. She wondered if they took care with them or if they were already broken.

Even if they did take care, did she have intentions of living in France with Uracca? Right now, with Helissent waiting for her surprise from Malcolm, she was leaning towards answering that in the positive.

The inn's doors burst open, and a brownhaired woman flew out and wrapped her arms around Malcolm's neck.

Something tight seared across Andreona's chest. She was jealous, not only of the free way this woman touched Malcolm, but that he returned her embrace. In all their stories to each other, he hadn't mentioned this inn or this woman. Why was she a secret and why did this all feel so awful?

'Helissent, this isn't safe,' he said. 'When are you going to know it's dangerous to fling yourself at every man?'

She pulled herself away. 'Will you all tease me

forever? I told you Reynold was good, but none of you understood. Are we to speak French in the open now?'

'There's a reason soon to be explained,' Malcolm replied. 'And despite his conspiring with us, Reynold's hardly tamed. Further, I wasn't talking of danger for you, but for us. Your husband is right behind you and is now glowering at me.'

A smile upon her face, Helissent turned towards the man who had exited the doorway. It was then Andreona saw her burn scars covering one side of her face. They did nothing to mar her beauty as she gazed at the man who, despite the dry air and dark clouds above, had his hood partially concealing his face.

Malcolm turned and held out his hand. Andreona felt foolish for holding back and walked to his side, but she couldn't quite take his hand. If even she was supposed to take his hand.

Helissent looked her over. 'This isn't Finlay.'

'Why does everyone keep saying that?' Malcolm lowered his voice. 'Do not worry, he was alive, a bit beaten up, but doing well. He's heading to Evrart's, then to Louve at the Warstone fortress to heal.'

Helissent's husband placed his hand on her shoulder. 'I want to hear this. It's almost safer to talk out here than inside—we are full.'

Helissent patted Rhain's hand. 'But we'll find

room. We have some men travelling—we can move them to the barn.'

'We can use the barn,' Malcolm said.

'You can? How interesting,' Helissent's brow rose, her eyes turned speculative. 'I'm Helissent and this is my husband, Rhain.'

Husband… So foolish to feel this relief, foolish to think Malcolm had a mistress. Everyone else he talked of was married, why didn't her thoughts immediately think that Helissent was too?

She knew why. Because she was falling for Malcolm, a man who spoke a rumbling language, held secrets and was angry at the world. A man who hadn't kissed her since the forest, nor said that he wanted to again. Was it because of the danger, her grief? Or was it simply her?

'I'm Andreona.'

'Ah, you come from France?'

'The Basque Country,' Andreona said. 'I am Gorka's daughter.'

When Helissent's expression was nothing more than curiosity, she turned to Malcolm.

'They don't know who that is,' he whispered like it was their secret. Half blinded by the softness of his breath against her ear, and the light in his eyes, Andreona didn't understand what he was saying…until she did. How could no one know her father?

That wasn't a reasonable response, she knew.

Of course, there were people who didn't know, but for her it was staggering. Her entire world was her father and his domain.

'It'll rain soon,' Rhain said. 'Come, let's go inside to our chambers, we can eat and dine in private. I'll see what I can do to ensure you a room.'

'Give those men from Aylesford free food and ale if they move to the barn,' Helissent said. 'And maybe return a coin or two for their accommodations.'

'I'll be a pauper by the end of this,' Rhain said. 'But I want to discuss, without prying eyes, what's around your chest.'

'Words I never thought I'd hear,' Malcolm quipped.

Chuffing, Rhain walked back to the entrance, whispered to two women wearing aprons and gave them coin. Then he went to a table where some men drank ale. From their smiles and nods, Andreona guessed they were willing to give up their room.

When Rhain joined his wife again, Malcolm placed his hand at her back, something he'd never done before, something both thrilling and comforting, Andreona followed the couple through the crowded inn. So many people, their expressions weary or far too cheerful from ale.

Large trenchers laid out on every stout table, meats heavy with sauces, turnips crisped from honey and fire. She'd recognised most of the foods, but not the golden glistening stacks that were practically on every table.

'What are those?' she asked.

Malcolm grinned. 'Honey cakes.'

Helissent looked over her shoulder. 'There'll be some for you.'

'I knew I was your favourite.'

When Rhain growled loudly, Malcolm laughed.

Because she was close, Andreona felt that laughter, which did odd things to her heart—perhaps her angry-at-the-world man wasn't so surly?

Hers? No, that wasn't possible. Had he made her any promises or kissed her again? The hand at her back was simply to ease their way through the crowd and down the long hallway. When they came to a spiral staircase, he let that slight touch go so she could ascend before him. Somehow, though, she knew where his eyes went. Part of her wanted to speed up so his eyes weren't simply *there,* or slow so he'd accidentally bump into her.

Where was this tension coming from? She wanted more of it. Looking down, she spied him looking up and the heated look before he hid it almost made her stumble.

At the top, they entered a room filled with a few chests and tables and chairs. It was a large cosy living space with loads of comforts, a door was closed at the end, which could only be the bedroom.

'Where are the children?' Malcolm asked.

Pushing his hood off his head, Rhain turned towards them.

For a moment, Andreona forgot her manners, her footing, the ability to draw a breath. Golden hair, golden eyes. Rhain was like a layer of gold across an enamel box and only became more beautiful when a wide smile broke across his lips and his chest filled with fatherly love and pride. That was an expression she coveted more than any box.

'The boys are in the kitchens,' Rhain said. 'It helps the baby to sleep and the other doesn't know any better.'

Helissent smiled. 'They'll join us in a bit, we should take advantage of this reprieve. And Fingal's there with his brother because the fires remind him of me.'

Rhain's eyes softened as he looked to his wife. 'Everything reminds me of you.'

This man was beautiful, but that look Rhain gave, the one they shared together, was blinding. There was no adequate word for it and Andreona felt her eyes prick with tears as she looked up at Malcolm.

Who was looking at her, his frown fierce, his eyes dark before he looked away. And no matter what was shared the rest of the evening, babies and laughter, cakes and information, he never looked at her again.

Not even when they walked into a small room with a single large bed.

Chapter Nineteen

Out of all the people who knew of the Jewell of Kings, the dagger, the parchments and the Half-Thistle Seal, Rhain was, in Malcolm's eyes, one of the least bothersome.

Rhain had had nothing to do with the Colquhoun clan...until he had crossed paths with the Warstones. But that was mostly Helissent's fault when she'd engaged with Reynold. Rhain hardly stood a chance and Malcolm silently commiserated with the man afterwards.

But now? Rhain was the most aggravating. If they didn't have to rest for the night, he'd leave immediately. All because once Rhain put down his hood, Andreona's herring-coloured eyes riveted upon him and stayed, until Malcolm wanted to break his nose. Instead of conversing with Rhain regarding the dagger and his intentions of how to get them safely first to the Mei Solis estate in England, and then to his clan, he'd retired along with Andreona.

Fortunately, a room had been cleared for their use. A lone candle on a table, fresh folded linens and the steam of water in a basin at a table. It wasn't their finest room, but it was better than the other inns along the roads they travelled. Best of all the door was thick, the lock sturdy.

There was enough protection here that he could sleep soundly. He was so tired.

'We'll stay for a day or two here, I think.'

'Then on to your Scotland?' Andreona said, picking up the lone candle and carefully walking to the few sconces anchored to the walls.

Hardly his Scotland and not a land he wanted to return to now. He was seething with the need to storm away.

'No, we'll make one more proper stop and rest in England. We need coin.'

'At Mei Solis?' she said. He must have given away his surprise, because she added, 'It's an odd name, so it's easy to remember.'

'We talked of that, didn't we?' How much she knew simply by being in his proximity. Rhain and Helissent hadn't held back their words either. If he wanted to protect her from the danger of knowing these secrets, he'd failed miserably. But then she didn't know all, and once he returned the dagger to his clan and left, she'd be far away from this burdensome quest as well.

'Mei Solis is a large estate where Nicholas and Matilda live.'

'And they are?' Andreona blew out the candle and set it on the tiny table, then she went to the hot water and washed her hands and face with the linen there.

'Nicholas is Rhain's friend. There's coin there for necessities and we're out of coin. Rhain can pay for our bill, which I don't need to say I relish.'

She slowly laid the linen across the bowl, an odd poignant wrinkle on her brow.

'What is it?' he asked.

'You have all these people who support and care for each other,' she said.

Malcolm wanted to argue he had no one at all. That these people were merely keepers of secrets. That they used each other to protect their families from worse fates. That he had no family, or perhaps they didn't have him.

He did what he did out of duty or obligation. Of simply wanting done with this mess of intrigue and lies, of his family's false concern because of his past failures. But support and care? Never.

'You have Uracca and those others who know how to bind a net,' he said, trying to keep it light.

When he moved towards the water to wash his own hands and face, she shifted away.

'Do I?' she said. 'I wonder, after what Uracca did, if I had any of their true support or friendship. Maybe Bita hid something from me as well. How would I know?'

How had it been for him when he'd first realised his family didn't trust him with the truth? Malcolm couldn't stand the lost look in Andreona's eyes. Dropping the linen in the bowl, he gathered her in his arms.

At first she stiffened before she eased in his hold, her arms going up between them where she rested her face against her hands. She wasn't as close as he wanted, but if he was what she needed, he'd hold her like this.

She felt so fragile and delicate, yet significant. What did she do to deserve the lack of trust from her family? Ander, the eldest brother, was reported to be with no principles, Ximeno the same…although now Malcolm wondered what he was up to. Gorka, unwell and pompous, was no threat, except to his daughter.

There wasn't truly a loss there, but they were the family she had been given and she'd tried to find worth with them. Then there was Uracca… that had to pain her and he hurt for her.

When Andreona shifted, he released his arms. Rubbing her face a bit, she looked up at him.

'What was that for?' she asked.

He had no idea. There was no true comfort and support in the world he knew of, yet he appeared to be offering it.

'We should get some sleep,' he said. It was the truth, but he regretted the words. They weren't what she had asked and it brought to his attention the one bed they had in this room.

Now was the time he should offer to sleep on the floor, or in the barn. But just as he inexplicably kept touching her, he also kept quiet. The room was large, he didn't wonder how the men slept here, extra blankets and mattresses taken out to the barn no doubt, but he did wonder how they would. Was he willing her to make a decision?

The oddness of that was he was the one who stormed ahead without thinking. Strapped around him, he had this dagger he and dozens of others had obsessed over and searched for, for years. All his focus should be on how to return it safely to his clan. Except all his thoughts were of her.

He wanted to hold her longer, kiss those lips he'd only begun to taste that night in the forest. Except it was wrong when she grieved. When she was just now realising family betrayed as much as enemies.

They should sleep. Instead, he stood in the room, seemingly unable to do anything except watch her. Now he had held her again, now he mentioned they were to sleep, he couldn't.

Taking a few steps away, Andreona swept the short red mantle adorning her shoulders over her head and released the mint-like scent saturating her hair. Was it a scent she washed with? Was it her?

Her long curls swayed along her narrow back as she went to the peg and hung up the simple garment with its complex colour that all evening had highlighted the darkness of her locks, the grey-green colour of her eyes, the blush of her lips.

Lips that had moved, eyes that had tracked Rhain of Gwalchdu. That was what it was. Underneath it all tonight, that was what he needed to understand. Because he couldn't sleep, not knowing...not guessing and wondering about what she thought of another man.

'You find him handsome, don't you?' he asked.

Turning around, she brushed her arms to warm them. 'Did you ask a question?'

Why was he simply staring at her? He knew they were to undress, the bed large enough they'd barely touch and yet...

He'd done nothing except stand in the middle of the room watching her take off one small scrap of wool that kept her shoulders warm. He was jealous of that garment.

All night as they'd dined and drank, he'd

watched her observe Rhain accepting honey cakes from his wife or touching the back of her hand. She couldn't keep her eyes off the man, and he didn't like it.

Something hitched in his chest like a barb and hooked inside him. He'd kissed her, held her—had she ever looked at him with such open curiosity?

'You found him handsome, didn't you?' he asked again. Reaching under his tunic, he clutched the leather strap holding the dagger and whipped it over his head.

Sitting on the bed, untying her boots' laces, she gave him a small smile. 'Of course.'

She didn't pretend not to know whom he was talking of, and she made a sighing sound because she recalled another man…a man who was not him.

Holding the dagger in one hand, the leather strap dangling to the ground, Malcolm was undone. Whatever odd patience or hesitancy that wanted her to make a decision on the bed was gone. With her words, she'd sealed their fates.

Partly wary, strangely eager, Andreona gracefully fumbled untying her boots and freeing a hose from her foot. There was nothing for her awkwardness. As long as Malcolm of Clan Colquhoun stood in the room, watched her with those green eyes, she'd go about the rest of the night stumbling over her own breaths. Throwing one hose towards the boots, she began on the other.

'Why are you wearing any clothes?' Malcolm said.

Her hand stuck in the fabric, her foot hanging over her knee, Andreona looked up.

Malcolm was closer, much closer. His eyes were riveted to her half-bare foot, his hand gripping tight to the dagger.

'You never wear clothes,' he said.

She wore clothes all the time. Not that she liked it. She liked the freedom living with women gave her over the last year. When the workers left, it'd started as nothing but practical to save a gown, so they'd wear only their chemises. But then her boots were ruined and she had to wait for the cobbler, and she liked not wearing shoes.

No, clothes were fine, except when hose got stuck around her ankle and her fingers couldn't seem to take them off.

'You're wearing clothes,' she said. Hadn't he said they should retire for the night? Didn't that require the taking off of garments?

'Is that the way of it?' he said.

Was that the way of what? What were they talking about?

All night this man went from oddly possessive, with his hand at her back, to completely ignoring her. While she conversed with this loving couple for the first time, she tried to find her balance. Was she to know Malcolm or not? It was made all the worse for how Rhain lovingly gazed at Helissent and how attentive they were to each other.

She longed for the same connection as them.

Hugh and Alice, Rhain and Helissent—had she ever seen love like theirs? If Malcolm had friends like them, how could he not have wanted what they had and why hadn't he married? It made her achingly aware of the man who shared a trencher and goblet with her.

Aware that they didn't have the bond Rhain and Helissent had, but still, at times, almost feeling they had something. Or perhaps that was just her own errant thoughts and remembering their kisses.

When they retired for the evening, she had expected Malcolm to stay up all night as he had with Hugh, but he followed behind her, closing the door once she lit the few sconces around the room.

Her sense of self stretched strangely more as they talked of her family, then oddly, he mentioned Rhain. Now he wanted to discuss clothes?

Tossing the dagger onto a padded chair, Malcolm slowly went to his knees in front of her. Andreona wasn't certain she was breathing.

Firelight flickered across the thick wooden walls highlighting the faint red in his dark curls, the shadows along his stubbled jaw. His back to the sconces, his eyes held almost no colour.

'What are you doing?' she whispered.

'You seem to be having trouble with your hose.'

That was because he'd been so strange with her. Had he hugged her for comfort or because he wanted her to be quiet so they could sleep?

He said they should sleep, but now she was so awake, she couldn't remember what sleep felt like.

'I have no trouble with my hose. I'm simply taking one off and then the other.'

'Let me help you.'

His fingers entwined with her own, tugged on the fabric, which gave easily, and pulled it off her foot, which was still propped over her knee. She was achingly aware of the bareness of her foot, her ankle, her toes.

The fact her gown draped around her legs with an opening meant that at some angle, at perhaps the very one he knelt at, he'd have a view of the apex of her thighs.

'That's better, isn't it?' he said, tossing the hose towards the other one.

She wasn't certain it was, not when he didn't move from his position. The only way to get the rest of her clothes off would be to stand, and that, she was certain, wasn't wise.

'I thought we were talking of my family,' she said.

'They have no place between us,' he said, laying his hand across her ankle, the gentle touch so startling her foot jerked.

'Then you mentioned Rhain,' she said, her breath oddly choppy though he wasn't doing anything except warming her skin with the heat of his hand.

'He's not between us,' he growled.

He was between them? 'Why?'

Malcolm stroking his calloused fingers in circles around the bone in her ankle was making her weak and strangely capable, as though she could bravely touch him as well.

'Why are we not talking of them or why am I kneeling before you aching to take off your gown?' He raised his gaze to hers.

'Oh,' she said. He couldn't be more explicit and yet she had no reference for this.

'I thought we were to sleep.'

'Later,' he said, more of a promise.

'You haven't kissed me since that night. You... haven't mentioned that night.'

'And you thought I'd forgotten what it was like to hold you.' Malcolm wrapped his hand around her ankle and stroked along her skin. 'Those kisses will never be forgotten.'

'But nothing since—'

'Are you doubting?' he said. 'It's a very simple matter to prove since your feet are bare.'

He'd made them that way.

'Yours aren't,' she said.

He chuckled. 'They're not.'

Taking her foot in his hands, he pressed his thumbs into her arch. The feeling was so startling and remarkable, she moaned.

'Your bareness drives me mad, but your sounds...' He pressed into her foot again and again she wanted to make such a sound, but because he was watching for it this time, she held it back.

He seemed half-amused, half-determined, for what she didn't know. Whatever opposite feeling he was creating in her, it seemed he did the same to himself.

'Always showing a wrist here, an ankle there.' He set that foot down and cradled the other in both his hands. The secure hold he had, the slow sensuous way he rubbed his thumb along her instep, made her toes curl and her core clench.

How could he ask about Rhain when he touched her like this? Whispered words like this? This was more than the forest and they hadn't even kissed yet. She wanted to, but didn't want to stop whatever this was he was doing.

'This arch has been tempting me, Andreona.'

He swiped a finger under her foot, which jerked, and he flashed a smile.

'Tempting you?' she said.

Nodding solemnly, he set that foot gently to the floor. The wood felt cool after the warmth of his hands.

He placed both hands on her knees, his fingers gripping into the fabric releasing it only to tug again. 'Your gowns drag the floor and your feet are bare. I see your toes, the curve of your foot, your delicate ankle.'

How could his hands feel heavy and hot through the layers of her gown and chemise? 'You don't tie your gowns in the morning,' he said.

How was he noticing all of this? She'd fought him, tied his hands and brought him to the gates of her father's keep. All the while she was bringing about his demise, he'd noticed her laces. That thought, his touch, his words were unravelling something inside her.

'I slip the gown over my chemise and forget about them.' Her gowns were often too small for her, so it wasn't as though they would fall off.

Each slow stroke along her knees became more determined, more of her fabric bunching under his palm as he slowly lifted her hem. Tendrils of cool air drifted against her shins, her thighs.

'Your loose laces sway with your steps,' he said. 'Most days, I wait for that moment when they'll flutter to the ground, but you tie them before they do.'

These were things he wondered... 'When they get in the way, I tie them as well.'

'As simple as that?'

All of her hem was under his palms, which had stayed on her knees. More fabric between them, but his hands felt heavier, hotter. His thumb and small finger hovering over her skin giving slight brushes of skin on skin. His fingers long, rough, skittering desire through her.

'No hair coverings either.' His voice a low growl, his eyes intense.

'They cost coin,' she said, her nipples hardening, her core softening. And all because they talked of her clothing. This wasn't like before, yet the intensity was much, much more.

Green eyes heavy lidded, he continued in a voice gone raspy, 'Loose hair tumbling over your shoulders, snaring with the untied laces.'

'Not for long, I tie them then, too, I don't like——' Her words caught in her head, behind her lips, more difficult to say than to feel what was happening between them. 'I don't like when my hair is trapped or tangled.'

'Your tangled hair.' His head dropped, his hands going under the bunched fabric. The fine chemise, the woven green finally released and cascading back to the floor. Except his hands were anchored on her knees. Skin against skin, the outlines of scraped knuckles and blunt finger-tips under crushed green linen, looking far more intimate and secretive than they should have.

They both watched as he palmed down her shins and caressed up to the back of her knees and around. The splay of his fingers stretching towards her folds, which were dampening with anticipation.

His fingers trembling or maybe it was her legs. Using her body, he pushed himself up, their height even and he buried his face in her neck, inhaling her scent. She rested her head on his shoulder, her hand caressing up his side to the open neck, feeling the damp heat of his skin under his curls. But it wasn't enough, so she rucked up his tunic until he guessed what she wanted and yanked the garment over his head to throw it somewhere behind him.

One of the sconces sputtered out, leaving only two. It wasn't nearly enough light for her to fully admire the outline of the man before her, but it was more than she'd had in the forest.

This view, the colour and shape of his skin, the way his chest was carved from the sword, the beauty of his frame under that...or because of that almost deadly blow.

She hadn't had a chance to touch before. So she boldly matched the movement of his hands on her legs, sweeping downwards and then back up over broad shoulders, a smooth chest and tapered waist, muscles flexing under her fingers. His whole body thrumming, before giving a hard shiver when her thumbs brushed over his nipples.

Eyeing his reaction, he flashed a wild grin at her. It made him impossibly beautiful to her. She hadn't expected this tonight, didn't hope for it. Did she welcome it?

'This doesn't feel simple,' she said.

His hands pressed her thighs outward to make room for him. 'No, not simple at all. Not here, not like this, not with you.'

Of course, for him there were other locations, other women. Whatever he saw in her expression, a pleased look flashed across his features. 'Feeling possessive? That makes two of us.'

Was that what this was? She'd never cared for a man before and none had cared for her. Neither the possessiveness nor him feeling it made any sense.

He pressed a hard kiss to her lips, along her cheek and against both of her eyes. 'I love your herring eyes.'

She pulled away. 'My...what?'

'Herrings.' He shifted closer, she felt his hands

sweep higher under her skirts, she gained more access to his back. 'They are these little fish.'

'You like my fish eyes?'

Chuckling, he gripped her gown, yanked it out from around her, and tossed it to the side. 'Not fish eyes. Coloured like these little herrings flashing silver and blue and green and grey in the water. When sunlight hits them, they shine.'

'Oh, that's...better.'

'What is?' He kissed along her exposed collarbone, his hands sweeping higher. Her own slid along the tapering of his waist, gripping when his kisses turned to half-bites and soothing licks.

'What is better?' he repeated. 'Is it my touch, my kisses? My spreading your thighs and disrobing you? Or is it being in this house, under *his* roof?'

Growling, he ripped off her chemise, leaving her bare to him.

Andreona's hands flew forward, trying to find some purchase, but there was none. Malcolm trailed his fingers, his kisses around each breast until the tips were tight points he engulfed, laved with this tongue and tugged.

Why was he talking of houses and roofs? Of Rhain and what could be better? If she had to answer any of it, this was better, him over her. Her touching him. Everything. The scent, the slight dampness at the base of his spine, the way his hips moved as if he couldn't help it.

She didn't understand any of it, but her body responded to the urgency of his touch, his voice as he laid her down and hovered over her, his hands fumbling with his breeches and braies.

Hers tangling with his as she pressed tender kisses on his neck, his chest, an arm, anything she could touch and reach and feel. Anything that was him.

'This is better,' she said. 'You're better.'

'Andreona,' he groaned hoarsely against her neck. It wasn't a question. Not when his questing fingers cupped her sex, her damp folds plump as he gently circled and pressed, dipped and stroked.

Not when she felt the heavy weight of him against her thigh and their lips met for more kisses.

Desire burst maddeningly inside her with every light flick of his tongue and harsh sweep of his calloused hands along her hips, around her thighs. The softer the kisses, the more his unyielding body lay on top of hers. With every desperate sound she released, the more his caresses turned to clutching at her hip, his fingers seeking, dipping, stroking. A fluttering deep inside and she arched against his hand until he shuddered and pulled back.

There was nothing green about his eyes, nothing soft or promising in the way he looked down at her. She'd never been naked with a man, never kissed any other than him. And he was everything she wanted.

This wasn't imagining or hopeful dreams after watching two happily married people, this was between them. They were who they were and there wasn't anyone else. He seemed to know it because he gave no more quips or touches, but held perfectly still, and waited patiently.

Laying her hand against his cheek, she said, 'Please.'

Desire and need in the grooves along his mouth, in the heat of his eyes, Malcolm adjusted her leg around his hip and kissed her lips, softly, tenderly, pressed himself torso to torso, hip to hip, and shifted.

This wasn't like his questing fingers and her body didn't react with soft flutters, but something bone-deep and sure as she accepted his urgent thrust. A hitch to her breath at the burst of pain that quickly disappeared as he seated himself inside her and held himself still.

'Please tell me you are well,' he said, his voice tight with restraint, his breaths harsh with need.

Her hands, balled into fists at his chest, shook. It wasn't from pain, but from want.

'There's more,' she whispered, asking a question and not. 'Please tell me there's more. I feel—'

His face relaxed, a glimmer to his eyes like a challenge. 'There is. Much more.'

'Can you…do it?' she said.

A harsh breath and she felt something pulse inside her.

When her eyes flashed to his, he grinned. 'That's not it.'

'What was that?' she said.

Shaking his head, he clenched his eyes. 'That was you shredding the last bit of control I have left. I need to move now and I'm not going to be patient.'

'Have you ever?' She flattened her palms, felt the pounding of his heart.

'You don't mince words, do you, lass.' He rotated his hips.

'Oh,' she said. 'Please.'

On a groan, he dropped his head, lavishing her with a kiss that grew in intensity, just like their touches and the position of their bodies.

Just like her emotions, which tightened and flew apart. Then reconstructed as she wrapped her limbs around this man who had taken her out of everything she knew and brought her somewhere else. Somewhere she sought, longed for, needed. Something that only began when the last shred of *her* control burst into something she knew was pure shuddering joy.

Chapter Twenty

Malcolm's breaths eased, his body weakened, shaken because of one tiny woman. He gazed down at Andreona. Her damp hair was trapped under her shoulder and he grabbed the locks to tug them free until they tumbled again.

She opened her eyes. Clear blue-green, with silver-grey streaking through. Every time he looked in them they were never the same, but he knew they couldn't be lovelier than now.

'You have strange topics to use when seducing women,' Andreona said.

Laughing, he winced and pulled gently away from her. She slowly lowered her leg and he massaged along the joints, her knee, her hip. Gently cupped and eased between her legs, watching for any sign of discomfort. When she gave him a soft smile, the last bit of uncertainty faded.

Smiling back, he plopped on his back and adjusted her against him. 'Topics?'

'You talked of roofs and houses.'

He wondered now how he managed to form words, and even so, it took him some time to even recall what she talked of. 'I wasn't talking of buildings, I was talking Rhain of Gwalchdu.'

'You ripped my chemise off when you talked of another man,' she pointed out.

To reveal all her beauty to him. 'Aye, I did.'

'You don't think those are strange words to woo a woman?'

'I wasn't trying to woo any woman, I was trying to woo you. And after a night at his table, I don't like you thinking he's handsome.'

It was her turn to be silent and he swore he could feel a smile against his shoulder. He didn't like feeling possessive about her, but if her smile was anything to guess on, she liked it, and something in his heart eased on that.

'Rhain is handsome,' Andreona said, her voice a soft pant he felt against his skin. 'But he is not you. He can't compare.'

Malcolm wanted to protest. Partly because he wanted more words on why he was better than a man who stopped women in their tracks. Mostly because she'd mentioned another man while she was cradled in his arms and his heart still pounded from the pleasure they shared. But

Rhain was the least bothersome of the people he knew, and he could find no frustration in him now.

Because in Andreona's eyes, that man didn't compare to him.

Malcolm knew he'd never be the same. Andreona had affected him with an innocent touch, her kiss in the forest...now he was altered. There was no life before her, at least not one he could remember or that felt so right. No feeling he'd ever felt was similar to lying beside her without a want in the world.

He shifted again, until he had one arm under his head, the other fortunate enough to be trailing his fingers along Andreona's arm as she lay curled into his side, her head tucked into his neck.

They fit far beyond the physical attraction they had, because she, too, had been betrayed by her family and would have reservations of trust like him. She couldn't possibly want to talk of her painful past and wouldn't pry into his. He never wanted to talk of his childhood with Shannon or what his brothers, Bram or Caird, had done.

With that understanding between them...with the knowledge they could be together like this with nothing more was stunning.

Maybe he was right to feel some sort of contentment when he took her along on this journey.

She'd never love him, nor he her. Neither of them should get past their complete understanding that people betrayed each other.

No, this was…good. Safe. Something in him knew it because he even felt jealousy since they'd arrived at Helissent's inn. Andreona was meant for him and him alone.

'Why were you watching Rhain all through dinner?'

'Hmm?'

'You said you found me attractive, but I watched you gazing at him all evening.'

'Is that why you attacked me?' she said.

Malcolm tensed. He… Had he asked if she agreed? He was half out of his mind with desire and need when he stormed across the room and—

She patted him on the chest. 'If you hadn't kissed me, I would have kissed you.'

He wasn't certain if that meant she'd agreed to what they did. 'We did a bit more than kiss.'

'I ken.'

Her teasing did more to ease his thoughts. 'You say that word like no one I've ever heard before.'

'I ken,' she said again, and laughed.

He gathered a long strand of her hair and played with the texture and length. This hair still tumbled like those Basque rocks from the hillside. He'd seen long dark hair, but none as wild as hers.

He loved her wildness, her innocence. He cherished her laying against him like this, letting their bodies cool in the night air. Knowing within moments, he'd pull her close and begin again...if she'd let him.

But something disquieted him. 'You didn't answer my question.'

She brushed her hand across his skin, traced along the line of the scar that carved deep across his chest.

Then he realised it wasn't the scar she traced, but the muscles and ridges along his stomach, and that his body was noticing...he almost forgot again.

'I like when you do that. When you touch me instead of trees,' he said.

She stopped. 'What?'

'That night in the forest when you were wearing less clothes than tonight.'

'You like me with less clothes?'

'You have doubts?' he said.

She rubbed her chin against his shoulder. 'If I do?'

He raised her hand to his lips and kissed each finger, licked the seam of her wrist then set it down on his chest, and entwined their fingers. 'If you do, we'll...have to compare.'

'Me with clothes and without?'

'Let's start with…without,' he said.

She settled into him. 'I could agree to that. But first tell me of this tree.'

He wanted to forget any trees, he wanted to continue kissing her, but settled on his hand wandering along her skin and his foot brushing against hers. 'That night, you kept going from tree to tree. Tracing the roughened patches with your fingers, caressing bark with your palm. It drove me mad with need for you. I was jealous of them…so I kissed you.'

'We did a bit more than kiss,' she said.

'I ken.' He emphasised the word.

She laughed. 'I don't remember touching the trees… I hardly remember the trees at all.'

He remembered everything about that night. Everything, but she didn't. Was it not as significant to her as to him?

'I only remember you,' she added.

Something happened inside Malcolm's chest. A heat…it seared and the warmth and soaring happiness that followed didn't feel much better.

This feeling was much more than the relief when Andreona's spirit fought against her father's cruelty. More than that quick elation when he scooped her in his arms simply because he had to.

This feeling encompassed all those and the

forest…and tonight…and the thousands of other ways they'd shared over the journey. This… wasn't good. He breathed in deep, let the unease permeate him a bit more, exhaled and let it out.

They were only words. What he felt was only a stronger contentment, nothing more than that. Certainly, her response hadn't meant anything more. She said she remembered him in the forest. Who else would she remember?

He had no worries except he hadn't had enough of her yet. Shifting on to his side, he propped his head with his hand. This shifted her from the warmth of his embrace, but this way, her curves were more easily accessible as she mirrored his own position.

'What else do you think?' He relished in the indent of her waist, the plump upward curve of her—

'I think I'll miss the dagger,' she said.

He removed the direction of his hand and raised his eyes to hers. There was heat there, but also, amusement. Oh, she knew she delayed the inevitable between them. He'd make her pay for that later. Especially since she'd revealed a subject he was loath to talk of. At least her beauty and warmth were a fine balm.

'How could you miss it when…?' He stopped those words. No, he didn't want to bring her father into this. Their pain had no place between them.

From her expression, she guessed why he stopped, but didn't prompt him for more and he swept his hand from her waist to her back and pulled himself closer. When had anything been more right?

'Everything you know has been in pieces,' he said.

'That is because you didn't want me to know of it at all,' she said.

So very true. He pulled the quilt up over them. If she wished to talk, they'd talk of this. She was still in his bed and she deserved truth between them since she'd risked her life more than once.

'True, but you've guessed much,' he said. When she nodded, he continued, 'And what I said of the story…is all there is. King Edward of England wants it because he loves legends. The Warstones want it because the dagger, along with some parchments, are meant to lead to some treasure. And, most likely, the King and the Warstones want it for both reasons.'

'There's a treasure?' she said. 'Of course, there's a treasure.'

He had only told her bits, but more couldn't harm her any worse. They'd made it to Dover, and perhaps they'd make it further still. 'We don't know where the treasure is, only that there's an indication of one. The King, the Warstones probably know of it, but we're not certain. My clan and others intend for none of them to have it. Right now, neither needs more power or coin.'

'It's a lot to take in,' she said. 'I found the dagger beautiful, spent hours imagining the objects that could fit inside. I would have liked to have taken it myself, but the craftsman purposefully replicated it for my...for Gorka, so it wasn't for me to steal.'

'Andreona, we don't need to talk of your father. We don't need to talk of our families at all.'

She rested her hand on his cheek. There was such warmth and softness in her touch. But they talked of her father, so why did it feel like she was comforting him?

'I know,' she said.

'You do?'

'But...if you want to talk of yours, I want to listen.'

The dagger was one conversation he could tolerate; his family, however, wasn't easy at all. He plopped on his back and looked to the ceiling. He could tell her some, however—after all, he knew of hers.

'They live in Scotland—my clan is Colquhoun.'

'You have used this word clan before, and clansmen, too. It is the same?'

'They are both another word for family,' he said. 'There's family and then there's those who are loyal to my family, like Finlay.'

'You're a noble?'

He chuckled. 'No…but similar. Caird actually is head of the clan now.'

'He leads your people?' she said. 'Is that what Laird means?'

She asked so easily, as if she hadn't a care for family ties or power. He found that perplexing after her family was ripped apart because of power struggles and her own worth questioned. He'd carried his resentment much too long to have any ease when it came to his family.

Maybe she had such ease because they talked of his family and not her own? Or maybe just knowing he had one would let her know he shared her pain. He could do this.

'Yes, when Bram married Lioslath to be Laird of Fergusson, Caird became—'

A touch on the end of his nose and he turned his head to her.

She tapped him on the forehead and the chin, and on his chest with the tip of her finger as well. 'You're gathering creases on your face. Perhaps, we don't need to talk of them. You've told me some…enough…for me to know it pains.'

He didn't realise the tightness in his chest until she said those words. She…understood. Fully. Completely. Without having to say any more, she knew this part of him was off limits, that it was too much agony and regret. He cupped her jaw, and kissed the tip of her nose.

She smiled, then settled back on the bed and snuggled under the quilt. She looked alluring and charming. But he, too, was under the covers...so if she meant to deter him—

'Legends, treasures, the Warstones are much to think about,' she said. 'And I still don't know everything. You tell me Hugh is a family friend, but though I now know of family names, I don't truly know who they are, not the way you know Uracca, or the other women.'

'I know their nets,' he said.

She smiled. 'There is more to them than that.'

So easily she smiled! Had she forgiven her friend? 'But see, that's what—'

She placed her hand on his mouth, 'I don't care if you tell me of these lairds and clan, or if you know everything about my family.'

He brought his thoughts again to matters he didn't want to address, but something of the blithe way she said everything alarmed him. 'Why?'

'Because I ask you questions, and you tell me enough, because...what we share isn't—'

What they shared? That sounded like she meant more than what was between them now. He didn't want any more than this.

He propped himself up because he needed

to see her as much as the candles would allow. Maybe they did need to talk.

'Andreona, I am not…on fair terms with my family.'

'I gathered that,' she said.

'I don't want anything to do with them. They have the gem and the parchments. Once I deliver the dagger, I don't intend to stay on Colquhoun land or have any conversations with them.'

She gathered the quilt to her and sat up. He was loath to leave the bed with her in it, or for her to leave him. He was achingly aware to just sleep beside her would be more than he could wish for. They simply needed to have a better understanding between them.

'I told you I wouldn't stop there. I thought you'd understand,' he said.

'I do,' she said. 'I left with you instead of travelling with Uracca.'

She had, yet it sounded like she wanted her friend again, when he didn't want his family at all. 'Because you went away.'

Her brows drew down. 'I didn't go away.'

How to say this? She was looking at him as if trying to understand and he saw the moment she did for she looked away. 'When we left your father. You were sad. It seems you're better now.'

'Better? How do you think someone can be better?'

'I'm not saying this correctly,' he said.

'No, you're not,' she said. 'But... I'm not angry about that, I like you trying, and I think I understand. I went away and you let me, I never thanked you for that.'

'Thanked me?'

'For being quiet, for letting me be just me. Being patient.'

He'd never been patient in his life, and by the time he'd realised she was hurting he'd been ashamed. Here she was...grateful? He didn't understand. Wasn't she seething or plotting against her family? Or Uracca, who was her childhood friend and yet schemed against her for a year?

No...instead, she seemed content. He searched her eyes, the plumpness of her lips. She seemed more than content. He extracted himself from the bed and pulled on his braies and breeches.

Her eyes dropped to his fumbling hands as if wanting more. There could be no *more*.

'We said too much tonight,' he said.

'I think we're just starting.'

Her looks, they seemed light...hopeful. They'd talked of her father—shouldn't she be feeling anger or bitterness? Shouldn't she be fighting against them as he did his own?

'No, this is enough. There doesn't need to be any more than this.'

'But of course there would be more—how

would there not…?' That hopeful look died and her eyes turned dark. 'You don't intend to just leave after the dagger is left—you intend never to talk to your family again.'

'Never.'

'And you thought I'd throw my family away like that, too?'

Throw them away? They threw him away by never trusting him, never believing he was worth the same as they were.

She yanked the quilt around her and stood. 'Did you think to throw me away as well?'

When he failed to leave her in France, he thought to leave her here. But with Rhain—that thought rubbed him wrong. There was still the possibility of returning her to the Warstone fortress.

They'd travelled this far. He'd been so relieved, content with her by his side, that he didn't think of what the consequences would be. He wanted her by his side, but not, not if she felt as if there could be more.

Maybe he was rash and hadn't learnt patience. But why did they need to change? 'I've been alone for many years. It's best to be alone, to separate from—'

'Out.' She pointed to the door.

He'd spent too long in Finlay's company. Where were his words! Perhaps if he started from the beginning, he could make her understand he wanted… What? If she wanted more, if she hoped for more, than he didn't deserve her.

He hadn't learnt patience, or to stop charging forward. He wasn't only affecting his own life by his deeds; he was affecting her. They were almost to Colquhoun land, but they still had far to go. At any moment, he could be killed.

He could promise her nothing.

And she knew it. The look of hurt and anger was there in the defiant tilt of her chin, but he could decipher nothing in those eyes of hers. He'd lost her.

'We'll leave on the morrow. In a few days we'll be at Mei Solis where we can get coin and be on our way to Scotland.' Grabbing his tunic, he opened the door. 'If you like that more than here, perhaps you can stay there.'

Malcolm slammed the door at her stricken expression before she saw the mirror of agony in his own.

Chapter Twenty-One

Having little choice in both her heart and her head, Andreona followed Malcolm through a driving rain that wouldn't cease and had given them little reprieve for a sennight. She felt the cold slashing of it against her back only as echoes of Malcolm's words to her. Each cold wet spike a repeat of 'separate' and 'gone'.

On and on they went as if he knew where they were going. Maybe he did. Maybe he also meant those seemingly practical, but cruel words he'd said to her and this was it for him.

She didn't accept them; she also didn't accept the seeming constancy of his ignoring her because she didn't avoid him. England afforded her a wide open beautiful landscape, but it was the broadness of his shoulders, the graceful effectiveness of his hands on the reins, the wind ruffling through his dark locks that drew her gaze.

And when the rain didn't let up, she watched the curls plaster to the back of his neck. She didn't care that they were nearing the border between England and Scotland. Nothing held *her* as much as Malcolm did...because she loved him.

Slowly and steadily they travelled onwards. He didn't push the horses; he didn't look back at her, not even when they rested the beasts. He merely took the reins and continued. Thus, so did she.

As the days drew on she felt none of the heat they'd shared at Rhain and Helissent's, not even that promising warmth they'd discovered at Hugh and Alice's. All that was slashed away drop by drop with the rain, with Malcolm's words.

Yet, like the weather, she knew it could change, if she changed it. She might not have control over the rain, but she had control over this and she wanted to show him very much.

This wasn't simply because he'd shown her a kindness after she'd learned the truth about her father, or protected Uracca when he'd stumbled in the tower. Because her friend was right, he had done that.

This was because...he was lying to himself. Just as she knew it didn't always rain, that it wasn't always this cold. Just as she knew that though she'd had hard times, there was good-ness out there in the world. She knew it, saw it, felt it. Malcolm had, too; he simply wasn't acknowledging it.

Malcolm meant more than any of her adversities before and she knew she'd regret it if she didn't try to help him as he'd helped her.

As they journeyed in one determined direction, as the sky turned from dim daylight to twilight, Andreona thought hard about how to reach this unreachable man. Except was he so unreachable? He'd told her more than he intended, but at the inn, he'd tried to tell her more.

She'd foolishly stopped him, could see the pain in his eyes, the way he tensed beside her. She believed they were of the same heart. She'd forgotten those troubled green eyes of his. Knew his pain, whatever it was, wasn't as simple as hers...

Simple. How odd she used that word. It wasn't easy, not at all, but she realised this time with Malcolm—with him allowing her to sleep, to have quiet, and when that became too much, he gave her the noise of children, the history of the abacus, the complexity of a wool industry and the recipe for a honey cake—this time with him had helped. It was what made it possible to feel as if the agony of their betrayal was simple.

Did that mean it didn't pain? Not at all. She'd always hurt when it came to her father and with Uracca and Ximeno her heart was bruised. That didn't mean she couldn't be with them again or think of them as family. That she could walk away as Malcolm had said.

Those words hurt terribly and she still did not understand how, after what they'd shared, he could have said them. From some past experience? Malcolm's green eyes, which were never soft, revealed he suffered some pain. Had no one given him time to heal? Finlay seemed a quiet man, but there was a difference to quiet and being ignored.

She just didn't know. So many thoughts while rain pounded against them both! Yet Malcolm seemed to know where he was going as he drove them deeper under a thick canopy until they neared a hut almost entirely hidden between the trees.

When he dismounted, so did she, but the rain made everything too heavy and he waved her towards the shelter. While Malcolm took care of the horses and their satchels, Andreona opened the door to the tiny hut, which was dark and dusty.

'What is this place?' She looked over her shoulder at the man lifting the saddles and resting them on a nearby log. Everything about this place appeared natural, but she could now see that the overhang was enough shelter for the horses and the log he placed the saddles on was placed for that purpose.

'A point along the road Finlay and I have used before. Nothing more or less than the other points we used along the way. Although we've now crossed the border into Scotland.'

But in France and England, they had stayed with people who knew him...people who cared for him. She'd even had a chance to meet Nicholas and Matilda at the oddly named Mei Solis. They'd stayed there for several days while Malcolm told Nicholas that some Basque women were on the way to his friend Louve at the Warstone fortress.

Then, too, both men laughed as they took coin from a chest. Something about stealing from a man named Reynold and how he'd deserved it. Malcolm had had to halve his amount into two pouches to make it easier to carry.

So many people, so many connections she didn't fully understand. Malcolm hadn't mentioned her staying with them and she hadn't requested it. His words, however, tainted the entire time they were there and once, late at night, she'd woken from a nightmare where he'd left her at the estate.

Afterwards she'd watched him carefully for any sign. He'd given none. In fact, he was as at-

tentive there as he was in front of Rhain and Helissent, Hugh and Alice.

He cared, he must, and yet he was very good at
this lying to himself. What she didn't know was
why. Fear, anger and, if so, at whom? She knew
why she stayed with him, but didn't he question
himself on why he travelled with her?

She was beginning to wonder if in these quiet
times, it wasn't only the people around Malcolm
who ignored whatever pain he was in, but he
himself did as well.

The rain forced most of their quiet between
them, maybe it was time for a bit of distraction,
of noise. She didn't have an abacus or any honey
cakes, but this hut and this rain might be what
they needed.

Though the hut appeared abandoned and de-
crepit outside, inside it was well insulated and
stocked. Wood, food, water...and comforts like
some linens. A few folded tunics and breeches.
Nothing she could use, but it was there.

It was certainly a point along the road and
more than expected, but it wasn't like the other
places they were. 'No, it's not.'

He paused in stacking the logs in the little
fireplace. 'Everything's too damp to light. We'll
only have smoke instead of a fire.'

She could barely see him. When the sun truly
set, it would be absolutely dark in the tiny room.

She hated that fact. Hated they would soon have a conversation where she'd only want to see his expressions, and she wouldn't be able to.

Because as hard as he was trying to ignore her, these four walls, the entire night-time with nothing to do, and her heart weren't going to allow him to ignore her any longer.

'This tunic might fit you,' he said. 'You should change.'

Her clothes weighed heavily against her and, despite the warmth of the season, she was beginning to shiver. The moment it turned dark she'd be cold. But she didn't want to change; she wanted this. She wanted this man.

'This hut is surprising, but it's not like the other places we've stayed,' she said. 'Those places had people who loved you.'

He ripped his tunic over his head and hung the dripping fabric on a peg. She'd never get used to the way he looked or the pain he'd endured to earn that scar and become the man he was. Maybe the scar was the key to understanding him.

'Love? I've been alone and that's how I intend it to be.' He sat down, ripped off his one boot, then the other, tossing them in the corner. 'It's best that way.'

He wasn't looking at her as he stood, his hands on his hips to rip off his breeches. Her heart was aching with his coldness, his words, but her body reacted to what he revealed. How was she to get through this? 'That's not true, either.'

He stilled. 'What?'

'It's not best to be alone.'

'What kind of reason is any of this?' He grabbed the folded tunic and whipped it out in front of him before pulling it over his head. 'And how could you believe anything else? Wouldn't your life have been better without your father's betrayal? Without the pain of your brother's lies?'

Words to hurt her if she would allow it. But this wasn't about her pain, it was about his. Because it was there, she could see it blaze out of those green eyes, in the rigid way he held his shoulders. The stance as he prepared to fight.

Anger laid siege to this man. He wasn't battling her, but himself. But why and how, she didn't know. She trembled with cold, with desperation to get through to him before they arrived at his home. She couldn't shake that one nightmare and felt he'd leave her in this Scotland where he told her he wouldn't stay.

'You said you want to be alone, that it's better that way,' she said. 'Yet we met Hugh and Alice. Rhain and Helissent. Nicholas and Matilda.'

'They're families who pass on the information needed to locate the dagger. They are the ones who led me to you. I would think you wouldn't want to talk to them because you resent them.'

'Resent them?' She envied them. Their small, caring touches and ease with each other. Alice's direct way with Hugh, Rhain's eyes softening as he looked at Helissent. Nicholas's constant touching of his wife's hair. Never in her life had she seen such love, and she wanted that, too, with this surly man.

'If they hadn't found the information, your life would still be the same. You'd have your tower you built and your friends surrounding you. Instead, you no longer have that future you literally built,' he said. 'You should change your clothes.'

'What I had were lies,' she said.

'And you think what I have isn't?' he answered.

No...he wanted to believe they were lies, but she could see the difference between Uracca wringing her hands and Helissent's exuberant embrace, Ximeno's heavy regret and Nicholas laughing so hard he had tears running down his cheeks.

What she had was terrible. Her father had uttered those words of her death so easily, it was as if he'd contemplated them all his life and simply hadn't got round to it.

She hurt, but how could he compare Gorka to Hugh and Alice? Of what they risked to have

William in their home? Or Helissent and the fire, Nicholas returning home to Matilda after losing his eye? Simply seeing that kind of love and loyalty existing confirmed for her that no matter what she felt now, the rain of her life would clear.

Whatever Malcolm had experienced, it must have been terrible, awful. Beyond what she could comprehend...or he hadn't given himself the permission to heal. Maybe this dagger and its danger had prevented that, too.

This rage he fought wasn't with them. Not truly, but something pricked him when it came to them.

'Can Hugh be something more than a messenger of the Half-Thistle Seal?'

'I have already told you he's friends with the man who married my sister,' Malcolm said. 'There isn't truly anything else.'

'Yes, but his greeting you was unusually violent.'

'We have a history.' A muscle ticked in his cheek. He walked to her, loosened her cape and hung it on the pegs near his clothes. 'He's English, I'm Scottish. We're not meant to get along right now.'

He looked over his shoulder to her. 'What makes you think there's a relationship there?'

She waved over him. 'You're all prickly about

them, yet you trust them enough for us to stay with them.'

'We stay because Hugh has information on the dagger…and because he has relations with our family. I told you he's friends with Robert who married my sister.'

He did. They talked of this that night in the forest. Wanting him not in the shadows, she walked towards him. 'When was the last time you saw your brother-in-law?'

'Years.'

That much time, yet he held on to whatever resentment he had against them. Hugh and Alice were English, but she didn't think this had to do with any boundaries…at least not entirely.

'Why are you looking at me the way you are?' he said.

Because he was so close and he was untying the laces of her gown and she remembered how it felt when he did that not as a practical matter, but because he wanted to. 'I'm looking at you a certain way?'

'Stop studying me.'

'Stop being interesting enough to study.'

He scowled. 'I'm not some box you need to open or some hollowed dagger you must peer into.'

He was, he was. He just didn't like it. 'Do you like your brother-in-law?'

'Not at first and he goes by Robert.'

Oh, she wanted to ask him questions on what that meant. She also wanted to know what he meant by 'he goes by Robert'. Had he...had he a different name before?

Green eyes looked to her, then to her hands. 'You're trembling.'

'My hands are cold—could you do the rest?'

He looked to the door. No doubt her Scotsman was wondering if he should brave the rain to avoid her request. On an exhale, he grabbed the laces at her sleeves and quickly tugged the fabric to loosen it. She was careful to keep herself away from him, careful to not push further than this...though she terribly wanted to lean into him.

'Is he good to your sister?' she whispered.

He pinched the lace on her other arm. 'Very.'

So it wasn't Hugh or Robert causing this man his pain. At least not exactly.

'What of Rhain and Helissent?' She tilted her head up, presented the bindings around her collar. 'These will have to be done, too.'

His nostrils flared. 'What of them?'

She could hardly think with him this close. 'How is it you know them?'

'Why all these questions?' He tugged at the ribbon around her neck. 'You asked me before when we stayed with them and I purposefully didn't answer.'

'What I remember is you purposefully not wanting to talk of Rhain,' she said. When a muscle in his jaw ticked, she added, 'I know they have to do with the dagger and they most likely have to do with the message, just like Hugh and Alice. But, like Hugh, you seem to be close to them.'

'Can we not simply leave my past alone? Our mission is to get the dagger to my family. To not be caught by the Warstones or anyone serving the King of England.' He stepped back and waved at her. 'The bindings are loose.'

Then she was to undress herself. The room was small; he could try to avoid her, but it wouldn't work. 'I care, that's why I'm asking.'

Green eyes narrowed.

She bent and grabbed her sodden hem. 'You've kept me alive, fed me, I have to care else...how am I to find a home?'

'Your home will be France, at the Warstone fortress,' he said with emphasis, to clarify, to demand she obey.

The fabric was heavy. She could feel Malcolm's eyes on her hips, shifting one way then the other as she got the fabric over her head. 'Hmmm,' she said, answering, but not. Making the journey to France, to a home she had never seen, didn't appeal, despite Uracca being there.

She loved him and she could tell him. She could, but there was a part of her that held back. Until he told her why he denied them, why he denied himself, she wasn't going to. She didn't fear he'd reject her, she feared he wouldn't recognise her love. Refuse it because he refused to believe others cared for and loved him. Hugh and Alice, Rhain and Helissent had years of knowing this man and couldn't open his heart. What hope did she have? None unless she understood, unless she allowed him to see these people differently than he did.

'If you are returning to France, why do you ask of Rhain and Helissent?'

In the dimming light, she couldn't see any of the streaks of red through his hair. Streaks that reminded her of his temper. Calm humorous waves, then that zip of irritation. He kept her on her toes, this man.

'We'll be staying with them again on the way back, won't we?'

He grabbed a linen square, handed it to her. 'Rhain has known Robert, my sister Gaira's husband.'

That was a tenuous relationship. Whatever, or whoever, was at the root of his rage, of why he fought everyone and everything, couldn't possibility be him.

'And he's part of this Half-Thistle society?' she asked. She went to the doorway, wrung out the linen where the floor was already soaked and then attempted to squeeze dry her hair again.

'Helissent's inn provides a perfect position for information exchanges.'

She didn't care for Dover, but she did like Rhain and Helissent. She'd remember the sweetness of the cake and the warmth of Rhain's smile towards his wife when he accepted them.

Malcolm lit a candle.

'Are there more of those?'

'A few, but in this space, it isn't wise.'

She might be able to move, but he hadn't, not really, since they entered. His head brushed the ceiling.

'So when Robert was Rhain's friend?' she asked.

'That was before my sister married him.'

It couldn't be Rhain who had caused Malcolm his pain, caused him to forgo acknowledging people who cared.

Maybe it wasn't people. Maybe...

'How do you like your family?'

'How do you like yours?'

Oh.

Malcolm took one step, two and sat on the

bed, laid his elbows on his knees and bowed his head. She didn't know how to take his reaction. His words hurt her again. Although he had warned her not to keep prodding, still she could only rally so many times.

'I think the rain's letting up,' she said.

Thunder shook the timbers.

Even with his eyes closed his mouth lifted. 'Neither of us is going anywhere.'

'The horses?'

'The tree canopy is all there is.'

'But what of the lightning?'

'They've been through worse.' Exhaling roughly, he said, 'Why is it every time there's some moment, we have rain?'

She eyed the pegs near him, the dripping clothes and the linen in her hand. 'I don't understand.'

'The day I met you it was raining. When we stayed with Rhain and Helissent, it was thundering then as well.'

He equated the day they met with what they did that night? Why?

'I'm sorry,' he blurted suddenly and with a tinge of remorse, but mostly desperation.

'We can't do anything about the rain.' Eyeing him, she walked to the peg, hung the sodden linen and then took another few steps. Far enough away from him, but not standing in the puddle near the door. The bed was the only place to sit.

He slid to the foot, eyed the expanse he made on the bed and her. She shook her head at his offer. It was too close, too soon.

'If it's any consolation, Finlay tried to talk to me, too, about the people we met on the journey to the Basque Country,' he said.

So, apparently, it wasn't only her he was unwilling to share himself with.

'I told him nothing,' Malcolm continued. 'I'm not used to sharing who I am, or where I've been with anyone.'

'Because you've been by yourself.'

'Because no one I've ever met deserves it… and that includes my family.'

And yet what was she to make of him telling her some of his family?

'You know what my family has done to me,' she said and then stopped. Talking of her family wouldn't get her anywhere, but this small space offered little to do.

'Do you want something to eat?' she said instead.

He placed his hands on his knees and squeezed. 'You do that, you know.'

Malcolm wasn't pleased, his temper showing again.

'What do I do?' Maybe he'd be hungry after she got the provisions out of the satchels.

'Feel sad or angry and then…smile, look for something to do.'

'Life is about survival, which doesn't wait for emotions,' she said. 'There are many things to do when it is up to you to feed yourself.'

'But you don't complete these tasks because of survival, but because of distraction.'

Is that how he saw what she did after the days when she understood what her father had done? She never thought he could be wrong.

'I can feel while I wash my clothes or gather kindling.' She tugged at the leather bindings. Everything was wet and difficult, but there was little else to do and eventually they would be hungry, and that lone candle couldn't last all night. 'There's no point in dwelling on anger or sadness. It only gets worse if you do. I always found it best to sort it in small batches. Easy to defeat then.'

He snorted.

It wasn't a friendly snort and not one she had to accept. She wasn't weak. Though she did wallow in her sorrow and grief, in her pain and hurt with her father's betrayal, but then, as she had done all her life, she…lived.

And she didn't need to take Malcolm's temper or his surliness—she knew her worth. And that was why she stood while Malcolm became restless, while she asked questions, while he became more agitated.

That was what people did when they cared. If there was a fight, even one like this, she stood by his side. The fact she was the instigator of the fight and his proponent wasn't lost on her. But that was his misfortune since he'd been avoiding his worth for too long.

He was worth more than all this anger, but it was what he made himself become. Didn't he see the other bits of him? His impatience, which was endearing when he wanted to give her a gift and couldn't wait.

How could she fault him then when he'd done it for her?

'What is it you do when you're in a temper?' She wanted to know his answer.

'You know what happens to me. My anger turns to vengeance, my—'

'What does your happiness do?'

His eyes searched hers. The darkness was upon them and the flickering of the lone candle was all Andreona had. It didn't let her see much, but she didn't need the light to know she had surprised…and made him wary.

'I don't have happiness.'

Chapter Twenty-Two

'Everyone has—'

'No!' he roared, stood, then reined himself in immediately. Pulled in whatever he was feeling to bite out the rest of the words. 'It was ripped from me, slashed right before my eyes, which blurred with blood and sweat. I was helpless to stop any of it while I watched it murdered. It never came back. It's gone.'

That was…specific and unexpected. What had happened to him?

His agony in every word went right through her and the healing spots she had didn't have a hope to stay that way. She felt weak, her stomach nauseous. If she could have run out through the door, she would.

The storm echoed his anger. More thunder, more lightning, and the rain slashed against the hut.

Swallowing her bile, she dared to ask, 'What did your family do to you, Malcolm? Was it Bram? Caird? Gaira?'

'It was *all* of them!' He heaved in a breath. 'Bram ordered me to stay home when there was a battle at Dunbar. I thought perhaps it was the distance, or the danger. But he never told me why and others from our clan and the next had already left. I had my pride—I knew my skills. I was worthy of a battle. And if my entire family were going to be cowards, if they risked having our lands stripped because we didn't heed the call of John Balliol, then I would go to represent them.

'That's where I earned this.' He thumped his chest right over the scar that carved deeply over his heart. 'I fell to the crushed grass beneath me. I should have died there. I should have been stabbed through to ensure it. Instead, I got buried under a few more men, then the scavengers came and no one wants to battle with those.'

She leaned back into the corner, knew the wetness there would seep into her clothing and any sense of getting dry would be for naught, but she couldn't hold herself up any longer. Birds had picked at his body?

He gave a knowing look. 'That's the scar on my thigh you've traced with the tip of your finger.'

She'd done it in fascination, in…love at being

able to freely touch him. After everything they'd experienced together, her touching his legs felt safe. That dip she circled was oddly comforting. And all the time she was causing him pain. She swallowed hard.

'Caird found me under it all, dragged me to a healer and I healed.'

No, he hadn't. She wasn't certain she'd survive the talking of it. The fact he stood here. What battles had he fought, was still fighting and it was all because of…? Oh…

'Bram staying on your land had something to do with the dagger and jewel, didn't it?'

He smirked. 'You understand how insidious the gem is, don't you? Bram was ordered to stay on the land and wait for a package. It never arrived. We believe it was the gem he was waiting for. The Englishman thought it rather humorous we didn't know what we were waiting for, but inevitably we came across it anyway. Like fate… or a curse that couldn't be avoided.'

She knew that, but felt she was missing something.

'Your family did something else, didn't they?'

'If Bram's harm to me was mistrust, Caird's was betrayal.'

She wasn't going to ask any more questions; Malcolm was breaking her heart. Her father and brother had betrayed her. And though she wished it were different, with her brothers, she never thought of them as separate, they were never siblings in the truest sense, but more an extension of her father. So, she had been betrayed in one stunning betrayal.

Malcolm talked of his siblings as if there were multiple betrayals, multiple injuries. How much was one man to endure?

'And Caird?' she whispered when she couldn't bear the silence.

'He met Mairead of Clan Buchanan, who had pursued the dagger to repay a family debt to her laird. Her brother Ailbert was killed because of the dagger he had found at the market…though most likely he'd stolen it in desperation, not realising what he stole from the mercenary.'

Given the value of the dagger and jewel, she thought that likely as well.

'Malcolm,' she said as softly, as carefully, as possible. 'What did Caird do?'

'He married her. After everything our family did or I suffered, he married one of *them*.'

She didn't know what to say, there wasn't anything she could say because after all this…she still knew nothing.

He looked sharply at her. 'The Buchanans took my happiness. Took the life I was meant to have, took my future. What you see is not what I was to be. Every slight afterwards was only compounded because of it. Bram mistrusting me with Dunbar secrets and Caird's rescuing me was because of what happened with the Buchanans.'

She was confused, but knew she was close to understanding this man. It wasn't the stumbling steps he took given the room was too small for him to pace. Whatever was causing him agony had had Malcolm running his hands through his hair, threading his fingers and wrenching it from his head, only to release it and begin again.

They weren't quiet, nor were they ignoring his pain, but she felt no closer to the truth.

'Why was it terrible that Caird married Mairead of Clan Buchanan, Malcolm? What did the Buchanans do?'

'They killed Shannon. Odd name, I know, for a Scottish lass, but her mother heard it once and liked it. So there you go. It fit her...she was unusual.'

No fire and almost no light in the small hut, but Andreona knew even if there were both it wouldn't make a difference in the sudden cold washing over her skin.

'Our home is near Loch Lomond. The Buchanans are to the east of it. We're down to the south in Dunbartonshire. It's a fair bit to travel to, but with a horse, specifically, one of my father's horses, it was certainly possible...

'They were drunk, the three men, truly drunk.

One didn't hold his horse and was stumbling about while the others held the reins to bring that man's horse with them. They played with us, all in fun at first, but it turned dark and I wasn't prepared for it. Shannon was older than me and looked it. I fought them with everything I had. It wasn't enough. I earned bruises and cuts. Couldn't see out of one eye and two fingers on my right hand were broken.

'I couldn't stop them. I couldn't do anything as they took her, they took and when they sobered enough or when they realised what they had done, they slit her throat.'

'How did you—?'

'I survived because I was already on my horse to flee for help. I only saw what they did when I looked back. I don't even know what happened afterwards. I…the horse took me home.

'My father had passed by then. So Bram and Caird went. I should have gone, but I fainted and didn't wake until they brought her back.

'Her family never blamed me, not once—they knew going there was her idea. How she loved it so, but it was my horse. She'd never have made it without my horse. She'd never have been killed, but for those Buchanans.'

'Did you know who it was?'

'No, talks were done and repairs were made as much as could be. Reaving was all we had until Caird married into the clan and settled our differences.'

'Reaving?

'Stealing. It can be done in fun, but this wasn't,' Malcolm said.

'How old were you when it happened.'

'Twelve. Thirteen?'

He'd carried this burden for that long? She needed more time with this. More thought. All these weeks with him and she knew something heartbreaking had to bring that look to this man's eyes, but this? No...

'So you hate Buchanans, and your brother loved one enough to marry her,' she said.

'It wasn't only Caird marrying that made the difference between the clans, it was the dagger. Mairead's family owed the Buchanan Laird. The dagger was supposed to be payment or at least to hold off punishment until coin could be exchanged, but when that dagger reached Buchanan land, it wasn't the true dagger.

'Best we can guess is it was switched when The Englishman, Howe, and some of his men surprised Caird and Mairead. The Englishman took the dagger that night, but he took the fake. And because the determined Englishman took it, no one looked at it closely enough to realise.'

'Not The Englishman's men, but one of my father's mercenaries,' she said.

Malcolm nodded. 'That will be interesting to tell Caird and explains how the dagger made it as far as the Basque Country. Another mystery solved.'

He sounded weary and there was a part of her that wanted to stop simply because he was tired and hurting.

When he was twelve, he lost Shannon, then later Bram didn't tell him of Dunbar, later still was Caird marrying a Buchanan and this Jewell of Kings.

These were her love's griefs held on to for too long. But everything seemed confusing to her. Some...convoluted, tenuous relationship between cause and outcome. Maybe she couldn't blame him. Years of spying, of seeing things that weren't there, of connecting dots that shouldn't have been connected. Maybe he had been trained to do exactly this.

Why hadn't his heart simply stopped? If it hurt, why did it beat and allow him to come up with these thoughts? Why didn't it stop torturing...? Oh.

'You loved her very much, didn't you?'

'Shannon and I were children.'

That wasn't an excuse. Children loved with their whole being. Maybe more than adults could. Adults weighed the cost of connections. Children didn't know how to do that. And if Shannon had done the same towards him, how could that not be anything but pure happiness?

Except...

'Love weighs more than hate, Malcolm. That includes the love in a family...if it's there.'

'How could you talk to me of loving a family when you've had yours?'

'*If* it's there,' she repeated. 'My family doesn't love. I know that now. Seeing Nicholas with Matilda, or Rhain with Helissent—I've never seen that before.'

Another gust of wind hit the hut; a horse neighed. Malcolm looked longingly at the door as if he'd risk it anyway.

'Your family isn't the only who doesn't love,' he said very carefully. 'I thought you would understand. I've told you every wretched moment with my family. You should understand why I want nothing to do with them. Only a fool would forgive them. That way lies suffering and pain.'

These words were Malcolm's deepest regrets and emotions and he was just spilling them out to her. She wanted to gather them all up and hurl them out in the storm.

How could he be so wrong and so...hard on himself all this time?

'My family never was there for me. My father wanted me dead, my brother gave me coin to run away. But your family was there for you—for Shannon, too.'

He choked on some words he wanted to say. His green eyes shone before they went cold with disdain. The room felt colder, damper, less likely to hold back the storm.

'Maybe it was wrong of Bram to not tell you, but he did it because he cared and was trying to protect you from treason,' she said, forging on despite the way Malcolm looked at her. As if she was adding to his pain.

'Your family made mistakes, but they tried to rectify them because they cared, Malcolm. You've been loved.'

'No.' He gripped his hair and released it. 'Perhaps your anguish is too new—maybe when it finally festers in how you were thrown to the side and discarded, maybe when you realise your family's agenda was more than your life, maybe then you'll—'

'Be like you?' she interrupted.

He faced her directly, his body like the storm before his eyes narrowed and he laughed. 'My father never tried to kill me. You have to resent your own for that.'

He knew where to hurt her and the fact he did it, the fact she let him, was telling on how close they were. She loved him. And if in this time he needed to hurt her, she'd take it. Not forever, but this pain needed to come out and this hut wasn't strong enough for Malcolm's anguish.

She was.

'You were ordered to be killed, then lied to. None of your family stood at your side. You had no one. Why are you championing them now? How are you able to forgive them anything?'

He said it with such vehemence, she almost believed him, until she remembered.

'I had you.'

He became utterly silent, utterly still. She wasn't even sure he heard her until he turned so slowly, it was almost like the turn of a day.

Chapter Twenty-Three

Malcolm's heart pounded. It was the only feeling he was truly aware of. Everything else, the fact he stood, the blinking of his eyes, the way the cool air brushed the back of his neck, blurred.

Andreona wouldn't let this go, but why would she care about Alice or Rhain or—? Care. He wanted to laugh.

'You were with me,' she said. 'I wasn't ever alone.'

She'd leaned against the far wall while he had sat, then risen, and stood for a conversation he would have avoided all his life until he couldn't. It was the relentless rain, the thunder that shook the ground. It was the dark lit by a lone candle. It was *her*.

'Agreeing for you to travel with me doesn't mean there was friendship.'

'No, but there was. Because I felt it.'

'You're mistaken.'

She shook her head, a gentle smile on her lips. Curse the low light in this hut that he couldn't see those eyes of hers.

They were the keepers of the secret. One that could make and destroy countries, men, lives for generations. She needed to not be anywhere near him. But he wasn't fooling himself she needed to be away from him because of the Warstones or The Englishman. He wasn't a child any longer and, if three men or more attacked, he could protect her.

The danger wasn't any of that. It was him.

How much darkness can one man carry on his shoulders and in his soul? He wasn't made of sinew and skin. He merely resembled a man, but he was made of injustices, grief and pain. He was nothing but death and betrayal. An ugliness that was reflected by the wide swathe of a scar carved across his body.

But the scars inside were far deeper. Permanent. Forever. For the one healed across his skin didn't kill him. The ones inside had.

'At first light, we need to leave,' he said.

Upon a sigh, her shoulders raised, then lowered before she strode towards him. He knew she wore only the chemise, knew their clothes would be damp in the morning and the only way to keep warm was this one bed. And as she got closer and brushed against him, lifted the bed's quilt, shook it away from them and laid it back down, apparently so did she.

'Do you want on the inside or out?' she said.

Her voice was a whisper, but sure, confident.

Crawling underneath the quilt, she slid the little distance to the wall to make room for him.

How could she do both confidently and retain a light in her eyes that was pure? Not in any maidenly way, but…true? Truth was what he felt since the beginning. An innocence and trust that wasn't corrupted. Not naive or without reason, but simply right.

Those eyes of hers told him so much and if he felt down to his bones that that was truth, then…? Then nothing.

He shook himself, laid down on the bed and pulled the covers around them both. He expected her to stay against the wall, but when she curled against his side that felt right as well.

Yet her words had sliced through him, cut deeper than any sword piercing his flesh. A phantom cut that no bandages could stem the flow of; no stitching could piece together what she'd ripped apart.

He had been one way and with one touch, with a few words arranged in such a way they had never been done for him, he was another.

He had no words for her, he had said all he

needed to. She was wrong. She couldn't understand because she wasn't from his family and wasn't there all those times when they'd revealed their duplicity.

That helplessness he'd learnt and earned when he was twelve, he carried it everywhere. If he climbed a tree, Bram would be there to catch him. Fall off a horse, Gaira was there to mend him. Learning to read, to write? Failing when the letters didn't make sense? Irvette was there to show him how they all made sense.

He wasn't the youngest. He should have mended himself, taught himself. He was old enough to climb a tree, he was old enough to get himself down.

But at twelve, he'd taught himself and his family how weak he was. He never forgave himself and they never let him forget.

Bram holding a secret and not letting him know what it was, Caird suspecting, and holding his tongue. All of that was to protect him because of his weakness.

And his actions since hadn't helped. Off to Dunbar to prove them wrong, only to get sliced across the chest. So physically weak he couldn't push the men who fell on him off, couldn't bat away a bird from pecking at his flesh. His family had rescued him again.

Andreona had grown quiet, but she wasn't

asleep. Was she thinking of what he said, or giving him time to think of her words, which thrashed around like knives inside him?

She had to be wrong, but her tone had been tender, her mannerisms reasonable. Certainly, he couldn't say she didn't know what she spoke of because he had a direct account of her family. He also was there when she'd grown too quiet afterwards, and when she tenderly smiled at Bertrice.

He'd watched the blow of betrayal hit her and the way she got back up. So he listened to her and her experience forced him to think more than he would have coming from anyone else. Was he learning patience, or…was he learning that if he was right, did she necessarily have to be wrong?

He could admit people made mistakes. He certainly did. This whole quest for the dagger showed how much blind fortune had helped him. And maybe she was somewhat correct that along the way, people helped and maybe he couldn't have done it at all without them.

But as to his family, as to them helping and fumbling with well intentions, once she met them, she'd know the truth.

Until then…until then they would share this bed in this hut. She'd curled her body around him and she felt right.

So he shifted his body until he faced her, thrust his hands in that tumbling hair of hers, slammed his lips on hers, felt the joy of her startlement and the satisfaction when her lips responded. When *she* responded and held him the way he was holding her. As though she needed him as much as he needed her. When that occurred, the world was right again.

Everything was right, even when their pleasure abated and sleep weighed heavily on each of their tangled limbs. The light in her slumberous eyes was as much truth as he wanted there ever to be. Why did there have to be anything else?

Another thunderclap shook the hut and Malcolm remembered the one deed he'd meant to set right. 'We forgot to put the thistle on the door.'

Andreona mumbled against his neck and he was loath to get up.

'I think it's in the satchel on the floor,' he said. 'I'll put it up.'

A grateful sound, a nod, her body tightening into his until he wished he could always keep her there.

But he had to stand and step into the cold rain because that's what his life had always been. When the world became right, good, and he'd found his way... When he found something true that he wanted to hold on to, something else would slash against him and reveal—

'I love you,' she said. Her words clear, direct. He heard, felt them.

'I do,' she added. 'I know you want to deny it or say you can't love me because of whatever happened in your past. But it's true and I hope you'll let me show you. Because that's what you've shown me, Malcolm. This entire time, your caring for me, it's love.'

He stood there, wondering what to say or how to say it, stood because he felt if he did anything else, what she said wouldn't be true.

With a small smile, she closed her eyes, and snuggled deeper under the cover. 'Don't get too wet,' she said.

Andreona loved him and, for one bright moment, he wanted it. Before he opened the door and thunder lit the trees, revealing—*reminding* him—there wasn't anything left of him for her to love.

Chapter Twenty-Four

⁓⁓⁓

That following morning had been almost too clear and blinding with sunlight. If the ground hadn't been soaked, and her gown not damp, Andreona wouldn't have known a relentless storm had allowed her to voice her thoughts to Malcolm. Whether he had listened to her or not, she didn't know because he kept his silence as they went about readying for another day's travel.

If the thistle hadn't been on the door, she would have thought she'd dreamt he'd done that for her. If her lips hadn't felt swollen and her body deliciously held, she would have dreamt he kissed and held her, too. Those deeds had to mean something, didn't they?

She'd told him she loved him, saw the shudder go through him at her words. She'd said them when she meant to, not in anger or when they kissed, but simply, easily, because it was that easy to love him. He didn't need to say them back and she hadn't expected it. After all his injustices, it would take time for him to see she was right and the world was still good.

It'd been a sennight since then and on and on through this Scotland they travelled with Malcolm mostly silent, except for his eyes, which kept seeking hers. There were times she thought he'd say something, but then that darkness would flash and he'd turn away. They didn't talk further on what was said. She knew all about the need for silence.

She wished, however, that they could talk of a few subjects. Like the fact they'd crossed some line and were now on Colquhoun land. She worried about meeting his brother and Laird, Caird, and his wife, Mairead. About Robert and Gaira and their children, of seeing what his life would be like after she left...if that was what was to become of her.

When she began this journey, she had wanted to simply get away. Then, as she'd got to know Malcolm, she wanted to know him more...and stayed longer than that until her body, her heart, were irrevocably his.

Maybe he'd let her stay at his home for a spell, though that threatened winter travel. She couldn't stay with him for a full winter. It was confusing enough. Not the way Malcolm ignored her during the day, but kept holding and kissing her at night.

Many a time she was tempted to bring up his family again, but what more could she say? Nothing differently. The days were spent talking of ways of avoiding being noticed and securing themselves sleeping areas. At times, he'd talk about the weather, which had remained pleasant since that night in the hut. Oddly, he'd appear irritated when she commented on the blue skies.

With barely any words exchanged between them, Andreona searched for answers to what was to become of her, of them, in this vast Scottish land. It was different than the sharp slopes of her home and the beauty of the beaches. But it was a mix of their travels. It held vastness, trees, hard rocky ground and occasionally salty sea air.

The colourful greenery looked prickly and fierce; the grass was tall but bent in the gusting wind. It was as if Scotland was both generous and harsh. Malcolm loved it despite him saying otherwise. It was the way he sat on his horse, the extra breaths he took. But perhaps she searched the land more closely because she was the one who spotted the riders first.

'Is that your family?'

Malcolm whipped his head to look behind her. His eyes widened and he cursed. His reaction could be for family or for an enemy. All she saw were five men, a flash of black, of red. One man in the middle. Older, his body thinner. He wasn't a warrior like the others so obviously were.

Malcolm yanked to a stop while the riders kept towards them.

'Stay here,' he ordered before he charged forward a few paces and raised his hand in a gesture for the men to halt.

She didn't trust any of them and eased her horse forward next to him. But whatever Malcolm did worked.

'I told you to stay behind,' he said, not taking his eyes off the riders.

'I'd refuse either way.'

'Either way?'

'If they're family or not,' she said.

He eyed them speculatively, his hands flexing on his sword. 'We're outnumbered.'

'Not family, then.'

He swung his gaze to hers. She was always struck by his colouring. By the darkness of his hair streaked with red, the green of his eyes and that scar that defined every feature as if simply showing off the beauty and fierceness of the man.

And then she knew. This…this was why his eyes were never quite right anywhere else. She always thought the green should be gentle, not turbulent. It should be soft, not so full of rage. But his eyes were like these Scotland Highlands:

generous and harsh. Right now they were struck with concern and determination.

'They are messengers. Murderers. They are Warstones.'

'Here!' They'd come so far and evaded danger for months. 'Shouldn't your family or the Buchanans be here to protect?'

'Doesn't matter when they are not.'

'But these Warstones are waiting,' she said. 'What does that mean?'

'I don't know, but I must talk with them.'

'I'll go—'

'No. It was the mistake I made...' He shook his head. 'I'll not do it for you.'

A mistake... He meant Shannon. Didn't he know, it could never be like that again? But she couldn't make that promise. Not when the men held still at the top of a hill with the wind battering them. Cloaks billowing out, horses sidestepping in agitation.

What a fool she was not talking since the storm and that tiny hut. How could she have kept the silence between them when there were more words to say? It was the blue skies making her think they were safe. She hated them as much as Malcolm did. It wasn't their pasts that were the only danger between them, but the fact every day he strapped a legend around his chest and these men wanted it.

'I want to help,' she said.

'There is only one choice for us…for me.'

She didn't want him to make that choice. 'You mean to sacrifice yourself, don't you? You ride up there, negotiate, and if that doesn't work—'

'Negotiations won't work.'

So they'd cut him down and take what they wanted, what they'd always wanted, and she'd be riding away and they wouldn't bother chasing her. Hadn't Malcolm told her there was no hope when it came to the Warstones? He had and she thought them stories no one could truly believe. But they were true. Now she knew their viciousness, she understood the man with the bow could merely release one of his arrows into her back. And she'd deserve it, too, for abandoning Malcolm.

'But they're holding still!' she said. 'If they mean to kill us, they could have already done so.'

'Why expend the energy when you don't have to? The small frail man in the middle is Sir Richard Howe, The Englishman. He'll have thought of every scenario to this, planned every scheme. He knows who carries the dagger and what I'll have to do. When I reach them, wait a few moments, then ride, fast, in the direction we were going. You're sure to find someone to protect you.'

'But you told me The Englishman lies and is cunning. Even if he negotiates, how will you know the truth? Why don't we both ride to protection?'

'The archer with them no doubt has skills enough to end me and I can't risk you.'

He *was* risking the life she wanted with him. Stubborn fool, and, if those Warstones didn't fight fair, neither would she. 'You'll make me you, then. If you ride out there... I'll be the one helpless to save you.'

This wasn't the same. She wasn't a child, like Shannon. He pulled in a breath sharply, his eyes sheening. But he'd told her she was safe with him. Did he care for her at all? Didn't he know what this was doing to her?

'Don't look back like I did,' he said. 'If I hadn't looked back, I could have pretended she was alive.'

A few of their horses were stepping forward and being pulled back. They didn't have much more time. She couldn't swing a sword or release an arrow. She could fight with her fists, but these men wouldn't fight fair. She didn't feel like fighting fair either.

'How close to your family are we?' she said.

'They're over that hill to your left. They can't see us here.'

If she went there before he reached The Englishman, if they could see a stray woman, maybe she could get help.

'You can talk, can't you? Stall?'

'You'd never reach them in time. Don't come back here.'

'Once you ride in that direction, you can't stop me.'

'I don't want that for you. I don't want you to see it, Andreona.'

She didn't want to see him killed either. 'Talk for as long as you can then so I don't. If that doesn't work, fight. *Stall* them. You've told me of these skills. You can do that, can't you?'

'Are you telling me what to do?' he said.

'A bit.' Very much so. She wanted to say other words to him. More meaningful, lasting, but he knew them all. She'd told him she loved him when she meant to tell him, when he heard her because there was nothing but them. She refused to say she loved him now when it would be tinged with anger and desperation. So she said the only thing she could say that meant anything at all in this situation.

'Good death to you.'

'What?' He stared at her, his mouth agape.

'A good death to you,' she repeated.

Malcolm's heart was ripping apart in his chest. Rage and wrath and desperation were his breath. He knew, after everything in his past, he knew he was never meant to keep Andreona despite her saying she loved him.

As if those words could make a difference! No matter how hard he wished, or that he wanted to say them in return…to *mean* them like she deserved. No, he wasn't meant to have any good. He was meant for betrayal and darkness and grief. Yet, as she looked to him, he wanted to fight against his fate.

He loathed the Warstones. Hated them mostly because this moment on his family's land should have been only them and their presence was taking away his focus on Andreona. And her strange words he couldn't have heard correctly.

'What are you saying?'

'I wish a good death to you, Malcolm of Clan Colquhoun.'

'I don't want a good death,' he said.

She gasped. 'You want a bad one?'

'I don't want to die,' he clarified because if he could stop any of this he would.

'That's not something we have a choice about, do we?'

What did these words she was telling him mean? He didn't want to die on a day he faced a man who'd plagued his family for years. He'd be damned if he didn't try to avenge them and his sister Irvette. And on a battlefield, when facing a mortal enemy, that wasn't a thought he made lightly.

'I'm not dying *this* day,' he vowed.

'You don't have that decision either.'

Kings, royalty, countries and legends plaguing his every breath and this… There was hope in those unusual eyes of hers that reflected everything good and strong. Everything he…needed. He needed *her*.

'Dammit, woman, canna you simply wish me fortune?'

Her brows drew in. 'I did.'

Malcolm lost the rein in his right hand and snatched it before it fell. He was completely confused, completely… He loved her. Of course he did—else he wouldn't have told her all he had. Wouldn't have held her even though he thought her wrong.

She wasn't wrong. He was. She wasn't alone, could never be alone because he wouldn't leave her, not then, not now.

He loved her and she…was wishing him a good fortune.

'Well, why didn't you say so?' he said.

Wanting to rip her from the horse and crush her to his body, wanting to say the words needing to be said by him. But most of all, not wanting to argue any longer, for them to simply be who they were, he winked and didn't look back as he rode towards Sir Robert Howe, The Englishman, his family's greatest threat.

Chapter Twenty-Five

Malcolm rode towards the Warstones, praying they'd stay away from the woman he loved. True to her word, he heard Andreona's horse's hooves pound and fade. She was riding away, just as he'd asked her to, or did she think she could save him? He wasn't certain he was meant for saving.

Why realise he loved her now when his true battle was ahead? In his right hand, he had a blade ready to throw. If the archer released his arrow her way, Malcolm would release his weapon. He'd be dead straight afterwards, but at least he could believe he tried to protect her.

And he'd die knowing he loved a woman and she loved him. Oh, her expression when he'd winked! That he could find any merriment now was because of her. A man could die with those wide surprised eyes.

He stopped well before the hill they were

on. The Warstones had the advantageous position and he needed to even the odds. Sir Richard's gaze turned from Andreona's fleeing horse down to him and he laughed. 'Fair enough, Colquhoun!'

He rode forward. Three of the guards kept to the top of the hill, while the other two flanked. The man with the bow stayed on the hill. This didn't bode well. But then, he didn't expect to live anyway, although he'd always hoped he'd know what direction death came from.

When they all came to a stop, Malcolm said, 'You'll regret it if you pursue her, Howe.'

Howe shrugged. 'It appears I have everything I need right here.'

He'd hoped for some surprise, but the wind whipping at them would outline the dagger strapped to his chest.

'It's a little inconvenient to ask you to strip given the briskness of the day,' Howe said, 'But why don't you go ahead so we can proceed on with the rest?'

Stall, Andreona had begged him. 'What would be the rest?'

Howe smirked. 'Colquhouns are usually uninformed, but they are never obtuse. What do you think you do by asking such an obvious question? Stall until someone gets here? We've been here for days waiting for you. By the time she gets to your home, she'll never make it here in time.'

As he knew. 'Wise decision waiting here.'

'There was no other place you would travel.' Howe shrugged. 'And I'm tired.'

Sir Richard Howe had never been a handsome man. Pasty skin, jowls, green protuberant eyes. Now, however, dark circles were under those toadish eyes and his skin was sallow. Always frail—he was gaunt.

'You're ill,' Malcolm said.

Howe laughed low. 'Don't know if it has been the trials of the last few years chasing you, Reynold and Balthus, or if perhaps one of these mercenaries who have kindly been donated to me by the elder Warstones has been slowly feeding me poison.'

'So not protection.' This was worthy news.

'Oh, don't get me wrong, Colquhoun, the goal has always been to get that dagger and Jewell to the Warstones, but it's taking me too long. I'm sure they have other orders to hurry me along as a result. The longer it takes, the more poison I get. I'm afraid I can't wait much longer.'

'So I am to die.'

'Of course.' Sir Howe waved his hand and pulled hard on his mount to move back. The other two dismounted.

Interesting, it would have been to their advantage to use the horses, but then…they probably wanted safe and healthy horseflesh for their return.

With his gaze on the three eerily still mercenaries at the top of the hill, he dismounted. All it would take was an arrow and this whole confrontation would come to an end. But perhaps that was too simple. It was the Warstones, after all, and they no doubt had something else afoot. To wait to see if these two wore him down or killed him most likely.

A long dagger in his left hand, his sword in his right, Malcolm faced the two men. Flanking him, they came at him hard and fast.

His one advantage was they hadn't cleared the hill, or The Englishman, and though they'd hit the rumps of their horses, he hadn't done his. Oh, he'd make the call for the horse to run rather than harm it and any worthy mercenary would wait and not hit good horseflesh.

In the meantime, he could fight them one at a time. And as long as he kept his back to one of the obstacles, the hill, the horse, there would be no clear way of taking advantage.

Stall, she'd said. Knees bent, his sword held to his hip, and dagger outstretched. His opponents equally dressed, both carrying similar weapons—who to choose? Malcolm looked to their shoes—one had decent, the other did not.

One more skilled and well paid versus the other. He'd rather have stalled with a pleasant conversation over ale, but this would do.

The first was over too soon. The man focused on his far-reaching sword, Malcolm stepped forward, thrust with his sword and sliced his dagger deep across the man's thigh. He fell immediately.

The second didn't look to his fallen counterpoint and held his position of right foot forward, sword out and hilt tilted left. Malcolm cursed. This fight would count. He struck. Malcolm shuffled back, kept his weapons separate. The man took notice and smiled. He was no fool.

He'd love to keep his focus on the man before him who could likely kill him, but he had to look to The Englishman, to the men on the hill, to the man holding his leg to stop the flow of blood. The man got too many strikes in, too many chances. He glanced to Howe and saw the man look on. No smirk, no interest...merely boredom.

Enough. A slice to the arm, another. Malcolm shuffled and forced the man between The Englishman and the fallen. Easy enough if Howe moved, but he didn't. The mercenary realised it, too. Malcolm blocked his sword and struck with the dagger through his stomach. A clean kill.

Stepping back rapidly, Malcolm heaved a

breath in. Three on the hill and The Englishman who didn't look well, but could do anything.

Howe dismounted, crossed to the sitting man clutching the deep gash in his leg and ran his sword through the struggling man's back. The man choked out a sound before Howe ripped out his blade and the body crumpled sideways.

'I've lost the ability to watch dying men struggle, Colquhoun.' Howe sighed.

Malcolm looked to the two dead men, then the three on their horses at the top. Blood pumping through him, he had an opportunity to kill The Englishman, but those three stayed still. Because Howe was alive? Or were they waiting for something else?

Malcolm eyed Howe and wiped his dagger on the fallen man's tunic.

'I think I know who has been poisoning you.' Malcolm indicated to the hill.

Howe stared at the men who stood as sentinels on the hill. 'One mystery solved.' He turned back to Malcolm. 'But I see another coming towards us. We have company. Come, give me that dagger around your chest and I'll go.'

There was no logical explanation for the men on the hill not to come to Howe's aid. Nor was there a reason why they didn't kill him and be done with it. But the three on the hill wore the Warstone colours, the two dead did not. So they were mercenaries in Warstone training and easily expendable. Did that mean Howe was as well?

'I'll not hand over the dagger so easily. I'd rather keep fighting until they reach us.'

Howe didn't raise his sword and kept his gaze on the approaching riders. 'The woman you picked as a mate isn't like the others. Neither red haired nor Scottish. Neither from good family nor connected. At least the others gained something. Gaira with Robert's skills, Caird with Buchanan alliance and Bram with Fergusson's. You brought nothing.'

Andreona was everything. 'I could kill you still.'

Howe scrunched his face as if he had a bad taste. 'But I'm not raising my sword, the three on the hill aren't raising theirs and you—'

Howe's gaze widened and, if possible, he paled a bit more. He kept his eyes so focused on what was behind Malcolm, it would be easy to kill him. Instead, all Malcolm wanted to do was look as well, but he was loath to turn his back on The Englishman. The other three could come charging down and cut his head off before he could realise how close they came.

But there was something in The Englishman's wide gaze that was no longer maniacal madness and hate, but a softness. A *longing*. It was so unexpected, it compelled Malcolm to look.

There were more riders coming over the hill. Caird, Robert, a man who was larger than a horse and a woman by his side, with hair whiter than snow. And if he wasn't wrong, eyes the colour of this man who shook before him.

'She's the archer, isn't she, your daughter,' he said.

'And the man at her side was her downfall, her husband, Eldric of Hawksmoor.'

The man who was friends with Hugh of Shoebury, a friend of Robert of Dent, Gaira's husband. Andreona was right, there were too many connections, and too tenuous to hold on to. And yet, here they were together.

Andreona would say that was an advantage, but another one was possibly revealed as well. By his tone, The Englishman wasn't fond of his son-in-law.

'You don't like him?'

'I would care to avoid him.'

'But not Cressida.'

A flash of pain crossed his features. 'I tried to kill my daughter several times.'

'But Cressida didn't kill you. She…forgave you.' And here he was standing, not killing him either. This man was a sword of the Warstones, but he was far worse to his family. He'd killed or had ordered killed Irvette, his sister. The sweetest of them all was dead because of this man.

Rage coursed deep and Malcolm flashed to the three men who were no longer still, but conversing with each other. They stayed there.

'I want to kill you.' Malcolm sheathed his dagger. 'Stab you through the back three times as you run away as my sister died.'

'I know.'

'Irvette was no stranger to you. You raped her, then had her murdered in the most brutal of ways.'

Howe flung out his arms to present his chest.

'Yet now we're family, aren't we?'

Howe eyed Malcolm's sword and dropped his arms. 'I am no relation to you.'

Malcolm didn't wish it either. 'I don't know why you complain, you forced it. My sister had your child, Margaret, *Maisie*. Raised by another, a good man, but my niece has your blood. And she's here as well, isn't she? Your flesh and blood are both here on my land. What is the irony in that? We're enemies, yet Colquhoun feed your family and we're related. Is that why you waited for me here? Not because it was easy, but you'd like a visit?'

'Don't, Colquhoun. I know not what the three men at my back's orders are, but it couldn't be outside the Warstones' intentions that you die.'

'I already expected to die when I approached you.' Malcolm sheathed his sword.

'That's too direct and messy.'

'You didn't want to harm the dagger around my chest.'

He smirked. 'That, too.'

'Now what? One daughter is safely in our clan and the other rides towards you. What's it going to be? King Edward's wrath when he discovers you, who pledged fealty, have been subverting his cause to gain the Jewell of Kings? Especially now after his loss at Stirling…because, yes, I heard he lost it. Or will you return to the Warstones and risk their madness? Either way won't go easy because you're not getting the dagger or the gem. You're left with nothing.'

Howe looked again behind Malcolm, who couldn't hear any horses coming close. Did they wait like the men on the hill? His family and their logic to analyse a situation… He had no patience for it. He knew if it had been him, he'd have ridden in here, sword drawn.

Except hadn't he learned some caution? When it came to Andreona, he'd learned more than enough. He couldn't wait to tell her he loved her. Knowing her, she probably already knew and was waiting for him to realise. Why was he so late to realise? He was a fool…but not like this.

'You lost the dagger twice,' he said. 'Why did they ever forgive you?'

'I would say slow poison and the unreachable

tasks they've given me reveal their exacting punishments,' Howe said.

True. His own journey to find the dagger and unite it with the Jewell had been a dreadful burden. But the difference between him and Howe was that he knew, he understood now, his family wouldn't betray him or hate him if he never returned with it. Howe, however, was likely to be killed either way—because he failed again, or because he knew too much.

'I wouldn't want to be you,' he said.

Howe sighed. 'I haven't wanted to be me for longer than that. There is no risk to the Warstones' madness. There is simply madness.'

'What do you mean?'

'Four perfect sons. Four strong siblings. But Ian and Guy are dead and Balthus and Reynold contrive against their own parents. Terrified, I haven't actually seen the elder Warstones for years. Though…given the three on the hill who haven't come to my aid, their malevolent reach is far enough to kill me.'

'They're gone,' Malcolm said.

Howe turned. The hill they had stood on was empty. Malcolm had watched them ride away. There had been no need to reveal it and his family approached.

Howe dropped his sword, but kept his eyes on his daughter. 'To end here is fitting.'

Chapter Twenty-Six

Malcolm heard one lone horse approach. He wasn't surprised it was Andreona. Aware of The Englishman's curious gaze, he said, 'When you tell me you'll bring help, you meant it.'

'They were already coming from the other side of the second hill. I'm grateful they didn't shoot an arrow at me.'

So was he. What had his family said? What had she replied? He wished he hadn't missed that. Her first introductions and he wasn't there. Yet another reason to set all this aside.

'Then my family abandoned us and you've come to my rescue.'

'They wanted to wait until you were done.' She kept her eyes on him, as if Howe didn't exist, but the horse, sensing her unease, shifted under her. 'Are you done?'

Andreona had learned some of his impatience,

while his family seemed to have too much. They should have held her back where it was safe!

'Walk to your daughter, Howe,' he said, while he kept his gaze on her. He was relieved they moved away from the men he'd killed. She might be on a horse, but she was too close.

'Face all of them without weapons and without a way to escape?' Howe said.

Malcolm stopped gazing into eyes he preferred and at The Englishman instead. 'I don't think you're worried about the others, or your lack of weapons. They're not strangers to you. There's Caird, my brother, whom you threatened. His wife, Mairead, must be at home. Since she scarred you, you likely don't want to see her. Then there's only Eldric and Cressida, your daughter.'

'Facing her without a weapon isn't intelligent. And that bastard won't let me anywhere near her.'

Howe was nervous. Not for death, but for rejection. Malcolm whistled for his horse. When it stilled in front of him, he grabbed the reins. 'That bastard is Eldric, her husband, and, yes, I suspect he'll be territorial. But I'd suggest using his name for a more friendly reunion.'

'Are you playing with me? That's not like you. Why haven't you run your sword through or raged at me?'

It was there, all of it was. His anger, his wrath, but whereas before it had flamed uncontrolled, now it was tempered with more pressing matters, like talking to Andreona. Would she want to stay in this land that looked nothing like hers and so far away from others she knew? 'I never thought this game with the Jewell was worth playing and doesn't deserve my concern.'

'You brought it here, the dagger and the Jewell are together, and not so far away they can't be reached. I may not last a season, but you and your clan won't make it a year. You think you're done, when you've made it worse.'

'You do need to work on softening those harsh edges, Howe. Those threats won't be taken lightly. And you know it won't stay here nor will you see them again.'

'Not to use it?' The Englishman waved around them. 'All of this, all of these years of struggle, and you'll waste it?'

Andreona laughed, but it wasn't light nor her usual smirk. She was up to something. Oh, to keep her away from this man!

'I do believe they are very pretty baubles, they won't go to waste,' she said.

Ah. There she was, always getting up again. If she could hold on a bit longer, he'd get them out of this. Malcolm mounted his horse and adjusted in the seat. 'They are pretty, aren't they? I wonder if we should use them for something else?'

'To put in one of my boxes, perhaps?' she said.

'You *are* playing games,' Howe said.

Not his game! 'You don't have much more time.'

'So that's it, I walk over there and you forgive me for what I did.'

'No!' The denial was forced through his throat. Curse this coward, this murderer for pushing, for bringing these memories forward so he must talk of them. The man didn't deserve these words. 'I loved my sister. *Never* will I forgive you. But your death is no more mine than it's Bram's, or Caird's or Gaira's, for they loved Irvette dearly. You harmed Mairead, so perhaps Caird is owed a bit more of your punishment. However, you made Gaira suffer because she saw her sister's body. Then there's Cressida, your own flesh and blood, whom you've harmed more than all of us. She's certainly capable of killing you and Eldric probably wants to make that right, so don't forget him. There's Maisie, though. Her first year in this world and you forced her to smell the charred remains of her father. Her true father... the one who intended to raise her. Then to kidnap her. She jumps, you know, when someone surprises her. You did that to her. You should die for that alone!'

'I'm right here, Colquhoun.'

Malcolm shook his head. Reynold or Balthus

would want answers; The Englishman would be of use to them. 'Maybe I've learnt patience.'

Howe raised his hand. 'Enough. I understand. You do know I'm dying.'

'I know.'

'Then hurry it up with what you all want of me. I'll give the last remaining breaths to you all. That seems fitting as well.' Howe stumbled around the dead body. Cressida and Eldric urged their horses forward and away from Caird, who stood waiting. For what and where did those three Warstones go?

Andreona shook. Conversations with Death couldn't have been more terrifying. 'So that's The Englishman. He's dying, weak, and yet so cold.'

'I think he lacks a soul, yet he wants to see his children.'

'You didn't kill him,' she said.

Malcolm shook his head. 'And he didn't kill me, so no good death today.'

'I only meant good fortune.' Tears threatened. 'I meant for you *not* to die.'

'I know. There is much you can teach me of you and your world. If you'd like.'

What did he mean? After she had said so much and he'd denied her everything except his body, this week had been days of shuttered expressions and clamped jaws. 'Is that white-haired woman his other daughter?'

He gave a rough exhale. 'It's another story.'

'It seems you have a lot of those. Bram's, Caird's, Gaira's, Rhain's and Hugh's—I'm only concerned with one.'

Unsure which one, not quite trusting the light in those green eyes, which were almost soft. When had his eyes ever been soft and *warm*? She looked away. 'He chose to walk towards her, not away.'

'He's not a good man. He killed many for nothing other than spite.'

'But she's seeing him.'

'With no chance of his harm spreading. It's a gift to him she's giving. One I can't understand.'

Andreona understood all too well, and it pained her heart. 'That's because it's not a gift for him—it's one for herself.'

'Seeing that man—'

'To forgive him is to let go,' she said. 'It's to let in happiness.'

His brows drew in. 'Is this what you want? With your own— Dammit, my brother comes now?'

The man had much longer hair than Malcolm and no dark at all. He did have that same raw build, but where Malcolm's was more elegant, this man was broader. Still, by the tilt of their heads, and the stubbornness of their expressions, they were related.

'Your timing could be better, Brother,' Malcolm said.

Caird huffed. 'Not a greeting or a thank you on our quick arrival? No graciousness because we let you have conversation with that ass's midge?'

Just Caird's voice alone brought him home. There were no words to express his gratitude or the sheer joy of returning. To be on Scottish land, near his family's estate again after all these years, for everything to be almost over. He was glad he sat or else his knees would give.

'You look old,' he said, 'and you let three of them go.'

'You've got wrinkles around those pretty eyes and Robert is trailing after the three.'

'Robert would take such a risk? And they're from laughter, not age.'

'Robert won't be seen. Dressed as he is, they wouldn't recognise him from any distance.' Caird's gaze turned reflectively at Andreona. 'If he's smiling, it's because of you.'

Andreona wanted to laugh, cry. Just a few words exchanged between them, and she knew they were true brothers. Malcolm had sacrificed this by being away, and yet...was he intending to stay away? How could he, when Caird's eyes were lit with joy?

'Caird, this is Andreona from the Basque Country,' Malcolm said. 'She was the owner of the dagger and decided to come along to put it where it goes.'

'How long did you have it?'

'Years.' She almost hated to say.

Caird fake-shuddered. 'I think there's more to this story.'

'There is,' she said.

They all looked to where Cressida, Eldric and The Englishman stood. They were off their horses. Eldric was half in front of his wife, his hands in fists. But no raised swords or words.

'He's not invited to dinner,' Caird said.

'No, but I wish we had a cellar with bars.'

'Who's to say we don't?' Caird said.

'Then why didn't you get those others? They'll only notify the Warstones.'

'It's all we can do. Kill three, six will arrive to see what has happened. And if they don't take the hint to keep going east, Robert will end them and we'll face those six who'll arrive in their stead.'

Malcolm looked to Andreona. 'He's the methodical, patient one. Unlike me, who is too hotheaded to know better, but can be taught.'

Was Malcolm teasing or telling her something important? He'd said more words to her now then he had since they'd argued. Caird's head swivelled between them. She didn't know what to say to him.

Caird eyed Malcolm's chest. 'You've got the dagger.'

Malcolm grinned. 'You want to see it? It's the correct one.'

Caird's eyes narrowed, but there was a happy light to them. 'Never. But it'll go where the… other item is.'

'You can talk in front of her. After all, it was a Basque mercenary who switched the dagger when you were fighting The Englishman. He gave it as a gift to her father.'

That was a diplomatic way of telling their tale. Caird gazed at Andreona speculatively, 'And you brought her here. That'll make Gaira and Mairead happy.'

Why would that make his wife and sister happy?

'She doesn't know yet, Caird.'

Caird raised a brow. 'About…anything?'

'She knows everything except for the most important.'

Caird grinned and, if possible, his smile widened and Andreona swore there was a sheen to his eyes before he swiftly looked away and blinked. With a quick nod to his head, and not even a backward glance, he said. 'Then you'd best get on with telling her, Brother, and I'll take care of here.'

There wasn't anything left for Malcolm to tell her except for words she wanted him to say, and even with all that happened, she wasn't certain he would say them still. As for her, she'd said all she needed to him. The Englishman coming didn't change matters, other than she'd rescue him over and over, but that was because she loved him. But then Malcolm knew that. As to the rest, Andreona appreciated Caird didn't elaborate what his tasks were. As relieved as she was it wasn't Malcolm crumpled on the ground, she didn't, couldn't help with the rest.

'I know the place to take her,' Malcolm said.

They rode in a different direction to everyone else with Malcolm frequently looking over at her. Andreona wondered what he was looking for or if she should say anything. What was she to say? He'd been hurt, various parts of his tunic torn and darkened with his blood, he'd paid them no mind, but she worried how deep his wounds were, if they needed to be stitched. When he stopped, she didn't understand. His home was not here.

Instead, there was a great tree with roots that tumbled up and out. Nothing else surrounded it.

With a look to him, she dismounted and shook

her legs, which had hardly any strength to them. None of her body had strength, or substance. She was as bending as the grass. What she did have were emotions thrashing her insides like boulders in the ocean.

Those rocks were all that was left of her. Emotions that tumbled one way: fear for Malcolm's safety, her desperation to try to save him, her relief that her desperate gallop across the field towards goals she didn't know would be there was not in vain.

Then the rocks going another way towards joy when she'd seen other riders, his family, Eldric and Cressida, Caird. She'd shouted words at them and they'd understood her. Or perhaps, now she thought about it, they already knew what was happening as they raced past her and she whipped her horse around to follow and watch Malcolm fight alone. Malcolm, who was safe and watching her stare at a tree. A tree...

'What do you think?' he said.

She stared at this man who told her she was mistaken, that he didn't care for her, didn't care for anyone. While she'd watched Finlay talk Malcolm out of his black moods, Hugh punch him for not trusting him and the family he thought he didn't want come racing over the hills.

And then she watched him risk his own life

by facing The Englishman and his mercenaries alone. What did she think? Too much!

Noticing her confusion, he smiled and waved in front of him. 'About the tree.'

She didn't want to talk of the tree. 'Are you hurt?'

He looked down, grimaced. 'Scratches, that's all. I can't even feel them except—'

She knew there was more, pulling his tunic this way and that she saw nothing else, so she spun and looked towards the horizon. Where was the danger? Where was another obstacle keeping her away from this man? A hand on her arm stopped her.

Malcolm stopped her and it wasn't really his touch, though that was warm and gentle. It was his eyes that were calm.

'Except,' he said, cupping her jaw with his hand until even her thoughts inside eased. 'I wish I was more presentable to you when having this conversation.'

Presentable? He was alive. Closing her eyes, she brushed her cheek against his rough hand and he let out that growl that was half in his language and all him.

She shook herself and leaned away.

'Don't,' he said. He took her hand and sat her upon this tree with its long branches and roots twisting and knotting into a perch above ground.

She looked at him, at the tree. When he only gave her a smile, but didn't release her hand, she looked elsewhere for answers.

'This is…unusual.' She brushed her free hand against the worn bark.

'It's always been my sister's favourite tree and place to sit, but I think I'll claim it today…as well as you.'

She couldn't have heard him correctly. Pulling her hand free, she set them in her lap. 'Malcolm, if this has something to do with the fact I brought your family…they were coming already. I had nothing to do with that.'

He was staring at her clutched hands, his brow drawn in. Did he want to take her hand?

'I don't know what I'm to say. I've said everything else and you've been quiet since then and then all this happened,' she said. 'I'm still shaking.'

'I'm sorry for that. I'm sorry to make you wait. I'm sorry because *I* was mistaken,' Malcolm said. 'Not you. But… I won't always be right.'

There was so much to talk about with what he said, but the last…

'Do you think you need to be?' she said. 'Right, or correct?'

He leaned his elbows on his knees, alternated his feet on the ground. 'Caird can't get up in the morning without studying the day first. Gaira wants to make the world fair. And Bram? I don't know what my father was trying to teach him, but there were lessons on the land that summer. Supplies were short and, because Bram had miscalculated, we went hungry. He…made a point to make everyone know the consequences of their actions. Including me.'

She laid her hand on his leg to still it. 'I'm not asking about your family—I'm asking about you. It's impossible to always be right or correct, or to not make mistakes. Not to be—' She stopped, breathed in a bit because this was hard to say not only for his sake, but for hers. 'To be vulnerable.'

'That's not a choice for me.' Malcolm laid his hand on hers.

Whatever warmth, whatever she'd been thinking was between them, wasn't there. He'd brought her here where there were no distractions and she'd thought he wanted to talk. To tell her his feelings, but he hadn't any. Standing, she tried to yank her hand away.

'It wasn't a choice for me the moment you touched me,' he said.

'I wasn't intending to give you a choice.' She kept pulling on the hand he wouldn't release. 'I was trying to hurt you.'

Chuckling, he covered her hand with both of his. She gave up.

'No, not the time where I came in to surprise you, but the moment you surprised me,' he said.

His knowing look gave his meaning away. 'Didn't we agree not to talk of that again? I don't know what my hand was doing!'

He shook his head slowly and then even more so. 'As startling as the touch was…it was true, Andreona. I felt truth then. Do you know how long it'd been since I had…' He let her hand go. 'Since before Shannon. And then when at Hugh's, when we kissed, at Rhain's when we touched, and your words to me?'

She missed the warmth of his hand covering hers. She also thought, perhaps, she lost what he was saying. She did, however, know what she had said to him. Words he didn't repeat.

'I have no choice,' he said. 'Because you're the only choice I want.'

'Oh,' she said.

'Will you sit with me again?' He gestured before him.

She stepped forward and he gathered her down to him. Back to chest, her legs atop his, both of them looking out at the vast sky, the grass swaying to the light breeze.

After everything before—the storm raging last night, Malcolm's fight, those strange men up on the hill waiting—being held like this, feeling Malcolm's breath, to feel this peace.

'I think I'll always be a bit impulsive, quick to temper.' His voice was rumbling against her.

'And I'll always wanting to look into boxes and distract myself with matters until I get my feelings sorted,' she said.

He rested his chin on her shoulder and she felt his soft kiss on her neck.

'I love you,' he said.

After all he had said and done? 'I know.'

'You do have me,' he continued. 'When your father left, you had me.'

'I know that, too.' She'd always known that; she had only hoped he would recognise it.

'It hurts to love you, Andreona.'

She didn't know what to say to that.

'But what does it say about me that, despite the pain, I do it anyway?'

She turned in his arms to face him fully. 'It says you love me,' she said.

'With all the thorns, the knowing you could betray, mistrust, or abandon me. Despite knowing there can be loss, I do.'

After hearing that her father had ordered her death, she'd felt such devastation, loss…but also simply feeling lost. Then to go from that to this joy. That's what was piercing her now with Malcolm's words. Simply joy. Did he not feel that way, too?

'Love doesn't have to hurt, Malcolm.'

'It does when I've been empty for so long. It hurts because it overflows and my heart doesn't know what to do with it all and it's making a mess inside my chest. I have trouble breathing around you.'

This man. Their journey hadn't been easy, but now they were here, it was the easiest thing ever. She'd have to show him how easy it was. Just as soon as she could look up at him without her tears blurring her vision. The very moment, she could talk through the little hiccups and sobs leaving her throat and chest.

'Andreona.'

'I'm happy, Malcolm, give me a moment.'

He curled his finger under her chin and lifted her eyes to his. She knew her nose was red, her eyes puffy from too many tears.

'This is happiness?' he said. 'It doesn't look much better than love feels.'

'I'm simply overflowing, that's all.'

'You, too?'

'My chest is all messy inside.' She patted his chest and rubbed there a bit, right over that scar, right over his heart. 'I like your eyes here in this land of yours. This Scotland.'

His brows drew in and he managed to look pleased and confused. 'How about the rest of me?'

All their travels and all her years, there was no other man who called to her like this one did. 'You'll do.'

He growled and kissed her. When he pulled

away, she blurted, 'We'll need to find Finlay and Uracca to bring them here.'

'Here?' he said.

'I haven't actually met your family.'

'They'll give you no other choice.'

'Do you think Howe will stay?'

'No. If he cares at all, he'll leave or maybe Cressida won't let him. But that's up to them. Either way, he's not well because they've poisoned him. He doesn't have long and will have to accept his fate.'

The Englishman wasn't a good man, but there was still something sad about it all, but it was Malcolm's tone making her wonder.

'Accept his fate like you have done?' she said, only half teasing.

'Since you've been my fate?' I didn't accept it—I relish it.'

He brushed his fingers against her cheek. 'We'll send messages with the Half-Thistle Seal and bring everyone here to decide the fate of the gem and dagger. But they're together again and our part in this tale is done.'

She buried herself into him again, her face in his neck, her arms trapped between them. 'Not right now, though.'

'No. Not right now.' Malcolm tightened his arms around her. 'This forgiveness thing isn't easy.'

Forgiving her brothers, her father for manipulating her life and making it a lie. For betraying her the way they did because it suited them. Yes, she could argue it brought her Malcolm and it was all worth it, but that didn't make it easy.

'No.'

'But it's easier with you and me like this.'

He rubbed his chin against her head, she felt his heartbeat against her hands, the rhythmic movement of his lungs. But when he drew in a ragged breath and she knew his thoughts burned with legends and enemies, she pulled away.

He looked down at her. The light breeze lifted the curled strands behind his ear and she wondered if he'd ever admit that his dark hair held the colour of red as well.

'How do we do endure with this life we face?' he said.

That was easy. Everything was easy when it came to a love like theirs. One she knew would weather any slashing rain or quests. Any enemies at their back or any doubts they might have of their worth.

'We live our love just one beat at a time,' she said, 'one breath every moment. Then we're there.'

'Like now?' he said. When she nodded, he added. 'Then we're already there.'

They were.

Epilogue

 ～⁂～

October, 1299

Andreona leaned against her husband's side.

'How are you holding up with this?' Malcolm put his arm around her back.

He'd insisted they marry and she hadn't given any protest. How could she protest, when he knew in the short time they'd been together she'd leaned against him only partly for warmth, but mostly for comfort.

'Better now,' she answered and he hummed.

They stood outside Colquhoun keep and up on a small hill where family was slowly gathering around a platform that had been built for this day.

The air held all the iciness of an upcoming winter. She was dressed warmly enough, but she wasn't used to the damp air or the cold. Scotland was nothing like the Basque Country, but she wouldn't give up the beauty surrounding her for all the oceans in the world.

She wouldn't give up the man who stood next to her and blocked the wind either. Malcolm brought her closer to him and she rested her head on his shoulder, buried her hand underneath his cloak and rested her hand on his stomach.

When she lightly brushed against the bumps and planes of a torso she was lucky enough to know about, Malcolm looked down at her with a knowing eye.

Embarrassed, she shrugged, but when he raised a challenging brow, she stroked a finger along each indent. Something she knew he liked since he'd mentioned he had to kiss her that night in the forest because he wanted her hands on him and not the trees.

She could do that.

'Ready to run for the hills?' he said. 'Surely the clan is driving you mad now.'

'You keep asking me, but your family is lovely, Malcolm, and you can't change my mind.'

'They're nice to *you*,' he said.

She knew he teased, but there was much about this land that haunted her husband. Though he was far less restless now than he had been when they'd first arrived.

'Are you certain you don't want to run?' she said, also keeping her tone light, but with the soft understanding in those green eyes of his, she knew he understood her full meaning.

'Not a chance,' he said. 'They won't be able to get rid of me now. And Caird owes me time in the lists after his cheating from yesterday.'

'How is your arm?'

'Sore, but if you tell him, you better start running.'

'As if I could run fast enough to escape you.'

'That's the point.' He winked, then turned towards Gaira and Robert and gave them a nod in greeting.

Even plaited in multiple strands to be held back, Gaira's red hair took Andreona by surprise. She'd never seen such hair before. The infant girl cradled against her and under the cloak had the same shocking amount of it and she smiled, hoping she would smile back...but no such chance.

Gaira grinned. 'I keep hoping, too. But our boy smiled at me first, so if little Irvette doesn't smile at Robert any day now, I think we'll all be a *ragabash loun*.'

Laughing, Andreona said, 'Where are the other children?'

'Look behind us. The true question is where aren't they?' Gaira said.

Andreona craned her neck. She could just see beyond the clan where all the children were playing. She was still learning their names, but there appeared to be more than yesterday if that was possible!

Flora, one of Gaira and Robert's twins, was surrounded by clamouring little ones as she swung Nicholas and Matilda's daughter, Julianna, and angel-haired Maisie around, while boisterous Alec, another of Gaira's, Caird and Mairead's boy, Ailbert, Rhain and Helissent's golden-haired boys, Fingal and Hamish, and several other boys and girls were screaming and running mostly because Flora's twin, Creighton, was playing some dangerous form of chase through the icy mud and tall grass.

Grinning now, Andreona gazed in wonder as Malcolm's extended family surrounded them. There wasn't a chance she'd exchange his family for hers or for anyone else's. There wasn't a chance she would change this moment for all the moments she'd ever have. To have this much bounty, to know this many people, and to have this many people love you in return? It was a fortune that overflowed.

'Winter isn't here yet, we could make a trip,' Malcolm offered.

'It feels as if winter will be here soon.'

He kissed her forehead and she leaned into it. 'That's only because you aren't used to it yet. But if you'd like, we'll stay for this winter, but I want to negotiate when spring comes.'

'I ken, but I'll not be changing my mind,' she said, using his word, which she always mangled because he liked it. She also knew he liked her arguing against him leaving his family. If her husband wanted to play games and laugh rather than dwell on past pain, she'd welcome every bit of it.

Over the last few months, Andreona had watched with joy how Malcolm was folded back into his clan. He still grumbled and complained, but there was an ease about him, a warmth to his eyes that wasn't there before.

For months now, Bram, Caird and Gaira had spent long into the night talking over their childhood and what had happened in the years Malcolm was away. Andreona tried to give them privacy, as did Lioslath, Mairead and Robert, but sometimes Malcolm wanted her by his side as his siblings did their respective spouses. There were tales to tell and it was easier to say it all at once.

So much family…and now she had letters from Uracca and Finlay who'd made it to the fortress, as well as Dionora, Mencia, Bita and Gaieta. They wrote how they were settling in a fortress far larger than any they'd seen. Thus far, they were having a terrible time hiding her Roman surveying tools and the little boxes from a boy named Thomas, but that could be remedied later.

She wished they could be here, but someone loyal to their cause had to stay with the fortress, and so that burden fell to Finlay. She wondered, too, with Uracca's letters, if something was happening between her and the gentle Scot.

'Here we go,' Malcolm whispered and Andreona turned her attention to the present.

Reynold of Warstone approached the newly built platform and helped up a petite woman, Aliette, his wife, who stepped close and didn't let go of his hand. Their children, Grace and Guillemette, were off the platform. A petite pregnant woman named Margery bounced and danced Grace about, while the infant was held by her husband, Evrart, who was scarily large, but somehow adorable as he one-handedly cradled the baby against him while his fingers brushed across the top of the little head poking out of the furs she was bundled in.

'We're not announcing another wedding, are we?' Louve of Mei Solis, now of the Warstone fortress, shouted. 'I have coin, but between these weddings and births, I'm running out.' Bied, his wife, playfully hit him on the shoulder. Probably because the Warstone fortress, according to Malcolm, held more wealth than entire countries.

Rubbing his shoulder, Louve grinned at Bied, but whatever they shared, this time, she poked him in the chest and he patted her swelling stomach.

'Not a wedding, you fool.' Nicholas of Mei Solis laughed. 'This is about the change in our meal for tonight and how we need two roasting boars, not merely one.'

'Who's hunting that down, Lioslath or Cressida?' Bram said, already pulling out his purse as if to place bets.

'More jests? Don't you dare,' Lioslath said grabbing her husband's hand, and not letting it go.

'Who says I'm jesting?' Bram grinned at her. His hair was as bright as his sister Gaira's. It must have fascinated Lioslath, too, because his wife curled one of her fingers around a few strands and tugged.

'She's pregnant,' Lioslath threatened.

'And you're not?' Bram's hand went to her stomach, which was quite swelled.

'I say whichever it'll be, will be the largest,' Cressida said.

'That would be me—' Nicholas, who shared scars from past battles, ridiculously puffed out his chest, while Matilda, his wife, tried to slap her hand over his mouth '—who can take it down,' he finished.

Andreona laughed. It was good to see this happy couple again.

'I thought I was the largest?' Eldric of Hawksmoor challenged.

'Even though I could take you down?' Cressida said.

'That's because I want to be taken down by you,' Eldric said to her before turning to the crowd, and declaring, 'Though I am the largest.'

Everyone looked towards Evrart, expecting him to retort since it was apparent he was larger than them all. Except the giant of a man blushed while Margery giggled.

'Are we certain we're now talking about the largest man and not a boar?' Lioslath quipped.

'Oh, I was talking about boar,' Cressida announced, 'But on some days, who can tell the difference?'

The crowd laughed.

'At least we know who are friends,' Reynold announced.

'Certainly not yours!' Rhain of Gwalchdu called out from the back.

'Don't listen to him, Reynold,' Helissent said. 'He doesn't mean it.'

Grinning, Rhain whispered in his wife's ear, but she kept shaking her head. Andreona so wished she knew what was being said.

'Is this all of us?' Reynold said. 'Please tell me this is all of us.'

'Those who matter, Brother,' Balthus of Warstone said, both of his arms being tugged in opposite directions by two energetic boys, while his wife, Séverine, juggled a dark-haired disgruntled baby, which Andreona now knew to be Marguerite.

Reynold's expression grew pensive as he shared a look with his youngest brother. Andreona knew so much more about these men simply by being near them in the last month, but not enough to truly understand the depth of the horror they'd endured, what it took for them all to find peace and love, and the women by their sides who gave them the courage to do so.

'There will be wars won and wars lost, but what we have gathered here together, what we have standing shoulder to shoulder, is forever,' Reynold proclaimed, his voice resounding over the near-silent crowd, his eyes going from one to the other, even her own. Since he'd arrived, Reynold was an enigma to Andreona, but his love for Aliette, Grace and Guillemette was clear for anyone to see.

Andreona's eyes pricked with tears. 'He means us. All of us.'

Malcolm gave a hard swallow and nodded. His eyes shined though he didn't look down at her, she suspected because Bram and Caird were looking towards him, all three brothers sharing their own silent bond.

There was so much love between this family, so much loyalty and faith in this clan. She'd never known such joy before.

'Then we have this dagger and gem,' Reynold continued. 'Some scraps of parchment are still not deciphered. I don't need to say these seemingly simple items stay together, or that they need to be moved often. It will all come down to how and when. There will need to be a schedule that won't be a schedule.'

Someone laughed. Another groaned and Reynold nodded in understanding.

'I know you've all volunteered to find secret locations, to keep the danger away from your hearths and homes.' Reynold looked to Aliette. 'Away from our *hearts* and homes.'

'And trees and books,' she said softly. If Andreona hadn't been standing close she wouldn't have heard.

'Never those,' Reynold whispered to her before he straightened and the soft expression he gave was gone.

'New Half-Thistle Seals are being made because one of you cleverly thought of making additions so it isn't only a Scottish thistle depicted.' Reynold looked to Andreona and she felt Alice's, Helissent's, Matilda's and even Gaira's eyes on her. They had loved the idea of thistles on their doors to keep out bad spirits and, as they talked and shared, the idea had come to Andreona that she, too, could contribute. However, it had taken these remarkable women to get her anywhere near Reynold, Bram and Caird to make the suggestion.

When she had, Reynold had closed the book he was reading and stood up so enthusiastically she almost stepped back. Her small contribution was apparently a key they'd been trying to solve.

'Not only does this new seal symbolise the blending and combining of our families,' Reynold continued, 'but it will also make it difficult to reproduce and trace to any one source. But we will be that source if we agree.'

'Will we, our children, and their children keep these secrets?' Reynold asked them all.

Andreona affirmatively answered as did everyone. Malcolm's hand clenched her shoulder. His eyes held the gravity and determination that these vows meant. Vows she also knew she'd die to protect. This family…her family now…had made far too many sacrifices, survived too much danger not to protect these objects. While the Warstone parents or monarchs lived, there would always be some peril surrounding the legendary gem and treasure.

Andreona rather liked it. The gem and hollowed dagger fit perfectly together, but the parchment with its coding and the scrollwork continued to be a mystery to be solved.

Séverine, Balthus of Warstone's wife, was busily trying to solve it all. Andreona liked to talk and sit at her side. She loved simply to imagine the possibilities the objects meant.

'Will we protect these items with our lives?' Reynold voice rang out.

The clans, the families, shouted in agreement.

'Will we protect our families with our hearts?' Reynold said, his hand now clenching Aliette's.

'No enemies or family will take it away,' Balthus vowed.

'Or friends,' Eldric of Hawksmoor said.

A question in her eyes, Cressida whispered frantically to her husband. When he whispered back, she smiled and nodded. Andreona wondered what that was about.

'There's a man… Terric,' Malcolm whispered. 'He's a notorious thief and smuggler they met along their journey. You can bet if he knew of the treasure he'd be after it, though Eldric insists he's trustworthy and loyal.'

'Is that possible?'

'I have proof thieves are trustworthy…and very beautiful,' Malcolm said, his eyes returning to Reynold. Andreona, almost blushing because Malcolm meant her, looked to the dais.

'Then we are one in this?' Reynold asked, his grey eyes determined and yet seemingly overwhelmed. Maybe, he, too, couldn't believe the love and strength he'd found with this new family.

Then his gaze rested on the man who stood next to Malcolm and Gaira.

Maybe Reynold wanted affirmation from the one man who hadn't called out or made jests. The one man whom, oddly, had been born in England and found a Scottish woman named Gaira and four orphaned children. Who had, by might and promises, brought them safely home and, in turn, had made this his home.

Robert of Dent's eyes went to Hugh. Alice, his wife, was buried in his side much like she was with Malcolm.

'I still don't wish for your death, my friend,' Hugh called out.

'And I don't wish for any of yours.' Robert of Dent gazed around the crowd, his family, his friends, and turned to Reynold to vow, 'We are determined.'

Claps and cries as all agreed and the crowd broke out in noisy voices while Reynold and Aliette descended from the platform to gather their children and talk to Margery and Evrart.

Malcolm shook Hugh's hand and a few others. Accepted slaps on his back, one harder than the other, from Caird and Bram. More came up to them with nods or greetings, and she herself made promises to Gaira and Alice to see them in the kitchens soon. Soon, but not now.

Andreona wasn't ready to leave the comfort of her husband's side and so waved to them all. And Malcolm didn't ask if she wanted to go, nor did he release the arm he had protectively wrapped around her because he knew she wasn't standing here simply for warmth, but for comfort.

It wasn't because she was overwhelmed with the vows they'd made or the danger it portended. It was because with this much joy, sometimes a few more hugs were needed.

When it was mostly quiet, and she revelled in their shared breaths and heartbeats, she remembered they hadn't finished their earlier conversation.

'I never stole anything from you,' Andreona whispered.

'What is this?' Malcolm said.

With her arms around him, Andreona looked up. Malcolm's cheeks were ruddy, his dark curls blowing this way and that. The wind had picked up since they first came here, but he stood still and patient because he knew what she needed: a little more time to themselves.

So he suffered with the wind and the cold and blocked her from feeling any of it. Could her husband be any more beautiful?

'Earlier, you implied I was a thief,' she said.

'You are! Of me, my heart, my soul, everything.' He tsked and shook his head. 'And you say that's nothing.'

Oh, this man.

Floating on the brisk wind there were shouts and laughter, the smells of roasting fires, the beckoning chatter of welcoming voices. Surrounding them there were possibilities of more days like this with family.

'It might be everything to you. *Might*,' she added when he grinned smugly. 'But I want more than your heart and soul.'

'And you call yourself not a thief,' he said. 'What more could you possibly want?'

'Well, those things,' she said as agreeably as she could though her nose was turning red and a couple of stubborn tears fell. 'Along with some years and forever.'

Malcolm caught them on his thumb. 'Oh, Andreona, you have that, too, and if there's more than forever, it's yours as well.'

She wanted to retort or say something witty. Instead, her tears only flowed that bit harder and she turned her face into his chest, right over his heart.

'I'll take that, too,' she said.

* * * * *

COMING SOON!

We really hope you enjoyed reading this book.
If you're looking for more romance, be sure to
head to the shops when new books are
available on

Thursday 20th January